Praise for Elaine C. Brewster

"Creative writing is the hallmark of this exemplary author. Elaine has taken historical facts and weaved them together to create a page turning novel. Readers will delight in walking into the past and encountering romance, struggles, sacrifice, and unexpected kindness. Hats off to Elaine for writing a riveting novel on a beloved ancestor."

— SUSAN EASTON BLACK - HIGHLY ACCLAIMED AUTHOR, BYU PROFESSOR, WINNER OF THE KARL G MAESER DISTINGUISHED FACULTY AWARD

"*Walking with Emma* is a heartfelt story about a young woman who leaves the strictures of Victorian England and travels to America in the 1860s with her family in order to join other Latter-day Saint families in their quest to build Zion. I was intrigued by Emma's character and her family's experiences since my own ancestors underwent such a journey during this same decade. A story of self discovery and fierce hope, readers will enjoy this immersive historical tale."

— HEATHER B. MOORE, AUTHOR OF *ELISABETH: MOTHER OF JOHN THE BAPTIST*

"Well written and uplifting. I appreciate Elaine's strong testimony of Jesus Christ that comes through her writing."

— DARLENE GOULDING, MEMBER OF DAUGHTERS OF UTAH PIONEERS

"Walking With Emma is a warm, engaging story that brings the 1860s to life through the eyes of a young woman. Brewster weaves rich historical detail into a deeply personal journey, capturing both the frightening uncertainties and the quiet faith that sustained the Horespool family as they traveled from London to the United States. Through hardship and hope, the family's loving dynamic shines, making their belief in reunion and gathering with the Saints in Zion feel both heartfelt and real."

— JENNIFER MOORE - BEST SELLING AUTHOR OF REGENCY, HISTORICAL, AND VICTORIAN ROMANCE GENRES

"I really enjoyed your book because of the way difficulties were met head-on and continued to move forward. I am very impressed with Elaine's writing and ability to tell this story in such a way as to draw the reader in and make them part of the journey."

— DAVE ASAY, PRESIDENT BMAF (BOOK OF MORMON ARCHEOLOGICAL FOUNDATION)

"I enjoyed *Crossing the Ocean* very much. Elaine's writing is descriptive and very engaging. Her research is impeccable, and I enjoyed the many details, as I had ancestors who also crossed the ocean."

— DEBBIE YOUNGBERG, LITERARY CRITIC AND HISTORIAN

CROSSING THE OCEAN

CROSSING *the* OCEAN

BASED ON A TRUE STORY

LIBRARY OF CONGRESS CONTROL NUMBER: 2026901209
PAPERBACK: 979-8-9945424-0-8
DIGITAL BOOK: 979-8-9945424-1-5

PRINTED IN THE USA

"Yes, my native land, I love thee.
    All thy scenes I love them well.
    Can I leave you, can I leave you,
    Far in distant lands to dwell?"

— "YES, MY NATIVE LAND" - WRITTEN BY SAMUEL
FRANCIS SMITH

Contents

Prologue
POPLAR, ENGLAND

SUNDAY, DECEMBER 22, 1852

Nine-year-old Emma stood in the dim, narrow hallway of her London home. It wasn't London, precisely; it was Poplar, a suburb, but she'd heard people call it London as often as Poplar. Her home was a double townhouse—numbers 148 and 149 High Street—joined by an arched door on the main floor. The double house had three stories, high ceilings, ornate doors, and wallpapered rooms. Emma wandered out from the nursery where her brother and sisters were, wondering what was happening with her mother.

Earlier, the new nurse had ushered the children into their bedroom. The paunchy woman had lined up Emma with her eleven-year-old sister, Elizabeth, seven-year-old Will, and five-year-old Hattie, spearing them with her fierce eyes. She'd rubbed her beefy hands on her dirty apron, making Emma aware of the raw edges of the woman's clothing. Emma wanted nothing to do with this woman.

The nurse's straggly hair strayed from her cap, and a frown accompanied her low Cockney accent. "Now children, yer father's gone and broke 'is leg on the ice on 'is way to the bakery this mornin.' He's in 'ospital right now, so there's no one to take you to your uncle's. Yer just goin' to have to stay 'ere while your mother works her baby out. Don't come out of this room. No matter what you 'ear; don't you come out!"

Spit flew from her mouth with her forceful command. Emma and Elizabeth backed up a step, and Will and Hattie pressed back against their older sisters as if they were a firm, protective wall. All four stood with wide eyes, unable to say a word.

The woman barked, "Do you understand?"

Emma and then Elizabeth stuttered, "Yes."

The little ones nodded ferociously.

She slammed the heavy wooden door unceremoniously on the children, and they stayed in the nursery as they had been told. They wandered to the fireplace. It had been lit earlier, but now as twilight approached, it waned, and the December chill permeated the room.

"Let's put some more wood on it," Emma suggested, grabbing the poker and stirring the few remaining embers.

The two sisters were used to doing everything together, but making a fire was not something either had ever done. There had always been someone older, like the nurse, to do it for them.

There was only one large piece of wood left in the bin. Elizabeth put it on, but it smothered the tiny flames Emma had stirred up.

"Oh, *that* didn't work!" exclaimed Emma.

"It's the only wood," Elizabeth said.

Emma looked in the wood bin for something smaller that would allow the smoldering fire to grow. Dust, wood shavings, and tiny pieces that had fallen off larger logs lay in the bottom. She scooped up what she could with her bare hands. "Ow!" she exclaimed as a splinter caught her finger. She dropped the tiny pieces like hotcakes, and the other children rushed to look at her hand.

"It's all right," she said. "I can get this out."

After showing the splinter to the other three, she pinched the side of her hand until the small piece of wood poked out. "Here." She held her hand up to Elizabeth, who inspected it, reached over, and gingerly pulled out the intrusive piece of wood.

"Maybe we'd better not try that again," ever-practical Elizabeth said, holding Will back from scooping up the leftover wood pieces.

"I'll do it, Will. I'll be more careful this time." Emma looked around the room for something she could use instead of her hands. She saw a wooden horse on its side. How silly; that wouldn't work. Her eyes lit on a book. After considering for a moment, she discarded the idea, realizing it was too thick to gather the fine particles. A doll's blanket gave her an idea. She went to her drawer and pulled out a scarf. Going back to the wood bin, she mopped up the tiny wooden bits with the thin material, careful not to get them on her hands, and dumped the contents onto the fire. Around the edges of the large log, some of the dust and pieces caught fire. The flame lasted only a second before the dust was consumed.

"Well, that didn't work either," Emma said disconsolately while Will and Hattie shook their heads.

Ever hopeful, Elizabeth said, "Maybe the log will catch fire if we just leave it."

Hattie reached out her hands toward the orange flecks clinging to the dying embers. "I'm getting cold."

The four children had been so intent on the fire, they hadn't noticed anything outside their room. Now they heard an agonizing scream, one so dreadful Emma imagined it stripping the trim off the door and leaving it in a broken heap in the hall.

Little Hattie burst into tears, and Will asked, half fearful and half hopeful, "Is there a lion in the house?"

Emma looked at Elizabeth in stunned silence, but her sister offered no encouragement, her eyes wide with fright. The cry had been feral and frightening. Of the four, only the older girls realized the screaming had something to do with a new baby. Emma didn't know exactly what, because she'd been told nothing in advance, only to stay in this room.

Emma thought, *There must be something I can do to make this better. I know, I'll tell them a story.* She was already the best reader in the family, and her siblings liked her tellings of the stories she read. "It's time for a story," she said more brightly than she felt. She herded them onto the bed even as another scream echoed down the hallway.

"Oh, good!" Hattie exclaimed, not heeding the cry and settling close to Elizabeth. "Is it Rose Red and Snow White?"

"Yes. How did you know, you smart girl?"

"Because Mama tells it. Snow White has dark hair like you, Emma, and Rose Red has yellow hair like you, Elizabeth." After pointing at each, she leaned again against her older sister.

"And they had a little sister named Lily Flower with brown hair—like yours!" Emma playfully chucked her nose, making Hattie giggle. Emma sighed in relief. Their circumstances felt a bit more normal now.

"Rose Red and Snow White lived with their widowed mother in a cottage in the forest."

"What's a widow?" asked Will, who was, for once, paying attention to the story.

"It means their daddy had gone," Elizabeth explained.

"My daddy's gone," said Hattie.

"No, dear, he's not gone. He's just in the hospital," Emma quickly corrected. "He hurt his leg, but he'll be home soon. Shall I go on?"

After the girl nodded, Emma continued, "One night, a knock came at their door."

Just then, another tremendous cry burst down the hall.

Will startled and pulled back. Hattie whimpered again and curled closer to Elizabeth. Emma looked again at her older sister. If anyone could calm their younger siblings, it would be her. Emma's strengths were in school and ideas, but Elizabeth's centered on the home—things like tending, nursing, and healing. Emma's eyes pleaded with her to find a way to explain the horrendous cries issuing from their mother's bedroom.

Answering Emma's beseeching look, Elizabeth began, "A baby is coming to our house. A little brother or sister. And it takes a lot... well, it's hard. But it will be all right." She hesitated and then nodded to Emma to continue.

Emma went on, "When the sisters opened the door—"

"There was a bear!" Hattie exclaimed, immediately getting back into the story. "This is your part, Will. Mama says everyone has a part."

Will looked mildly interested, this being the only part he contributed to. "Yes," he said, almost by rote. "But he was a nice bear. He only asked to warm himself by their fire."

Emma nodded. "They let him come in, and the sisters brushed the snow off his fur coat."

Hattie fluffed her hands out in brushing motions.

"He slept by the fire that night and went away the next day."

"But he came back!" Hattie said earnestly.

"Yes, he did," said Emma. "Every night, all winter. Now, in the spring, Snow White and Rose Red were walking in the forest—Lily Flower was too little to go anywhere yet, so she stayed home—and they spied a dwarf whose long, white beard was caught in a tree. They freed him by cutting his beard..."

"And he yelled at them for ruining it."

Smiling, Emma finished, "The bear found out how mean the dwarf was to the sisters, and he *tossed* him from the land with his big paw."

Hattie's arm swung out, nearly knocking Will's nose.

"Hey! Watch out!" he cried.

Emma gently pushed the little girl's arm down. "As soon as the dwarf was gone from the land, the bear turned into...," she spread her hands out triumphantly as Hattie finished, "a prince!"

"Yes! You see, when the dwarf left, the spell left the bear. He'd been a prince all along!"

Elizabeth hugged her little sister, and Will, not interested any longer, flopped onto his stomach and traced a wavy line on the yellow patchwork quilt, his sandy-colored hair flopping over his forehead.

Meanwhile, Emma turned her ear toward the door. During her story, the sounds had stopped. Emma's curiosity finally grew stronger than the nurse's admonition to stay in the room. She climbed off the bed and walked to the door.

Looking pointedly at her sister, Elizabeth said through thin lips, "She said to stay in here." From the bed, her other siblings stared with wide eyes.

Looking over her shoulder, Emma said, "I'll just be a minute." Gingerly, she put a hand on the knob and opened the heavy door.

The hall was dark, quiet, and cold. Night came early in December, and the hall sconces were not lit. The flowers on the wallpaper, so cheery in daylight, now looked like creatures with jeering mouths. She looked quickly away and stared straight down the hall as the silence and the dimness almost overwhelmed her. She felt as terrified as if a giant bear's paw were pressing down. For one long minute, Emma stood stock still. Finally, mastering her imagination, she slid her feet forward one at a time. Step by step, she slowly made her way to her mother's room. From downstairs, she heard rustling sounds and metal clinking along with muffled voices. She ignored them and entered the bedroom.

There was only one lit candle sitting in its sconce on the wall that flickered as she walked in, making the wardrobe and the rocking chair seem alive. Imagining dwarves and demons, she held still again until she realized nothing was moving. She stepped farther inside and saw her mother lying on her bed in her pale nightgown with a babe next to her. Neither moved.

"Mama?" she called tentatively. "Mama?" she called in a stronger voice. There was no answer. That terrified her more than anything ever had.

Both her mother and the newborn lay uncovered. That seemed strange. She could see that the baby was a girl and barely wrapped in some cotton material. But where was Mama's quilt? Grandma Charlotte had made it, and it was colorful and warm. Emma looked underneath the bed and even on the opposite side to see if it had fallen. It wasn't there.

Emma didn't know what to do. The voices continued below, and Emma realized one was a man's. Was her father home? No, this male voice sounded rough, strident, and unfamiliar. Why was there a man in their house? Was it Uncle Jesse? It didn't sound like him. It had a frenzied quality that didn't remind her of Father's brother, and it didn't sound like anyone from her church, either.

Suddenly afraid, Emma turned and fled back to the nursery. She shut the door, her eyes shooting to the bed in search of her siblings. They weren't there! Then she saw them squatting by the fireplace. A bit of flame had finally taken hold, and they had climbed off the bed to warm their hands. She joined them, holding out her palms gratefully to the speck of warmth offered by the tiny flames.

Elizabeth asked how Mother was. Will and Hattie looked up with expectant, innocent eyes. Emma still didn't know what to say. Everything was strange. Nothing was right, and everything was wrong. She didn't know how to frame what she feared. Instead, she said, "They're quiet." Well, that was the truth. Then she added, "It's a girl. The baby is a girl."

"Baby Sarah," Elizabeth said softly, looking back at the fire. Her voice lacked color, like using a white pencil on white paper. "Mama told me, if the baby's a boy, it would be Jesse after Papa's brother. If it's a girl, she's named after Mama's mother."

All Emma could do was nod.

"I'm cold," Hattie said again.

The fire now did little good, but holding their hands toward that tiny bit of orange in the charred wood only let them pretend they were warmer.

Elizabeth got up and dragged the yellow quilt off the bed. Emma grabbed the pillows.

"Here, sit on these," Emma said while her sister arranged the quilt around their shoulders. The four snuggled as close as they could.

After a minute, Will said, "I'm hungry."

Is there any food here in the nursery? Emma thought desperately. While she was thinking, a different thought crossed her mind. No, there was no food, but what might bring comfort were the songs of Zion. Yes, singing the hymns they sang on Sunday might make them feel better. In her pretty voice, she sang:

> *The earth was once a garden place, With all her glories common.*
> *And men did live a holy race, And worship Jesus face to face*
> *In Adam-ondi-Ahman.*

The children joined in on the chorus word, *Adam-ondi-Ahman,* and when Emma couldn't think of any more words, she stopped. A silence descended over the house. No sound came through their heavy wooden door. The quiet felt like a dense fog blanketing their home, obliterating thought and reason and hope. Listening acutely, Emma realized she no longer heard the rustling and metallic clinking from downstairs.

Emma was just as hungry and cold as her siblings, but for her, the greater discomfort was what she had seen—her mother and the baby lying still on the bed. She couldn't say it out loud—she simply couldn't

—but she thought they were both dead. And she hadn't done anything to help. She had walked away, and then she hadn't even told Elizabeth. Emma liked to *do* things. She liked to help. Since she hadn't done anything to assuage or correct the awfulness in her mother's room, that surely meant that she was responsible. Somehow, she knew she was at fault for their deaths, at least a little.

Just then, she heard a man's voice coming from her mother's room. He uttered a loud, sharp exclamation, and then she heard footsteps coming toward the nursery. They sounded purposeful, not surreptitious, nothing to be afraid of.

The door opened. It was Uncle Jesse, his well-trimmed beard framing his handsome face as his eyes pierced the dim room. He immediately spotted the four of them huddled under the quilt by the cold fireplace.

"Oh, children!" he exclaimed with compassion. He knelt and gathered the smallest two in his arms. "What has happened here? What has happened?" he said to no one in particular.

"I'm hungry, Uncle Jesse," complained Will.

"I'm cold," said Hattie again.

"Where's your father?" he asked.

Elizabeth answered, "In the hospital."

"He fell on the ice and broke his leg," Emma finished.

"Well, you are all coming to my house, where you'll be warm. Aunt Jane will have a wonderful dinner for you." He stood, sounding assured and in charge. "Everyone, get your nightclothes, shoes, and coats."

Hesitant to leave the bit of warmth he had, Will asked, "Can we bring the quilt?"

"Yes, certainly," Uncle Jesse said absentmindedly. He flung the patchwork quilt over his arm as they grabbed their things and marched outside.

Uncle Jesse gently helped the children into his carriage with a consoling smile. Emma was the last to climb in. She overheard her uncle tell the driver, "It looks like the house was ransacked. The kitchen and parlor are thrown apart."

He started to place the quilt on their laps when a funny look crossed his face. "Here, use the wool blankets." He reached for two folded gray blankets and started tucking them around the children. "Wool is much warmer."

Emma watched as he went back in, the yellow quilt still over his arm. A few moments later, he emerged, pale as a ghost, and climbed into the carriage without the quilt. The coach immediately leaped forward, leaving the house, her mother, and the newborn babe behind.

Sisters

POPLAR, ENGLAND

MARCH 21, 1860

Emma and Elizabeth flitted happily about the upstairs bedroom. They leaned and bent over each other, almost in a dance, as they picked up and folded the linens Elizabeth had embroidered for her trousseau. Emma's sister was packing today and getting married tomorrow!

"Where do these go?" Emma asked brightly, holding up a pile of crochet-edged pillowcases.

"Let's put those on this side of the trunk, the dresses on the other side, and my underthings in the carpet bag."

Emma gently fingered the edges before laying them down. "You did a beautiful job with these, Elizabeth."

She smiled contentedly. "Thank you. It will be nice to use them!"

Emma folded a dress with bold vertical stripes of blue and white. Her sister said, "Why don't you take that dress, Emma?"

"It's yours."

"The style never really suited me. And the color goes better with your dark hair."

"I think it looks fine with your fair hair."

The sisters were remarkably alike, other than their hair coloring. They were so alike that their neighbors had a hard time telling them apart. Both were 5'3" and thin, although Elizabeth was a straight quill-thin and Emma was more a curving teacup-handle thin. Both had an energy about them that indicated they liked to get things done in a no-nonsense way, and both were seamstresses of considerable skill, having been taught by their stepmother.

Elizabeth thrust the dress at Emma, but Emma pushed it right back.

"It's fancy. When will I need it?"

"Sundays."

"And have little Freddy dribble all over it during meeting?" Her youngest stepchild was just eighteen months old.

"I'm sure William will take you to the theater or the opera sometime. You won't want to go in your flowered day dress. It's going in." She grabbed it, folded it carefully, and held it out with her head at a questioning tilt.

Emma laughed when Elizabeth rolled her eyes and said, "You win. Put it in."

Good, thought Emma. She would take as many wins as she could over the next two days, at which time her sister would permanently leave her life. They had shared so much over the last eight years since their mother had died—their father remarrying, four little brothers being born, two of those dying, and the front room in #149 being converted into a retail bakery. Through it all, Elizabeth had been her mainstay, her support, her listening ear. Elizabeth was gentle and genuine. She offset their father's stern aloofness and countered their stepmother's strict set of rules. Elizabeth kept her secrets and listened to her when others thought her ideas were unconventional. She could share anything with her. Who would she have now?

Determined for this to be a pleasant day, Emma continued the conversation. "It's not like you haven't been sitting already with children at the fellowship meeting!" Her husband-to-be had seven living children: Louisa, Eloise, John, Sarah, six-year-old Matilda, four-year-old William, and tiny Frederick James.

"They certainly fill up the pew!"

"You've been so kind to their family since William's wife died. Admit it, you were their favorite nanny."

Elizabeth chuckled, "I did help out as often as I could get away from the bakery. By the way, did you know Father hired a man to take my place?"

"Oh?"

"Yes. Benton Berrycloth."

"Brother Berrycloth from our church branch?"

"Yes!" Elizabeth smiled. "I let Father know how busy I would be taking care of the children, and he finally realized I wouldn't be able to continue working for him."

Folding a set of tea towels, Emma said, "I wish Father had realized I needed help when he had me take our money to the bank." Oh, why did she let that slip out? Emma hadn't meant to be negative, not today! She immediately wished she could call back her sour words.

Too late—Elizabeth heard her tone. Quickly setting her extra corset in the carpetbag, she pulled Emma to sit down on the bed with her. "Does the alley still bother you?"

Emma shrugged one shoulder, smiling slightly. "Only when I'm in confined, dark spaces." Hastening, she added, "And that doesn't happen often." She squeezed Elizabeth's hand reassuringly.

Elizabeth gestured to their room and the hall. "How about here? Does the dark hall bother you at night?"

Emma shook her head. "I make sure a wall sconce is always lit. And I try to remember what it looks like in the day, so I don't imagine it filled with goblins and gremlins."

Elizabeth laughed. "That's smart!"

Emma didn't like thinking about the alley, but the memory popped up at the most inopportune times. Her father's bakery business was in two locations. His main shop was near the docks, and the second was in their house on High Street. He'd needed their earnings taken to the bank every week, and he had settled on little Emma to do so. She'd told him she was frightened, and she told him she didn't want to. But he said Elizabeth was needed to clean up at the Dock Road bakery, Hattie and Will were too young, and their mother had to tend the little ones and prepare supper. To him, Emma was the only one left.

She remembered how the flat leather bag containing their weekly earnings slipped easily into the bank's after-hours slot. The trouble was that the slot was at the back of the bank, not the front, and she could only reach it by going through a long, dark alley. There were no lanterns, and the dim light and oppressive air between the tall gray buildings made her feel that the heavy stone walls might fall on her and crush her. The cobblestones caught at her shoes, and where there were none, the mud squelched under her feet, making her feel as if she were being drawn into the ground.

The dock workers in their section of town were out and about all hours of the night, so she was used to seeing people as she performed her task. The real people never bothered her, as they seemed to walk with purpose, with places to go and people to see. It was the fog and the shadows and the sounds in the alley that stayed and swirled and shifted into wolves or monsters or feral dogs, no matter how fast her little legs ran. Her imaginings were more frightening than reality.

Her father had drilled into her, "This is our weekly earnings. Do you understand?" Yes, she had understood. But that didn't remove the fear. She thought, *You'd think doing it so many times would have inured me against the terror. But it did the opposite. It ingrained it in me.* She felt foolish now, at seventeen—all these years later—that it still stirred such strong emotions inside her.

Elizabeth's eyes were tender. "I'm sorry it's still so hard."

"I'm sorry I mentioned it! It never should have come up at this happiest of times. Forget I said anything!"

Emma had never told anyone else about the alley because Elizabeth had been her only confidant. She was genuinely happy for her sister to marry, but she couldn't help thinking about how things would change for her. Bringing the story of the alley to mind simply reinforced the simple fact that after tomorrow, Elizabeth would no longer be a constant in her life.

With a sob, Emma cried, "I'll *miss* you, Elizabeth!"

"I'll be right up the street. I'm not going far." Her sister squeezed her hand, smiling.

"You and I both know things will change."

"You're right. Of course, you're right."

"You'll be in charge of seven children all day long."

"Six and a drooler." Elizabeth was trying to make her smile.

Emma rewarded her with half a smile and then softly said, "Who will I talk to?"

Elizabeth suddenly understood. "You've never told anyone about the alley, have you?"

Emma shook her head. "Will and Hattie were too little, Father was too busy, and Eliza had a hard time with her four pregnancies. And the two of them are so strict and not easy to talk to. Then, when the bank changed its policies, it was no longer necessary to take the money after hours. So, no, I never said anything." Emma felt her sister squeeze her hand, but she could no longer contain her deepest fear. She burst out, "What will I do without you?"

Elizabeth dropped Emma's hand and pulled her into a hug. "Oh, sweet Emma. You'll manage. I know you will."

Emma rested her head on her sister's shoulder. Allowing herself a moment of self-pity, she said, "It's not just the alley—it's everything. No one else really listens to me, not like you do. Will's in his own world, Hattie lives in her fairytales, and Mother and Father are always occupied. And Georgie and Richie are just plain little."

Emma let a few tears drop onto her sister's shoulder. How many times, since their mother had died, had Elizabeth held her, befriended her, comforted her? Their father had married two months after their mother had died, and their stepmother was not comforting toward Emma. Eliza was a good woman, just rather strict. All right, admit it: very strict. Easy-going but obedient Elizabeth had been Emma's buffer for almost eight years.

Hugging her tighter, Elizabeth said, "Emma, you do more than you realize. To me, it's *you* who eases people's burdens. Why, do you remember Thomas Purdy, just after his family moved into our area? He was six, and he fell at the shipyard and impaled his arm on a four-inch-long gimbal!"

"Ouch, yes."

"The other children made fun of him until you had him be King David in a church play. After that, all the children wanted him to be their friend." Holding onto Emma's shoulders, Elizabeth pulled her away to look at her. "Maybe you could give Will and Hattie more of a chance. They might surprise you. They're older now. And Emma, I really will be just up the street!"

Wiping the last tear from her eye, Emma smiled. "I know. I'm just feeling sorry for myself." Taking a breath, she said, "I'm done now. All right. Let's get back to packing for you!" Standing, she grabbed Elizabeth's pale orange dress with the small teal diamonds and started folding.

As Elizabeth went back to her linens, Emma teased, "Let's talk about your groom!"

This was a topic Emma knew Elizabeth would endorse wholeheartedly

Her sister caught up with the idea immediately. "Oh, William! He's wonderful! Emma, he is so good, and so kind—"

"—and quite handsome, too!"

"He is!" Elizabeth giggled. Elizabeth was a sensible girl—a solid young woman who was not given to giggling or hysteria. Yet, around Emma, she could often be quite giddy.

"It honestly doesn't bother you that he's a year older than Father?"

"It really doesn't. He acts so much younger, and that's how I see him. I'm an adult, and he is, and that's all that matters. Well, and that he's a faithful member of the church." She tucked in her last load of underthings and looked directly at Emma. "Someday, we will emigrate to Zion, and then we will be married in a temple of our Lord where there is authority to seal our marriage for all eternity! That's our plan."

She spoke more surely and smiled more broadly than usual. Emma could tell this was something her sister and her intended had already discussed, and she felt honored she'd share that deep desire with her. Emma emerged from her reverie, "Then we'd better get this wedding going! Remember that top drawer. That's all yours, milady!"

Elizabeth swayed in her pale green dress as she pulled a necklace, a jeweled mantilla comb, and a shawl from the high, shallow drawer. Placing the yellow paisley shawl on her arm, she gently placed the necklace on top of the dresser, its pale aquamarine crystal glinting slightly. She then handed the comb to Emma. "It's lucky that the nurse didn't see this, or it would be gone."

"Oh, it's Mama's! And you'll wear it tomorrow! Here's something new I heard—" She recited, "—'Something old, Something new, Something borrowed, Something blue.' Your necklace can be the *blue*. And Mama's comb can be the *old*. Let's see, what's Something borrowed?"

Almost shyly, Elizabeth said, "Eliza is lending me her wedding veil."

"The lace one she was married in?" The girls were almost ten and twelve when their father remarried; they were old enough to remember that beautiful veil.

"Yes! And Emma, the lace cost more than everything else she brought into her marriage combined."

"That just leaves us with something new. What about your wedding dress?

"Actually, I think it should be this shawl." She pulled the yellow wrap off her arm and held it up.

Emma gasped as the fringed edges danced merrily while the broad border of coral, red, and brown flowed in a chorus of paisley swirls. "I haven't seen this before."

"It's my engagement gift from William."

"Perfect! Elizabeth, you are going to be beautiful! You and William will be so happy!"

"We will! And Emma, I sincerely believe you will *know* when the right man for you comes along."

Breathlessly, Emma asked, "Do you truly think so?"

"I do!"

"I do want what you and William have."

"I believe one of your gifts is that of discernment. You've shown that you are sensitive to the Lord's Spirit."

"How?"

"Do you remember when we were left alone in the nursery when Mama died? We were all cold and hungry, and you were the one who had the idea to sing hymns. And you're the one who remembers the words. You sang and sang until Uncle Jesse arrived. I don't think that idea came from nowhere—I think you were guided to do that, and you followed that prompting. So, you'll know, Emma. You'll know when the right man comes along."

"Thank you, Elizabeth. You are such a comfort to me!" Emma

hugged her briefly, then pulled back and looked squarely at her. "But first, it's your turn. Let's finish getting you packed!"

Laughing once again, the sisters tucked the remaining items into the trunk and locked it. Their hearts were light as they looked forward to the upcoming day.

Pre-Wedding Conversations
POPLAR, ENGLAND

MARCH 22, 1860

The morning of Elizabeth's wedding dawned foggy and cool. Emma lay on the bed, looking up at the tall ceiling and breathing in the fresh scent of magnolia and blackthorn. As she hopped up to close the partially opened window, she saw mist rising off bricks and cobblestones below. It was mysteriously captivating.

"Overcast day," she announced, jumping onto the bed again.

"All the better for wearing my shawl," said ever-positive Elizabeth, sitting up and hugging the quilt to her chin.

Grabbing half of the quilt from her sister, she shook her head, which was blissfully free of pins this time of the morning. Her long dark hair fell in waves down her back as she breathed deeply of another scent. "Ah, smell that! Hattie must already be up." Hattie had lately taken to making muffins and popovers—something her father called 'quickbreads.'

Elizabeth inhaled deeply and then giggled. "I always love how bread smells! Mmmm! But Poplar won't get the benefit of that today because the shops are closed for the day."

"Both?"

"Yes! Can you believe it?"

"Hardly."

"Papa decided just to concentrate on the wedding today and worry about work tomorrow." Elizabeth was not a diva who needed to be in the limelight. She never brought attention to herself. Nevertheless, Emma noticed how pleased her sister was to have this special day set aside in her honor.

"Are you ready?"

"As ready as I'll ever be," Elizabeth replied.

"Then let's go see what our marching orders are."

The young women dressed as quickly as possible and pinned their hair out of the way. They were just trooping downstairs into #149 when they heard their mother call, "Girls! I need you."

"We're here, Mother Eliza," smiled Elizabeth.

"Good morning, Eliza," Emma said.

"Good morning, girls," Eliza smiled in return. Singling out Elizabeth, she asked, "How are you feeling?"

Emma secretly smiled. She knew their stepmother didn't like to be demonstrative, but her question showed love and concern for Elizabeth, nevertheless.

"I am well." Elizabeth grinned, raising a one-shouldered shrug. "Happy for the day! What do you need from us?"

Unsurprisingly, their stepmother had every detail mapped out. Being seven months into her fifth pregnancy did not slow the master organizer down a bit. "Elizabeth Charlotte, after you eat, you press these sliced almonds around the pound cakes. Then, use this lace template and sprinkle confectioner's sugar on top. Be careful not to jostle it, or the design won't be clear. Mary Emma, you glaze these sponge cakes and then place lady fingers around them."

"Vertically, correct?"

"Yes, vertically. We bought extra. I'm sure you'll have enough."

"My, these are tall cakes!"

"Your father certainly knows how to bake them! Now, Harriet Marie has already put in the muffins..."

"I can smell them!"

"...and as soon as we've eaten breakfast, she'll put in more for the wedding guests. After those come out, Harriet, I'd like you to play *Elephant and Castle* with Richie to occupy him. He'll be awake by then, and we don't want a three-year-old underfoot."

"Yes, Mama," the thirteen-year-old answered obediently. She enjoyed playing with her littlest brother, although truthfully, he wasn't old enough to play the game. He just liked the colorful cards and the large "Eh-phant," as he called it, in the middle of the board.

As the older two boys emerged, Eliza invited them to breakfast. "Here are muffins and milk, boys. We already prayed. George Alma, after you eat, go pick up anything left out in the common room. Stay *away* from the kitchen. No pranks from you today, especially while I am doing the sausage rolls!"

The blond-mopped six-year-old flounced into their common room, still holding a muffin in his hand.

Eliza called, "Come back here and put that down, young man!" Then, in a more reasonable tone, she said to her fifteen-year-old, "And William Francis, I'd like you to dust the common room and make sure our jackets and capes are by the door. It might be rainy today."

He nodded in acknowledgment. The sandy-haired boy glanced briefly at Emma. She knew he didn't relish interacting with others and was glad his mother didn't ask him to. It seemed he preferred staying in the background, saying and socializing little.

As Eliza assembled the sausage rolls, Emma asked, "Is Father at the main bakery?"

"He is!"

Emma's eyebrows scrunched together as she wondered why her mother had such a pleased lilt to her voice.

"He is making a rich brioche, and then he is decorating your cake, Elizabeth."

Elizabeth looked up from her almond pressing. "The tiered cake?" Tiered cakes were newly in vogue, and John was one of the first to embrace the style.

"Yes! I can just see his wrist swirling sugar ribbons and bows around the edges." Eliza flattened out a generous amount of dough for the sausage rolls.

"And rosettes," added Elizabeth, smiling.

Nodding, Eliza plopped meat into the center, then looked up mysteriously. "But that's not all. He showed me his design." Wrapping the dough around the meat, she said, "In recognition of your groom, who is a shipwright, he is creating five white Royal Icing dolphins leaping out of splashing 'water' on the middle tier!"

Emma's jaw dropped, and Elizabeth's eyes brightened. "That sounds wonderful!" Emma grinned at her sister, and they both giggled, setting to work again.

Preparations in the main part of the house were finished by one o'clock. Eliza directed everyone to their rooms to nap and rest before they needed to leave for the church at four.

Emma, Elizabeth, and Hattie went up to the girls' second-floor bedroom in #148, but there was no napping. The young women were too excited about the rest of the day ahead to close their eyes.

Thirteen-year-old Hattie handed a ribbon-tied paper roll to Elizabeth and then joined her older sisters on the double bed.

"What is this?" Elizabeth asked.

"Your wedding gift," replied Hattie modestly.

Elizabeth untied the ribbon. "Yellow, my favorite color!"

Hattie smiled more broadly. "I know."

Emma watched her sister unroll the parchment carefully. Elizabeth tilted it toward her. Emma saw handwriting so beautiful it could be calligraphy, and the edges were decorated in yellow roses and green leaves. "It's a poem," Elizabeth said, reading:

> "Rosy dimples, rosy lips,
> Roses to thy fingertips.
> Rosy-tinted all thy dreams,
> Sunlight in thy blue eye gleams.
>
> Blessing on thy Lov'd and thee
> We will plead eternally.
> We who love will love thee still,
> Wander wheresoe'er you will."

"That's lovely, Hattie," smiled Elizabeth, setting the parchment on her lap.

"Did you write it?" Emma asked.

"No," the younger girl shook her head, smiling. "I found it in the *Millennial Star*."

"Well, it's beautiful," reiterated her oldest sister. "But 'Wheresoe'er you will'? Where do you think I'm going? I'm just moving up the street!"

The sisters all laughed and fell back on the bed. Emma popped up, saying, "I have something for you, too." Retrieving it, she handed her sister a heavy rectangular box carefully wrapped in brown paper with a decoration of dried flowers on top.

Elizabeth admired the wrapping. "It's beautiful!" She weighed the package, pretending to guess. "Let's see, a set of square plates?"

"No. Try again."

"A shadow box framing my baby shoes."

"No. I used your baby shoes, and then Hattie did. There's nothing left of them to frame!"

"Hm, a very large doorstop?"

Looking hopelessly at Hattie, Emma smirked. "We'd better just let her open it."

"Go ahead!" Hattie urged.

Elizabeth carefully unwrapped the package to discover a fairy tale book by the Grimm Brothers.

"Oh, my!" Elizabeth exclaimed, rubbing her fingers carefully across the decorated cover. "It's beautiful. Wherever did you find it?"

"I had that book dealer in Covent Garden look for it for a few weeks. It was hard to find it in English. But look!" Emma eagerly riffled through the pages until a familiar illustration came into view. "Here's the story of Snow White and Rose Red. Now you can read it to your own children."

"Thank you, Emma!" The book was squashed between them as Elizabeth hugged Emma fiercely. Then she hugged Hattie just as intensely.

Setting aside the book, Elizabeth lay down on her back, followed by her sisters.

Looking up at the ceiling, Hattie asked, "So, who is marrying you, Elizabeth?"

Emma knew what was coming, and she tried not to chuckle as she heard the pretend solemnity in Elizabeth's answer: "Brother William Kidman."

Hattie huffed. "That's not what I meant. I mean, who is... um." She couldn't come up with the right word.

In unison, Emma and Elizabeth said, "Officiating the ceremony?"

"Yes! Who is doing that?"

Elizabeth said, "I wanted President Purdy to, but he doesn't have English authority."

"Church authority, yes, but not state," Emma said. Their neighbor, Samuel Purdy, was the president of the Poplar Branch of the Church of Jesus Christ of Latter-day Saints.

Elizabeth, wiping a wisp of blonde hair off her face, hastened to say, "He's not marrying us, but he and his wife are hosting the reception after the wedding."

Hattie said, "Oh, that's why we're going there." Then, she abruptly changed the topic, flipping her braid back. "You must have known William was the one for you when you found his birthday is the same as yours!"

Emma and Elizabeth burst into laughter. Hand behind her head, Elizabeth smiled indulgently. "You think sharing a birthday on April 25th was the clincher?"

Emma turned her head in her direction, the waves in her silky dark hair moving like water on the pillow. "You must admit, that's unusual, especially since you're so far apart in years."

Trying to justify her view, Hattie moved up to one elbow. Her thick brown braid fell over her shoulder as she argued, "It must have made you look more closely at him."

Glancing at Hattie, Elizabeth acquiesced, "I'm sure it did."

"But besides that, how did you know, Elizabeth?" asked Hattie dreamily.

"Ah, the question every young woman asks!" Emma chuckled, letting her thumbs idle in slow circles over her stomach. Emma wasn't going to admit anything today, but the question was one she had considered more than once.

Elizabeth replied seriously. "Well, William was the branch president before President Purdy—a couple of years ago. I remember hearing him give sermons and thinking how faithful he was in the Gospel. His testimony always inspired me."

Emma agreed, "That's a huge consideration for a marriage—finding someone faithful in the Lord's Gospel."

Looking at the stately molding circling the tall ceiling, Elizabeth went on, "But I think I knew William was the one for me because of how he treated his first wife and how he treated his children. He's a *good* man, a kind man."

Putting two and two together, Hattie said, "And so you knew he would be kind to you, too."

"Exactly."

Hattie's head fell to the bed again, and all three lay still for a moment before Elizabeth giggled, "Of course, considering how strict Papa was about us talking with boys, it's amazing that Emma or I have even spoken with the 'strong gender' at all!"

Emma's eyes closed momentarily, and she shook her head slightly. "It was before your time, Hattie—well, I mean you were still small— but Father called out one of our neighbor's sons, and Elizabeth and I never dared talk to boys after that!"

Elizabeth propped herself up on her elbow, telling Hattie the story. "It's true. Our private school was girls only..."

"As mine is," Hattie added.

"Yes. And this lovely young man named Michael..."

"Didn't he live on High Street?" Emma interjected.

"No, he lived around the corner on Lubbock's Court. Anyway, Emma and I were walking home from school, and Michael Culpepper came up to us. Thin, dark-haired, good-looking, just gaining his adult height. He was more Emma's age, so I walked on ahead, and she stood on the corner talking to him. I was just walking up the steps when the window flew open above me, and Papa called out in that stern voice of his for Emma to come inside right away."

"I was so embarrassed. We weren't doing anything wrong. We were just talking."

Hattie was confused. "Was it because he was a boy, and Papa didn't want you talking to them?"

Emma recalled, "Possibly. But I think it was because Michael went to the National Public School for Boys, and Father didn't think it ranked as high as our private one."

Elizabeth looked tentatively at Hattie. "Since Papa can't read well, he takes *our* education very seriously, as you've noticed."

Emma nodded, her dark hair brushing the bedspread. "Well, I got a reaming out at home, and Michael never stopped to talk again."

Hattie looked over, saying thoughtfully, "I'm sorry that happened to you."

Emma said, "Well, just you take a warning from that and watch what boys you're around!"

Elizabeth smiled coyly. "*You've* been around the Purdy boys, Emma. I've seen you dance with them at a church dance or two. How did *that* go?"

Emma sat up, looking at her sister, "For your information, *that* went just fine! As you know, Thomas is my age, and Samuel is a year older. We have all decided that we are much better suited as *brothers and sisters* in the gospel, rather than having any 'tendresse.'"

Elizabeth sat up, too, saying, "So, nothing exciting between you."

Emma grinned at her older sister. "No, nothing. But, Mrs. Bride-to-be, we've got to get you ready because 'nothing' is exactly what we have done so far!"

"You're right! Enough talking," scolded Elizabeth light-heartedly, rising from the bed.

Hattie's eyes shone with anticipation, and she clasped her hands excitedly at the thought of helping her older sister dress for her wedding.

The girls helped Elizabeth into her corset, petticoat, crinoline, and then the lightweight muslin dress she had selected. Eliza had offered to make something fancier—she *was a* dressmaker, after all. She'd been inspired by the dress of the Princess Royal, who married Prince Frederick of Prussia just two years before, but practical Elizabeth wanted something she could continue to wear on the Sabbath during the summer. The material she had chosen was cream-colored, dotted with tiny, understated yellow, pink, and white rosebuds and feathery green sprigs. It was beautiful in its own way, and the skirt swayed gently every time Elizabeth moved.

Suddenly nervous, Elizabeth asked Emma, "Are you getting every button in the back?" Then, turning to Hattie, she asked, "Is she missing any?"

Emma just smiled, knowing it was pre-wedding jitters. After tying a half-bow at her waist in the back, Emma plopped her down on a chair, where she styled Elizabeth's hair. They tried to get her to wear her hair in one of the newer styles, but sensible Elizabeth only felt comfortable with a bun. Emma, however, insisted on a high bun, also insisting on curling a few wisps at Elizabeth's cheeks with a narrow curling iron. Emma instructed Hattie to heat it on the panel at the side of their fireplace. "Check it until it's hot, Hattie," she directed while securely pinning Elizabeth's bun in place.

Carefully holding the curling iron so it wouldn't burn either of them, Hattie transferred the hot barrel to Emma. Then, before it could cool, Emma quickly created two feathery ringlets on each side of Elizabeth's face. It was a throwback to the styles of the forties—how their mother had worn her hair when they were tiny girls—but a wedding day was a good day to remember one's mother, was it not?

As Emma angled the jeweled comb in Elizabeth's high bun, she said, "Hattie, this was Mama Martha's. She wore it when they went to the theater."

Hattie reached out and delicately touched the jeweled scrollwork at the top. "It's so pretty."

Elizabeth smiled and nodded. Then she handed Emma a white lace concoction.

"This is Eliza's veil?"

Elizabeth's eyes shone as she said, "Yes!" It was a beautiful, filmy thing that drifted and floated just to her shoulders. None of them had seen it since Eliza and Father's wedding. Along with two small wall mirrors, it was one of the few things Eliza had brought to her marriage. She had resurrected it from her keepsake box and lent it to Elizabeth for this special day.

Looking in the mirror, Elizabeth couldn't stop smiling. Emma thought her sister looked fresh and new, innocent and beautiful. Emma couldn't stop smiling, either.

Slipping on her new shoes, Elizabeth was ready to go.

Emma looked out the second-story window at the gray day. At least it wasn't raining. "I hope your new shoes will not be ruined, dear sister!"

Emma had laughed when Elizabeth balked at buying new slippers. She'd said, "Eliza, I can wear my Sunday shoes. We've spent enough money on this wedding. After all, I'm just getting married and living up the street!" Eliza had answered, "All the more reason to give you a good send-off. You're only doing this once, daughter." Emma shook her head when her sister had sighed, relented, and become the owner of a pair of lovely new pale green slippers.

Emma and Hattie put on their Sunday outfits—not new, but perfectly usable—Emma's mauve and Hattie's green with ruffles. Then, after reheating the curling iron on the fireplace panel, Emma put a curl on each side of her own face (only burning herself once in her haste) while Elizabeth braided Hattie's long, thick hair and put a green ribbon near the bottom that matched her dress.

Hattie then ran downstairs to find their capes, leaving Emma and Elizabeth alone in the bedroom they had shared for so many years. Emma reached for Elizabeth's engagement shawl and, needing the nearness of her sister, placed it lovingly around her shoulders.

A panicked look crossed Emma's face fleetingly. This was the moment everything would change. This was it. This was the time she had been dreading. Elizabeth saw her sister's look and reached over. Securing her paisley shawl with one hand and holding Emma's hand in her other, Elizabeth stepped forward. Without another word but with determined smiles, the sisters stepped out of the bedroom of #148.

Wedding Day

POPLAR, ENGLAND

MARCH 22, 1860

"There you are, girls." Eliza sounded sharper than she probably intended. She was dressed in a rust-colored moiré Sabbath dress in which she had let out the seams to accommodate her coming expansion. A cream-colored lace collar, black crocheted shawl, and black snood over her strict bun completed her outfit. She looked at her husband and said, "We are ready to go."

"We're getting a late start," John said gruffly.

Emma thought, *Oh, Father, don't ruin this day by being so blunt.*

Will and the younger children were dressed and waiting impatiently.

John formally put out his elbow to his oldest daughter. "Are you ready, my dear?"

"I am!" Elizabeth smiled sweetly.

How Emma would miss Elizabeth! Her gentleness always had the ability to assuage and soothe their parents as well as help the younger boys to be obedient.

The family walked outside to the magnificent sight of two large carriages, each with a pair of matching horses. One pair was gray, and the other was black. They seemed spectacularly out of place in this workaday neighborhood.

"Where did they come from?" Georgie asked breathlessly. The boy who never stopped moving loved anything that moved fast.

Meanwhile, Richie looked up three times his height at the behemoths. Eyes wide, he grasped his mother's skirt, using it as a shield while staying as close to her side as was possible for a three-year-old.

"Grandpa Horspool sent them from Harlington," their father replied.

"Did he come, too?" Emma asked hopefully. She loved Grandfather William and the majestic animals he kept at his manor house. Being one of the older grandchildren, she had ridden most of the times they had visited their grandfather's estate in Harlington.

John replied, "No, he's older now and didn't feel up to making the trip."

Elizabeth added, "And Grandmother Charlotte died last year."

"Charlotte? That's your middle name!" Georgie loved putting two and two together.

Elizabeth smiled down at him, "Yes, I was named for her."

Will added, "As well as being named for the Queen."

Emma looked at him curiously. When no one else in the family had thought of the connection, Will had. She thought of how Elizabeth had told her to talk more to Will and Hattie. Indeed, it seemed there were depths to plumb in Will that had gone unnoticed before.

The family climbed into the first of the two carriages, and their father said, "Grandfather sent his groomsmen. They will drive."

He shut the door and knocked on the carriage's roof, and they started off in grand style. Emma grinned at the little boys, who fairly bounced in their seats, while Hattie waved gaily at everyone in sight.

"Back in the old days," said their mother, pressing down Hattie's overly enthusiastic arm, "the wedding festivities would have started at the bride's house, picking up people in the neighborhood until they came to the groom's house."

"Yes," agreed their father, straightening himself grandly on the leather seat. "These carriages certainly are a reminder of ceremony and formality. Very thoughtful of Grandfather Horspool."

Emma thought it far more than thoughtful. It was an absolutely stunning way to begin the celebration. Anyone passing by High Street or the church on East India Dock Road would know something special was happening.

Emma watched Elizabeth, who sat with a beatific smile. Her fingers toying with her shawl's fringe was the only sign of her nervousness. Emma knew this sister of hers—who had filled the shoes of their dead mother many times—to be utilitarian, practical, and efficient. Grandness was not her style. But right now, four magnificent horses must have made her feel like a princess, for Elizabeth couldn't stop smiling. Emma held her hand and grinned back at her.

The carriages stopped in front of the Kidman home, where William, waving merrily at Elizabeth in her carriage, followed his seven children into the large second one. The entourage proceeded to East India Dock Road, where the All-Saints Poplar Church was.

As they passed St. Anne's, Georgie asked, "Why couldn't Elizabeth get married in there? It's pretty." It was, indeed, a beautiful and imposing structure—perhaps the most notable landmark in the Tower Hamlets.

"Pwetty," Richie pointed at the beautiful white church.

"They can't get married there," Will volunteered. "William and Elizabeth need the non-conformist church."

Eliza and John looked pleasantly surprised. "Well, someone's been listening in Sunday School." He finished dryly, "Indeed, the Baptists, Wesleyan Methodists, and Latter-day Saints are all married and buried at the non-conformist church."

Eliza added, "It's called All-Saints."

Hattie, using a proper word this time, asked, "Who is performing the ceremony?"

Her father answered, "The Reverend Mr. Frost. He is a regular at the Dock Road Bakery. We often banter about our differing gospel ideologies. He's a pleasant man."

When they arrived, they all agreed that All-Saints was also an imposing structure. Will again volunteered information. "Did you know its foundations are of an even earlier century than St. Anne's? It's really old!"

"Apparently, our money for your private boys' school is being well used," Eliza responded.

Emma again noted his contribution. Will, it seemed, was a well-spring of trivia.

The carriages came to a halt in front of the church, and the two families tumbled out. William immediately found Elizabeth. Taking her hand, he bent his head toward hers, telling her she looked beautiful as they headed into the church. Emma walked behind the couple, delighted at the shy smile and blushing cheeks that defined her sister.

The Reverend Mr. Frost welcomed them and seated the families—the Horspools on the north side of the aisle and the Kidmans on the south. A few other people from the Poplar Branch and from the shipyard also attended. He attested that he'd had many conversations with baker John Horspool, and he mentioned William Kidman's high-quality work in the shipyard. He said that both families were valued in the community, and then he began his reflections on marriage before the actual vows were exchanged. "Let us review together I Corinthians 11:11: 'The man is not without the woman, neither the woman without the man in the Lord.'"

William and Elizabeth held hands, eyes sparkling, as the reverend's drone echoed to the heights of the ivory-stoned church.

At Emma's side, Hattie was gushing with joy. She saw the sparkle in the thirteen-year-old's eyes and imagined her romantic fantasies were being realized right before her. Grinning, Emma grasped Hattie's hand tightly, whispering, "I'd better keep you from floating up to the ceiling."

Emma was as happy as Hattie was. This was a glorious occasion. Holding her sister's hand, Emma leaned back in her pew, letting the beauty of the setting, the reverberation of the reverend's words, and the rightness of the couple before her settle over her. Why, if the church had burned down right that moment (heaven forbid!), Emma could see that Elizabeth wouldn't have known. Her entire being seemed melded with her husband-to-be; all she could see was William.

Emma glanced around. She saw Will looking noncommittally at the marble floor and saw the fond looks from her parents as they watched their daughter. Meanwhile, Georgie was poking Richie, pointing to a bird that had inadvertently flown inside the building. The poor thing fluttered high in the rafters, attempting to escape through a window, only to be foiled time after time. Richie pointed up to the roof, excitedly saying, "Birdie!"

"Shh!" Eliza put her hand on the boy's lips, looking across the aisle at Brother Kidman's children, as did Emma. They were all behaving, even eighteen-month-old Freddie, and didn't seem to have noticed the bird.

Finally, the authorized words of marriage were spoken, and Elizabeth was officially Mrs. Kidman. William leaned forward and tenderly kissed his new wife. Elizabeth beamed.

Emma thought it was the sweetest thing she had ever seen. Enraptured, she thought, *I can hardly wait until this happens for me, too!*

Then reality set in, and her second thought was, *"Yet, I will wait for 'Someday.' That's when discernment will tell me that the man I choose and who chooses me is the right one."* A subtle feeling of rightness came over her, bringing with it the surety that she *would* recognize him when the time came.

The newlyweds walked sedately to the entrance with their families and visitors quietly behind them. As soon as they reached the outer portico, a happy pandemonium broke out. Elizabeth and William were thronged with happy hugs, claps on the back, and cheery congratulations.

Then, the two families climbed back into the carriages driven by the four magnificent horses for the ride to the Purdy residence. William handed his new wife in next to Emma and then squeezed into the Horspool carriage himself. Across from them, their parents held Richie and even Hattie on their laps, with Will squashed into the corner.

"Up you go, Mr. Georgie!" cried William. "Right onto the lap of your new brother."

"You're not my brother!" he sang, with a devil-be-dare glint in his eye.

William tickled the boy, and Georgie burst out laughing. "Stop! Stop!"

"Not until you call me your new brother!" commanded the bearded gentleman.

"Never!" Georgie declared.

"Oh, dear. How shall we rectify this? Wife?" He looked at Elizabeth.

She held up her hands, letting him know this match was all his.

The wagon lurched over the cobblestones, jostling the occupants left and right against each other.

"Oh, my! This ride is so bumpy, you might be thrown out the window." The strong man lifted the boy off his lap as if he might fling him out the window.

"No, no!" shouted Georgie, to the delight of everyone in the carriage. He grabbed William's sleeve, amending, "I'll say it! I'll say it. You're my brother." Then, in a whisper, he added, "But you're really old."

William winked at his new wife. Georgie settled down, Emma chuckled, and Eliza said with mock seriousness, "What will the carriage driver think? Husband, perhaps we said yes to this match too quickly!" John merely shook his head and smiled at his wife and his new son-in-law.

The reception following the wedding was the event of the month. The Horspools and Kidmans entered Purdy's large home, and Elizabeth and William stayed in the foyer to greet the many guests. Having no assignment from their mother to tend to their brothers, Emma and Hattie walked together, looking at the crowd.

Hattie whispered, "Have you noticed the people here? Such a variety!"

Emma leaned over. "I'm astonished. Look at those three women dressed in satin, and the men with them in tails. But over there—I bet those are men who work with William at the shipyard."

"And their wives. They certainly are dressed differently from the silk-and-satin crowd."

"But no one seems put out by being near people outside their normal realm. They all seem perfectly happy to mingle. I bet some of Father's bakery clients are here, too."

"And members of our branch." Hattie wiggled her fingers, and

Emma nodded in greeting as they passed the Fletchers and the Athertons from the Poplar Branch.

Skirting past a knot of visitors who were engaged in a discussion of Bazelgette's sewer system—"Designed to eliminate the 'Great Stink' of the Thames from two years ago"— Hattie said, "It must be the power of President Purdy. Everyone seems perfectly happy."

"The Purdys are wonderful hosts. I'm so grateful to them for doing this for Elizabeth."

"Oh, look, Emma! Here's the food," exclaimed Hattie with relish.

John's bakery workers had brought over the baked goods while the families had been at the wedding ceremony. The cakes, pastries, breads, meats, and relishes were laid out on long tables on the main floor, and Emma heard many 'oohs' and 'aahs' when people saw and tasted the food. Growing up in a baker's family often meant long hours and hard work, but right now, she was glad that her father's expertise was benefiting her sister and was so appreciated by her guests.

There was a general press around the food tables, the guests having all been ushered into the Purdy's main floor common room. Emma and Hattie had just filled their plates when the cry was heard, "The Bride Cake! It's time to cut the Bride Cake!"

Brother Benton Berrycloth bustled forward and unveiled the tiered cake. He instructed the crowd, "Back up, please. Give it plenty of room and you'll all be able to see."

The guests obediently pulled back where they could see the marvelous cake in its solitary position in the middle of the table. Immediately, everyone had something to say about it.

"Isn't that the most beautiful thing you've ever seen?"

"Tiers. Who would have thought?"

"How is it held up?"

"Will you look at those fish?"

"What are they? Sharks?'

"No, I think they're dolphins."

"What are they there for?"

"I don't know, but it's beautiful!"

"I've never seen anything like it!"

Emma's smile split her thin face, lifting the dark curls at her cheeks. This cake was the most amazing thing she'd ever seen in her seventeen years, and she was so proud of her father and happy for her sister.

Elizabeth and William were brought in to stand beside it. As they were given a serrated knife, a teasing voice was heard over the others: "Don't cut into those dolphins!" It was Brother Bates from the Poplar Branch, a rotund shopkeeper with a rotund wife, six young children, and a smiling manner that made everyone think he was their best friend. John ordered much of his refined flour from him, and Brother Bates, in turn, sent customers to John.

William responded to the group, "I wouldn't be much of a ship-wright if I didn't know how to cut this intricate cake!" People laughed. A calculating look came into his eyes as he looked at Elizabeth. "Give me a minute to figure this out, sweetheart." Emma knew him well enough to know he was kidding—it was just a cake, after all. Elizabeth stood by, a little smile playing on her face as she patiently observed his bantering with the crowd.

Knife in hand, looking intently at the cake, William stroked his beard thoughtfully with his free hand. He introduced Mr. and Mrs. Campbell as important contributors to the Haymarket Opera Association, saying, "Pardon me," and moved around them. He looked at the cake from every vantage point, much to the delight of the watchers. "Excuse me," he said overly politely, as he introduced Mr. Barton, a manager of the shipyard, to the crowd.

Meanwhile, the group got into the fun, taunting him in a friendly fashion. "He can cut wood, but he doesn't know how to cut a cake!"

"He doesn't know how to saw through anything smaller than six feet!"

"Watch out for your home, Elizabeth! With a knife in hand, he might do almost anything!"

Emma's cheeks lifted in mirth like two red plums as she looked at the happy crowd. It gave her an idea of why people liked to be around William Kidman, and she was gratified they all were having such a good time, even though it was at his expense—his willing expense, as he was doing this on purpose. She chuckled as the group grew louder until William held up his hand and walked back to his bride. Elizabeth raised her eyebrows in question, and he answered with a nod. Then, both holding onto the knife again, they carefully cut through the cake on the opposite side of the dolphins. A roar went up from the group, and small pieces of cake were handed out to everyone. Emma noticed that the dolphins were carefully set aside on a white linen cloth.

After the Bride Cake was handed out, the women brought gifts to Elizabeth. She was moving into a house previously occupied by another woman, so she didn't need much, but it made her happy to have a few linens, dishes, and vases that were new and her own.

A new call went out. "For those who would like, we have dancing upstairs. You can go up this hall or up the stairs in the corner."

This was the cue Emma and Hattie had been waiting for. At thirteen, Hattie had only learned to dance at school, but Emma had been to several dances already. She was light on her feet—soaring like a water bird—and loved nothing more than swirling and swaying to music. For a chance to dance, she would have said yes to anyone who asked, even pudgy and off-beat Brother Bates.

Emma and Hattie eagerly went upstairs, where a large room had been cleared for dancing. The rug and the furniture had been moved, and a small band provided delightful dance music, mostly of a country variety. The main fiddler was cheeky Billy Purdy, only fifteen but already the leader.

The girls had the time of their lives. Will came upstairs but refused to dance. Thomas and Samuel Purdy, as well as men both old and young, saved the day. Emma danced the Scottish Caledonian Quadrille with Mr. Campbell's son, the Money Musk with Mr. Barton, and even Haste to the Wedding with Brother Bates. Emma grinned happily at Hattie whenever their whirling paths crossed.

At two o'clock in the morning (the music band having had only two breaks), people moseyed back to their homes. The next day was Friday, and the work of Poplar and the London docks would continue in full force. The littlest children had long ago fallen asleep on the couches and sofas that had been pushed aside, so they were picked up and draped in their parents' arms.

Emma reluctantly left the upstairs ballroom, laughing with her friend Thomas Purdy as they trooped down the steep corner stairs.

Hattie had come down the main stairs and was already next to Elizabeth while the bride stowed items in a wooden box. Saying goodbye to Thomas, Emma walked over to join them. "Are these the bride's gifts?"

Smiling, Elizabeth said, "Yes." In one hand, she held up a teal opaline vase embossed in gold and, in the other, a heavy brass rabbit paperweight. She put the brass rabbit down and, while wrapping the delicate vase in paper, said, "Look, Sister Bates made these." There were seven towels, marked Monday through Sunday, all embroidered in colorful huck toweling.

Emma said, "That was sweet of her. By the way, I danced with her husband."

"How was he?"

"A terrible dancer, but I still had a good time."

Elizabeth chuckled as she tucked the towels around the teal vase. Then she reached into the box and pulled out a flowered heart-shaped box made of thin white porcelain. "It's Royal Dalton!" Elizabeth whispered, carefully handing her the box.

"Who is it from?" asked Hattie.

"The Purdys."

"Oh, Elizabeth!"

"It's to hold my hairpins. Sister Purdy said she wants me to see something beautiful every day because she knows how crazy life will soon get caring for seven children."

"She has eight. She would know!" Emma smiled, handing her back the delicate heart box. "And we want to keep the new bride sane!"

"Amen to keeping the new bride sane!" Elizabeth agreed as she rewrapped the precious porcelain and placed it in the box.

Emma heard a tremulous tone in Elizabeth's voice that she hadn't heard before— something that belied the lightness of her words. Fear? Hesitancy? Before Emma could respond, Eliza and John came over. John was carrying a sleeping Richie, and Georgie kept leaning tiredly against his mother's skirt. "Hattie, Emma, it's time to go. Hattie, would you go gather our capes, please?"

Hattie left, and Eliza and John both hugged Elizabeth. It occurred to Emma that for her parents, this, too, was a significant goodbye. *Life will never be the same for them, either,* she thought. It gave her pause to think of things from her parents' point of view.

"I'll be just a moment," Emma said, and her mother nodded.

Emma noticed how painfully slow her sister was packing the items. She knew her well enough to realize her sister was nervous. It was now her turn to support Elizabeth.

Emma said, "This has been a wonderful day! All designed to help all of us accept the big changes in our lives."

"Such big changes," agreed Elizabeth, lips tight and eyes wide.

Taking both her sisters' hands, Emma whispered, "Remember all those wonderful things you said about William? Now, you get to see them firsthand, and you'll add your own stories. You get to live with him! Changes for sure, but wonderful!"

"You're right! Of course, you're right."

"Yes, I am. Change is good." Emma realized with chagrin that she was admonishing herself, not just her sister. "And remember, if you ever need a listening ear, I'm only...," she smiled as she inverted Elizabeth's advice, to which both chanted, "Down the street!"

They were still laughing when Emma went to meet her parents, and William came to collect his bride.

Inevitable Change
POPLAR, ENGLAND

NOVEMBER, 1861

Change. Emma didn't realize how many changes would occur in her neighborhood in the year and a half after her sister's marriage, starting with the birth of three little girls in the Poplar Branch—the Purdy's Mary, the Bates's Martha, and her own stepsister, Martha Jane. A sweet child, blonde Martha Jane was loved by everyone and was the apple of her father's eye.

Then, ten months after Elizabeth and William's wedding, twin daughters were born to them. Hattie was quick to point out that the Snow White and Rose Red tradition was still intact because Barbara was dark-haired, and Charlotte was light.

Deaths were changes, too—sad, but common changes. There was old Brother Bean, who was, well, old, and Sister Monahey, who slipped on her stairs. The one that affected Emma the most, however, was Elizabeth's oldest stepdaughter, Louisa, who died just after her fifteenth birthday following an arduous illness. Her devoted father was constantly by her side at the hospital, and he related to the family that she was not afraid. "The more she weakens, the more her testimony of the Savior grows," he told them.

Elizabeth told Emma how Louisa strengthened her family, how much she loved them, and how she gave tender little mementos to each. "Just before she died," Elizabeth related, "she said she looked forward to meeting her two sisters who had previously passed through the veil, whom she had never known." Choking, Elizabeth finished, "She knew she would be gathered to her Savior and to her mother."

Emma was filled with grief when the final news came, as well as gratitude for the strength in the Savior Louisa exhibited in her last days. Louisa was a stalwart example of faith. Emma couldn't help wondering if she would react with such faith when something truly hard happened to her.

Meanwhile, another eventful change was taking place right under her nose, but it had nothing to do with births or deaths. It was called the Gathering. The Saints of God were admonished by the leaders of the church to leave their native homelands and build up Zion in the Utah Territory.

Zion was something Emma had thought of many times. She had read about it often in the *Millennial Star,* the church's newspaper, published in Liverpool. She loved reading it, but as far as she knew, the only people in her branch to order the paper were her family and President Purdy. Each family ordered every other week and then shared with each other or with other members in the branch.

What a beautiful word was Zion! Almost since the beginning of the Church of Jesus Christ of Latter-day Saints, the idea of Zion had been broached by the Prophet Joseph Smith. According to the president of the mission in Great Britain, Joseph Smith had been translating the story of Enoch and had found it took him 365 years to create the city of Zion. But it was so successful, the entire city had been taken up to heaven—people, buildings, and all, apparently! Saved in heaven to be brought back in a future day when Jesus comes the second time, the city of Enoch would help create the Millennial peace.

Emma had brought up the topic several times with her parents. Zion was currently in the Utah Territory, and she wondered why they didn't pick up lock, stock, and barrel and move. It sounded so exciting. Every time she mentioned it, she received vague replies ending with

"Not now." She was happy when the topic was brought up on the way home from church that November day.

"What's Zion?" eight-year-old Georgie asked as he kicked through the crackling leaves on the way home from their chapel at 28 Penny Fields. He, Emma, and Hattie were sauntering in front of their father, Will, and Richie. Their mother had stayed home with seventeen-month-old baby Martha, who had a cold. "They were talking about it in church."

Before Emma could answer on one of her favorite topics, Hattie replied, "Zion is the pure in heart." Then, with a certain heat, she added, "It's people being *honest*." Yesterday, Georgie had taken one of her brown ribbons to wrap around a toad he'd found in the park, and he hadn't yet admitted it.

"Yes, it is that," agreed Emma, wanting to deflect a confrontation on such a golden, glorious autumn day. Kicking her own brown and yellow leaves, she said, "Did you know, Zion is also a place? In the early days of the church, that place was Missouri, and then Nauvoo, Illinois. Then, about the time Father was baptized, it moved to the West. Now it's in the Utah Territory, way out by *tall* mountains." Emma had only seen pictures of the Rocky Mountains, but they certainly looked impressive.

"I've seen pictures of them," informed Hattie. "They are very big!"

"Why can't Zion be here?" Georgie asked. It was a legitimate question.

"Maybe it will be someday, but for now, it's in Utah."

"Will *we* move?" This was the first the boy had paid attention to such a thing.

"I hope we will!" It still sounded so exciting and fulfilling to her. As if it were an illustration in a book, she imagined a long line of people from all the lands of Europe and the British Isles queued up to enter the newly built city of God. The city would be shining and clean, and the Saints would be kind and generous. They would move happily with energy and purpose. That's the picture she had of Zion.

Hattie asked, "I wonder why we haven't gone yet? Father joined the church in '46, and it's sixty-one now."

"The end of sixty-one!" Georgie said proudly, turning in a circle. Georgie tended to be quite literal, like his father.

Hattie skipped back to her father, tucking her arm through his. "Why haven't we gone west with the Gathering yet, Papa?"

"Yeah, Papa, why aren't we gathered?" Georgie asked.

"Oh, that's what you're talking about up there, eh?" He patted her hand. Georgie threw a pile of leaves at Richie, then darted away. Emma spun and walked backward, smiling as Richie ran to join Georgie in a leaf war. Georgie didn't seem to be listening for the answer to his own question, but she was interested in the answer.

Grabbing the back of Georgie's collar with his free hand, John towed the boy in. "It's a matter of timing, Georgie. So far, we haven't dared travel because of Mother's health."

Flipping her braids behind her, Hattie said knowledgeably to her little brothers, "That means all the babies she's had." Emma made a note to tell Hattie later that the little boys did not need that information.

Their father continued, "But while we're still here, we do what good we can for our local branch and for the missionaries. For instance, we contribute to the funds for the Elders when it comes time for them to return to Utah."

"They can't earn any money while they're here on missions," Hattie told her little brothers importantly. "So, how would they get home?"

Continuing, John said, "And sometimes we've even been able to help families emigrate who didn't have enough funds."

"Like the Johnstons?" Emma asked.

"Yes, and the Bagleys."

Emma turned around again, her mauve skirt swishing like a dance. She told the boys, "Father can help because our bakeries do so well."

"That's because *everyone* loves The King's Baker!" Hattie proudly announced.

"Well, and we feed the Elders." John cleared his throat, apparently warming to the topic of helping the local church.

Will added quietly, "And you let them stay in our house."

After their father married Eliza Bennett, they purchased the townhouse next to theirs, giving them #148 as well as #149 High Street.

That gave them a total of twelve rooms, and the extra rooms on the top story were used to house Elders who were working in the London area.

Currently, Elder Francis Marion Lyman, a twenty-two-year-old missionary from Utah, was staying there. Elder Lyman was a pleasant fellow with dark hair, broad cheeks, and a sturdy frame. His father, Amasa, was one of the Twelve Apostles—part of the reestablishment of Christ's ancient order within the LDS Church. Besides being one of the Twelve, one of Amasa's claims to fame was that he had been in the original company of Saints with Brigham Young that crossed the American plains in 1847, and it was that original company that had established the City of the Great Salt Lake.

Emma had noticed the Elders were among the few people Will felt comfortable talking to. It did not surprise her, therefore, that he knew some details about Elder Lyman's life. He offered, "Did you know that when Elder Lyman was just eight, he helped drive a yoke of cattle to the Salt Lake Valley?"

"I recall hearing something like that," said his father.

"That would be like you, Georgie," said Hattie.

"And when he was eleven, he drove an entire herd of cattle to California."

Emma thought those images would surely set a young man's imagination afire, especially when that fellow's normal excitement comprised winning a spelling bee at his private school. Elder Lyman was easy to talk to, with piercing eyes that seemed to let you know he wanted to get to know you. As for Emma, she had been drawn to him when he'd first had dinner with the Horspools. Then she discovered that he'd married at the age of seventeen and even had two little girls back home in a small Utah community called Farmington. Not being the sort to engage in fanciful dreaming, Emma stopped any silly romantic notions right then at the dinner table!

Will wasn't finished. "He went back and forth to California sixteen times. And on one of those times, he saw the cornerstone of the Salt Lake Temple laid!"

Emma hopped up to his side. "You are a fount of knowledge, brother."

"I listen," he said, somewhat defensively.

Walking up to the door, their father said, "I listen, too. And I heard that Georgie here needs to give a certain ribbon back to a certain young lady."

"Aww, Papa."

"I'll expect it in my room!" Hattie flounced inside happily.

Emma was happy that, in this case, her father's sternness would achieve justice for her sister.

Later that very day, during one of Eliza's tasty suppers of Yorkshire pudding, the topic of Zion and the Gathering came up again.

Emma said excitedly, "Let me read what I read in the *Star*." She leaped from the table and grabbed the newspaper. She read, "'Building in Great Salt Lake City proceeds with favorable rapidity. Zion is fast becoming an unmistakable living fact on the earth. While Gentile nations are conflicting with each other, Zion is growing and increasing in internal strength and becoming more and more entitled to the appellation of *the Home of the Saints*.' That's from an article called 'News from Home.'"

Her recitation was met with silence. That wasn't what she'd expected. She'd hoped for an enthusiastic response—an overwhelming, Yes, let's go! But what she sensed from her parents was hesitancy—the same response she'd been given every time in the past several years when she had suggested emigrating to Zion. She continued anyway, with shining eyes, "When the Savior comes to the earth again, don't you want to be with the Saints there in Zion?"

Clearing his throat, her father finally said, almost in an undertone, "You know we couldn't go earlier because of your mother's health. Five babies in seven years, and two of those died. Well, it would have been too much."

"I know, Father," Emma said submissively. "But Martha Jane is plenty old enough now. It seems like a good time to go."

Eliza joined the conversation. "I've been worried about the reports I've heard about the War between the States. It might make traveling difficult. What I read is that the U.S. Nation has been seized with madness and is rushing to destruction with headlong speed."

Emma rejoined, "All the more reason to go now. We don't want to wait so long that their war delays travel indefinitely."

Coughing slightly, Elder Lyman entered the conversation. "My father says that the world is going to hell in a handbag and suggests the Saints get to Zion while the going is good. Last year, over two thousand people emigrated from Great Britain, Europe, and Africa."

Will said, "His father is in the presidency of the European Mission, so, he would have a good perspective."

Emma smiled at her brother. He had never said as much, but his defense sounded like he was in favor of emigrating.

Elder Lyman placed his large hands on either side of his plate, and the group sensed whatever he said next would be important. "Come spring, I will finish my mission. When I leave, I've been asked to bring as many Saints as possible with me to Utah."

His announcement hung in the air. There was a finality to it, almost a challenge—a pronouncement that, once made, couldn't be revoked. Emma was electrified, and Will looked pleased. Her parents looked stunned, but not necessarily in a moving-forward way, and the younger children looked around the table at everyone else.

To break the silence, Elder Lyman said, "Miss Harriet, why don't you and I clear up these dishes?" As they both stood to help, he said, "Thank you for dinner, Sister Horspool. Again, it was splendid!"

Murmurs of agreement and thanks were heard as everyone moved from the table. Emma knew that she couldn't say anything else just yet. She would have to wait on her parents, as she had before, to see what they decided.

❧

OVER THE NEXT couple of weeks, Emma was aware that her parents often discussed the matter. She'd catch a brief word here (civil unrest) and half a response there (selling all...). She heard the rise and fall of their conversation behind closed doors, although she couldn't hear any words. There was a tension in the house that didn't ordinarily exist. Not a negative tension, but one of indecision. She also heard them speak with various branch members, some of whom had decided to leave Poplar and emigrate to the Utah Territory.

Wanting to do something herself during the interim, Emma fasted and prayed on her own. She was seeking the gift of discernment that Elizabeth had told her she had. She identified it as following the promptings of the Holy Ghost. She thought of times in her life when she had truly felt God's Spirit. One was her baptism in Bow Creek when she was nine (A lovely experience, although the River Lea flowing into it was so cold)!

Then there was the time when she was somewhat older, she and Elizabeth had been tending toddler Georgie, and he'd gotten lost. They'd looked everywhere in their big double house. Finally, she and Elizabeth had prayed, and Emma got the distinct impression that he was under the drapes in the south-facing common room. Sure enough, there he was, completely hidden by heavy velvet drapes. Relieved beyond measure, they woke him, and he told them it had been warm by the window, and he'd just fallen asleep. She knew that, without that impression, they never would have found him.

Another time, she'd been so sick that her father had given her a priesthood blessing. She had felt better almost immediately and recognized that as a gift of the Spirit.

On Wednesday, she sat on her bed gazing at Poplar Park, which she could see from her window. She mustered faith that God's Holy Spirit would manifest positive feelings to her if emigrating was the right thing to do. She considered what she'd been reading, thinking about, and praying over. What did moving really mean to her? She'd been looking through rose-colored glasses, yet now, when she thought of it, she felt tentative. She finally faced what she'd be leaving.

First off, she thought, *it means I'll leave my house, my neighborhood, my city, even my country. Why, I've lived in England my whole life! I'll never see Grandpa Horspool again, or Harlington and the horses. When it comes down to it, do I really want to leave? In America, would they expect me to speak in that horrible, flat tone they have? Heaven forbid! Do they dress differently there? Not as far as I know. Well, that isn't important; Eliza and I can always learn to sew differently and wear new styles.*

She let her mind run wild. *We'll be going to the Utah Territory— what kind of houses do they live in? Dirt? Log? Sod? Here we have solid buildings and established neighborhoods. Theater? Opera? Legislature? There is so much about Utah I don't know, even though I've been reading the* Millennial Star *for years!*

Just then, church bells chimed at the top of the hour in Poplar and nearby Limehouse. Their sound bounced against her ears like flies hitting a window. *Do they have bells in Utah? I don't think so.*

And the war. She read about the War between the States every week. The English consensus was that it was ridiculous and that someone should stop it. But the States continued fighting to uphold their point of view, so no, they weren't stopping. *We'll be heading right through the middle of it. And don't both sides conscript men for their army? Georgie and Richie are way too young, but Will and Father are of an age to be put into the Army. Taken against their will? That doesn't even bear thinking about!*

What about Father's job? Surely, they need bakers in Utah! Would he be able to bring the equipment he needs? He can't bring the large oven with the wonderful door because it's built in.

And Elizabeth. Here, Elizabeth is so close. Will she and William want to come? If I don't have Elizabeth to talk to, who will I have?

When she started listing the trees—*Do they have blackthorn and magnolia trees in Utah?*—she knew she was going astray.

Pulling back, she realized if she had faith, Heavenly Father would provide. Faith was the necessary element. What was essential was her testimony of Christ and what He wanted from His burgeoning church —this church that was barely thirty years old. She listed essentials in her mind: 1. Jesus had been resurrected. He was very much alive and had charge of His Saints. 2. He would be coming a second time, and when He did, He wanted a Zion where He could reside with people who believed in His Father as He did, and who were willing to be obedient to His Father as He was. 3. He loved all mankind. That's why he died—because he loved every single person. He wanted as many people as possible to choose Him and to join Him—thus the many "Come Follow Me" verses sprinkled throughout the scriptures.

Suddenly, with her heart pounding, Emma knew that she, Mary Emma Horspool, would always pledge to be one of His followers. She wanted to "Come unto Christ." As she pledged and prayed, a warm feeling swept over her that made her comfortable and happy all over. She felt complete and satisfied. *I feel like a cozy blanket has been wrapped around me at the same moment I feel like jumping for joy! How crazy is that— opposite feelings at the same time!* She felt this calm completeness was the answer to her prayers, and that emigration was something the Lord wanted.

She waited patiently until Sunday. After the church meeting, her father gathered the family together and formally announced, "Children, Mother and I have decided that at long last, we will emigrate to the Utah Territory. Come spring, we will go to Zion."

Emma beamed as a cheer went up from her siblings. Finally, it was their turn!

Family Preparations
POPLAR, ENGLAND

FEBRUARY 1862

It was the second Saturday in February, and Emma and Hattie finally had some time off. They had been helping their mother with the fancy ornamentation on her clients' dresses for three months, and the work, for now, was finished. Fourteen-year-old Charlotte Purdy had invited Hattie to sew reticules for their travels. The Purdys were also emigrating come May, and having a personal bag to carry on your arm was a good idea. Emma went along to read their latest issue of the *Millennial Star*.

"It's so exciting at our house," Hattie confided in Charlotte. "It's like getting ready for Christmas, but so much bigger!"

Charlotte smiled. "Same at our house."

"Yes," Emma agreed, looking up from the overstuffed chair where she was reading. "Ever since we decided to leave, everything we do is directed toward moving."

"It's true. Mother has long lists of things that need to get done—"

"Eliza always has lists," Emma inserted dryly.

"Starting with clothes. Oh, Charlotte, you can't believe how clever she is with our clothing."

Her blonde friend's bow bounced in her hair as she laughed. "She is a seamstress, so, yes, I can! Tell me what she's doing, and maybe we can use some of her ideas."

"Well, first, she is allotting two dresses for each of us."

From the depths of the newspaper, Emma intoned, "'One to wear and one to wash.'"

"Yes, but we get a third dress to store in the bottom of a steamer trunk, so we'll have something nice to wear when we get to Zion. Isn't that grand?"

Charlotte agreed, but amended, "We have so many children, I'm not sure we can do that, even though those chests are huge."

Putting down her paper, Emma said, "Speaking of steamer trunks, Eliza is out buying two today."

"Who is home with the baby?"

"Will is. Don't worry. It's Martha's nap time, so he doesn't have to play with her."

"He doesn't feel comfortable around tiny girls, does he?" asked Charlotte.

"Any girls!" Emma chuckled. Then, more thoughtfully, she continued, "I've wondered if being the sole brother for so long in a threesome of sisters made him a loner."

"Or maybe his personality is just reticent," Charlotte said understandingly.

"True. But I wouldn't mind his conversing a little more readily."

Lifting her work to look at it, Hattie said, "Back on the steamer trunks, I asked Mama to get the ones with rounded lids."

"Aren't they more expensive?" asked Charlotte.

"Yes, but they hold more. Plus, you can't stack anything on top of them, so *they're* the ones that are top and therefore, more accessible. Two good reasons."

Emma looked at her sister. "I know that's what you read, and I agree that makes perfect sense. But I can't help feeling we should get the flat-top ones. I don't know why, but that's what I keep feeling."

"Is that your discernment telling you?"

"Maybe."

Hattie sighed. "I guess we'll find out when Mama gets home."

Changing the topic, Emma said excitedly, "Eliza's doing something else very shrewd. She's separating the bodices from our skirts, essentially turning them into jackets. It's more work, but it will be more flexible."

"Oh, that is a good idea."

"She's also putting less fabric in the skirts, so they'll be less cumbersome."

Hattie paused, needle in the air, "One hundred ten inches at the bottom instead of one hundred forty-four inches, I believe she said."

Emma added, warming to the subject, "And she's raising the hems by *four* inches. She said, 'We don't want to be immodest, but we won't be walking on ballroom floors!'"

The girls laughed, and Hattie continued. "I told her I wanted each of us to have two aprons. Those things are bound to get so dirty. Hm, we probably need three!"

Emma said, "Eliza made a sweet little apron for Martha. She doesn't need one, but she'd feel left out if we all had one and she didn't."

"It's pink, and it has flowers on it," Hattie added. "It's the prettiest one of all!"

"As far as sunbonnets, I think one will be adequate," said Emma. "I dread wearing those things. I think they look awful."

"I think they're cute!" Hattie said, "and mine is going to be made from leftover material from the green suit Mother made for that rich Mrs. Campbell. So, it will be a very fancy one!" She giggled and then tied off her thread.

Practical Charlotte smiled, "Well, they are designed to keep the sun off. But I think they're cute, too."

Hattie said excitedly, "I told Mother that it would be easiest for us on the trail if each of us has a different color. So, my dresses are green..."

"Green always looks wonderful on you," smiled Charlotte.

"Emma's are blue, Mama's are tan, and, of course, Martha's are..."

Charlotte joined Hattie in saying, "Pink!" They laughed again.

Charlotte asked, "What about the boys? And your father?"

Hattie waved her hand aimlessly. "Oh, I don't care about them. They all have white shirts and a couple of pairs of trousers. The little boys are having some things remade from Will's and Father's old clothes."

"And two pairs of boots each," added Emma. "Boots will be really important with all that walking."

Charlotte shook her head. "There's so much to bring! And we haven't even mentioned food or pans or tools!"

Emma said, "I think mostly we need to bring clothes and what tools our fathers need to carry on their trade in Zion. A lot of the food and other things we can buy in Nebraska, when we get that far."

Hattie looked at her. "Mother said we'll take some bedding with us, too. You don't know what accommodations will be on the ships."

"Oh, look at this!" Emma pointed to an article in the *Star* titled 'For Those Who Emigrate.' "It suggests we bring cinnamon, cloves, or nutmeg, dried currants or raisins, and herbs like rosemary, basil, and thyme because the food on the ship is quite bland, and having something extra for flavor is wise."

"We'll have to remember to tell Mama," Hattie said.

Laying her project in her lap, Charlotte broached a delicate subject. "Is what I heard about your father true?"

Emma looked up from her chair. "That he's going early?"

"Yes."

"It's true!" Hattie exclaimed with some heat. "I hate that he's leaving before us."

"Is it safe?"

"I don't know." Emma shook her head. "It will make it harder on Eliza, but she and Father feel it's for the best."

"What will you gain?"

Hattie sat petulantly with her hands in her lap, her head turned away from the other girls. She flipped her braids behind her, something she did when she was nervous.

Emma answered, "They think he'll have a better pick of wagons and teams if he's there earlier than most of the others. From what we've heard, a *lot* of the Latter-day Saints will emigrate this year."

Charlotte nodded. "Well, that does make sense, then."

Emma added, "He's going on the *Kangaroo*. It's a steam ship instead of a sailing vessel, so he'll get there even faster."

"That does sound fast!" Charlotte said. Then, turning the lining of her little purse inside out, she continued, "I hope we can be on the same ship together!"

"Wouldn't that be wonderful!" Hattie enthused.

"Time will tell. Papa is trying to hire on as a carpenter, so his passage is paid for."

Emma went back to her reading, only half looking at the page. Instead, she wondered what this trip across the ocean would be like. As exciting as it seemed right now, there would surely be trials and unforeseen complications. She and Will were the oldest children, so Eliza would have to rely on them since Father wouldn't be there. Emma had a feeling that her past 'normal' of school endeavors, home, and sewing were about to have a drastic change.

❧

APRIL 1, 1862

Emma and Hattie bustled about her parent's side of their townhouse helping Eliza pack for John. Four shirts, extra trousers, socks and eight large handkerchiefs lay in a pile, ready to be put in his valise. It was three in the afternoon, and their father was leaving England. Tomorrow.

Emma skirted the two large steamer trunks in their common room, happy to be inside this morning. Rain came down in torrents, darkening the inside of their house and bringing a chill with it. Wind lashed up the street, tearing new green growth from bushes and trees and plastering them against their windows. Hopefully, it would be better weather tomorrow when her father was set to leave.

Flipping a braid behind her shoulder, Hattie tossed his valise on top of one of the trunks. She was still exasperated that her mother had bought trunks with flat lids. "I did my research," she complained. "I don't know why Mama bought these."

"I know," Emma said, appeasing her. "But she said when she got to the emporium, she kept thinking about what I said and then felt *strongly* that the flat-top ones were what we needed."

Prosaically, her sister acquiesced. "Maybe in the future we'll find a reason."

Eliza asked the girls to go find Papa's shaving kit.

Obediently walking upstairs, Hattie called, "Mama, where's his bag?"

Emma followed her, and found his shaving brush, cream and razor while Hattie located the bag. They finished packing, then carried his valise downstairs where they saw their father sitting in the common room talking with a gentleman. Not wanting to interrupt, the girls stayed in the hall.

Hattie whispered, "That's Mr. Campbell. He's the rich businessman."

"I know," Emma nodded, whispering back. "I danced with his son at Elizabeth's wedding."

Hattie's hand whipped up to cover her mouth, which formed an 'O.'

Mr. Campbell was dressed formally in a handsome black coat with tails while her father looked too casual in his shirt sleeves, suspenders, and vest. The men seemed comfortable with each other, though. It sounded like her father was in the middle of explaining the basic methods that Latter-day Saints had for traveling across the American prairie.

"One way is to go by "church train," said their father. "That consists of wagons owned by LDS members from the Utah Territory and sent from the West to pick up emigrating Saints who have arrived in the East."

"In other words, members of your church who don't have enough funds to finance the whole trip themselves."

"Exactly. A second way is called P.E.F. or the 'Perpetual Emigrating Fund.' Money is set aside to bring the poorest Saints out of all countries to Zion. The church provides the traveling money, and after the new immigrants start making a living in Zion, they repay the fund—thus making it perpetual."

"Both of those methods are very clever. Your church has really thought this through."

"Indeed. They have so many emigrating to the Utah Territory—over two thousand last year—they try to accommodate every situation. Now, the option that we will take is to go in an 'independent company', that is, a group of wagons owned by individuals."

"I imagine you have done well for yourself with the "King's Baker" shops," Mr. Campbell assessed frankly.

"We have. We'll buy own fit-out, which is precisely the reason I am going on ahead."

"Ah, getting ahead of the pack," nodded the businessman astutely.

"That's the idea," John said, smiling.

Standing, Mr. Campbell said, "Well, I wanted you know Mrs. Campbell and I will miss you, Eliza, and John."

"Don't you fear. Benton Berrycloth will be handling the bakery from here on. I believe he'll do a good job."

"I certainly hope so. Sometimes when I'm hurrying to work for a business meeting, my breakfast is simply the heavenly scent of bread that you provide all through the streets!"

John chuckled and reached his hand to shake Mr. Campbell's hand. To his surprise, Mr. Cambell thrust into his hand an envelope, nodding as he shook John's hand. Then he left.

Emma and Hattie walked into the common room. Emma asked, "Why did Mr. Campbell come visit?" followed by Hattie's curious, "What's in the envelope?"

Eliza, wiping her hands on a dish cloth, came in as he said, "Let's see."

He opened the envelope and spread out for their view one hundred pounds.

"My goodness!" Eliza said. "How generous of Mr. Campbell."

Scratching his head, John agreed. "Yes. What a surprise. A very pleasant surprise!"

"Do you think it's to help you travel better?" Hattie asked.

"Yes, I think that's exactly what it's for," he agreed. Handing Eliza the envelope, he donned his coat and hat and said to Emma, "Remember, I'll want you and Elizabeth at the bakery within the hour." Then he went out into the rain.

"Why does Father need you?" asked Hattie.

"I honestly don't know," answered a bewildered Emma. "I guess I'll find out when I get there."

The Gospel

POPLAR, ENGLAND

TUESDAY, APRIL 1, 1862

Emma put galoshes over her half boots, flung a shawl over her shoulders, and donned her serviceable black hat with feathers. Grabbing a lightweight cane-rib umbrella, she hoped the rain wouldn't ruin the feathers on her hat.

As she opened the door, she was surprised when Will called, "He's probably going to have you clean all his worst pots and pans from the bakery. Have fun!"

Emma rejoined, "You have fun hefting those heavy steamer trunks, brother." Then she was gone, happy that he'd said something to her.

The rain had finally stopped, leaving just a light patter on her umbrella. The wind, too, had died, and the worst she had to endure was walking around the newly formed puddles.

What did Father want with her? He was cryptic when he had told her last night to come to the bakery with Elizabeth. Her sister's house was on the way, and she was ready when Emma knocked. Her oldest stepdaughter, fourteen-year-old Eloise, had invited her friend over to help tend her five younger siblings and the twin girls.

"Do you know what this is about?" asked Emma as they swung down from the Kidman porch.

"Not a clue. Father stopped by on his way home last night. He was very cryptic."

"That's what I thought!"

"Maybe some last hurrah before he leaves for America."

"Or, like Will said, maybe just to have us scrub and pack."

Elizabeth laughed. "If that's what it is, we'll do it gladly!"

To their left was the park where they ice skated in winter and to their right were other houses and apartments like theirs. They passed the small fire and nursing building, a livery, and a neighborhood mercantile store. Turning onto East India Dock Road, the buildings all became business establishments and then thinned out as the road reached the Thames.

Just as Mr. Campbell had said, the heavenly scent of bread filled the air as they neared The King's Baker.

"Oh, smell that!" Emma drank in the delicious aroma.

"I'll miss it," Elizabeth nodded.

Brother Berrycloth opened the door to the sisters, and Emma breathed in the pleasant scent of sugar. She wondered fancifully if the delectable aroma of bread and sugar hovered in every corner of the workroom, even when nothing was being baked.

Their father greeted them. "Hello, girls. Thank you for coming." Emma expected him to be all business, even curt and abrupt. To her surprise, he was blithe and almost care-free. Beaming, he continued, "Today we are making a chiffon cake."

Well, the mystery of *what* was solved, but the *why* remained a puzzle. She would be patient and let it remain a mystery for the moment.

"Each one of us has an assignment," he began.

That sounds list-oriented, like Eliza, Emma thought. *Either she rubbed off on him, or he rubbed off on her.*

"Elizabeth, you measure the cake flour, sugar and other dry ingredients according to the receipt card on that counter. Sift them four times." She washed her hands, put on an apron, and went to work.

"Emma, you beat these five yolks until they turn a lemon color.

Then add oil and my secret ingredient—" He wiggled his eyebrows, and Emma almost fell back a step. She hadn't seen him do anything so silly and nonchalant since she was little. "—the juice of three oranges." He cocked his head as if this were the greatest secret of all time.

Holding back a smile, Emma stepped to the bowl containing the egg yolks after washing her hands and aproning and began beating.

"Benton, my good man, it's your job to check the temperature of that magnificent oven."

"Yes, sir! I'm getting it to a steady three hundred twenty-five degrees."

"And make sure the tall tube pan is clean and dry."

"Yes, indeed," agreed the cheery, balding man.

"While you were on the way, I beat the egg whites to stiff peaks. No under-beating the whites!"

"It took fifteen minutes," Brother Berrycloth told the girls proudly, "and that was using the special beating paddle."

Turning it over as he looked at it, John said, "This paddle is small enough I can take it with me. I'm sorry, Benton, you'll have to buy a new one."

"So you are buying the bakery, Brother Berrycloth?" asked Emma politely.

"Isn't that splendid!" he enthused. "I have funds enough for the mortgage and a few basic pans and baking sheets. The other things, I can acquire as I go along."

"And of course he gets the large oven with the beautiful iron door that shuts the heat in so evenly," John said wistfully.

Elizabeth chuckled, "It's built in, Papa. Of course he gets that!"

Emma finished adding the orange juice, still musing over *why* they were there. It seemed like such an odd thing to do the day before he left his home forever, and he easily could have done all of this by himself. Indeed, he usually did. But he offered no clues.

"All right!" John brushed his hands together, looking at his daughters excitedly. "Are we ready? Bring your bowls over."

He thoroughly mixed the dry and the wet ingredients to a puffy batter, and then, ever so gently, he folded in the stiff egg whites.

Lovingly cradling each spoonful with a graceful wrist action, he sang a nursery rhyme.

> "Mary, Mary, sitting on a gate
> Eating cherries off a plate.
> Grace, Grace, dressed in lace,
> Went upstairs to powder her face."

Emma was dumbfounded. Who was this man? This was a different father than the stern, starched person he was at home. He was so free and funny here. With perplexed eyebrows, she looked at Elizabeth, who just shrugged and smiled. Apparently, Elizabeth had known a different John Horspool all this time.

When the whites were incorporated into the batter, John scooped the batter into the tube pan, asking Benton, "Are you sure the oven is at the right temperature?"

"Yessiree, it is!"

John carefully placed the pan inside and gently closed the door. "I'll surely miss this lady." He lovingly patted the oven. "It was after I bought this oven with its magical door that my business here in Poplar really took off," he explained to his three workers, as he rubbed his hand on the gold scrollwork around the outside edges of the door, barely touching the hot metal.

"It was a good investment," Brother Berrywhite agreed.

"That it was. That it was," John nodded. "All right, the cake bakes for fifty-five-minutes. While it's baking, we'll wash, dry and pack what's left here that Eliza can sell."

Emma grinned. Will was half wrong, because none of the pans needed heavy scrubbing. But they *were* cleaning and packing, so Will was half right. She'd never admit it to him, though.

Everyone set to work, with John frequently checking the watch at his waist. However, the lovely smell of the golden cake let them all know it was done before his watch did. John put the cake, still in its metal pan, upside down over large metal funnel.

Winking at Elizabeth, John asked Emma, "Do you know why we do this?"

She looked perplexed. "In all these years, Father, I've never seen you bake a chiffon cake. I was always home at the confectionery. So, no, I don't know."

Leaning conspiratorially on the counter, he said, "It lets it keep its height as it cools."

"How does it do that?" Emma looked perplexed.

John spread his hands out to Elizabeth, letting her answer the question.

"If you just take it out and set it on a rack, it will settle. The cake will flatten."

"Amen," Father said appreciatively.

"Ahh!" Emma said, enlightened. Then she asked, "By the way, Father, who did you say this is for?"

Quirking an eyebrow, he smiled mysteriously. "You'll find out."

Emma looked at Elizabeth, and both looked quizzically at Brother Berrywhite and their father. The men turned their backs on the girls, finding themselves suddenly quite busy packing cooking sheets. The young women shook their heads, smiling at such secrecy, and went back to their packing.

Seeing Emma wrapping a glass plate, her father directed, "Leave that out, Emma." She complied and left it on the counter.

When the cake had cooled, John removed the base of the metal pan, and then, slicing carefully around the edges with a long knife, he gently removed the cake. Here was the moment of truth! It was goldeny-brown on the outside with hints of gold on the inside. He proclaimed it perhaps the best chiffon cake he had ever made. He hummed while he swirled icing all over it— a rich, creamy frosting made of confectioner's sugar, butter, cream, vanilla and a touch of orange extract.

"I only frost the most expensive cakes," he half-sang to the girls, while Brother Berrycloth grinned. Again, Emma saw a different side to her father, and envied Elizabeth all those years she'd been able to work with him.

Finally, he dusted the cake with gratings from the orange peels, so it looked as well as smelled heavenly. After sending Emma outside to find mint leaves in the small bakery garden, he picked and washed the three best ones and put those on top with three hard-icing peach-colored roses he had made ahead of time. That finished it off beautifully.

"Now it is time," he announced. The cake was placed on the glass plate and boxed up safely. He looked at his daughters and said, "We are taking this to the Reverend Mr. Frost."

Emma said to her sister, "Oh! The clergyman who married you."

"Yes, it sounds like it," Elizabeth replied.

"You have your walking shoes on, don't you, my dears?" asked their father.

"Yes, Papa, my shoes are fine," answered Elizabeth while Emma nodded and put her galoshes over her half boots.

As they walked out the bakery door, leaving Brother Berrycloth still packing items inside, Emma asked, "Why are we taking this to the Reverend Mr. Frost?" Elizabeth, also, was very perplexed.

"You will find out," came John's cryptic reply.

The sun had finally come out and dried the puddles. Emma didn't open her umbrella, and drops still fell occasionally from tree leaves, plopping on her hat or shoulders.

They carefully skirted the ruts made by the spring rain on the muddy road as they walked toward the non-conformist church on East India Dock Road. When they reached All-Saints, John knocked on the rectory door. The Reverend Mr. Frost appeared, not wearing his official Sunday garb.

"Oh, Mr. Horspool, Mrs. Kidman, Miss Horspool. How good to see you! Won't you come in?"

He ushered them inside, and John carefully lifted the cake from the box. It seemed to gleam gold and white like one of Queen Victoria's formal gowns. Handing it to the reverend, he said, "This is for you and Mrs. Frost."

"Baker Horspool, it's wonderful. An amazing cake!" He couldn't seem to keep his eyes off it. "Thank you! But why have you brought it?"

"Well, Reverend Mr. Frost, I am leaving for America tomorrow. I wanted to give you the last thing I baked."

Startled, the reverend looked up at John. "Why, that's very kind of you, John."

"I have always been pleased that you have taken such care here at the non-conformist church. It's been good to talk with someone who believes in equality and religious freedom. I've also been gratified that you accepted a couple of tracts from our church, and, of course, we were pleased to have you officiate Elizabeth's wedding."

John smiled at his oldest daughter as Mr. Frost concurred, looking at John and Elizabeth, "I was happy to do it for you."

"Before I go, I wanted to give you my testimony that the Church of Jesus Christ of Latter-day Saints is the true Church of God, and there is none other."

Mr. Frost collected himself, clearing his throat, and said, "Now, John, I'm happy that you believe what you do, but..."

"Mr. Frost," John interrupted, "when you and your good wife eat this cake, I want you to remember that the cake needs ingredients and heat. But without the heat, you'd just have batter, wouldn't you say?"

Confused, the reverend nodded, "Yes."

John went on, "The doctrine we share is that just like the flour, sugar, and eggs are all separate ingredients that combine to make the cake, the Father, the Son, and the Holy Ghost are three separate personages who combine their gifts to help us. Then the 'heat', Reverend, is revelation. Revelation is a living thing that comes through the Holy Ghost to tell us God's will. Revelation puts it all together. Reverend, I know you have received revelation many times in your life as you have acted in your calling here at All-Saints. I also know you can receive a specific revelation that what I have spoken is true. I have searched my heart, and I can tell you what I say is the truth."

The Reverend Mr. Frost, still holding the marvelous cake, marshaled himself and smiled at John. "Thank you, 'Brother' Horspool. That's what you're called in your church, isn't it?"

John and his daughters nodded, smiling.

"I will share what you say as my good wife and I partake of this beautiful cake. You have done me an honor in bringing it."

"Reverend, I would have it be more than an honor. I would have you learn of the Church. Even though I will have left England, there are still missionaries here in Poplar."

"I will remember, John. Thank you all for coming."

Reverend Mr. Frost bowed himself back out of the small front foyer, opening the door for them and clearly signaling it was time for them to leave.

As the three turned, Mr. Frost asked quickly, "Mrs. Kidman, are you leaving, too?"

She turned back with a smile, "Yes, soon. My husband is a shipwright and has been hired on a ship across the ocean. We will go with him and then across the plains to Utah."

A pained look crossed the reverend's face as his imagination took over. "It sounds like a long and difficult journey. I wish you the best." His voice did not match his words.

"Thank you, Reverend. I'm sure we will be fine." Elizabeth answered with a quiet strength that astounded Emma. She showed none of the hesitation or anxiety the reverend did.

Pasting on a smile, he returned, "I'm sure you will. Well, goodbye to all of you!"

The door shut and the three made their way toward their homes.

Elizabeth said, "That was a lovely thing you did, Father."

"I hope he does tell his wife when they eat that cake," Emma added.

"I hope so," John replied. "But it doesn't matter. We must each do our part in whatever way we can, and that must suffice. Their conversations and decisions will be theirs alone."

Elizabeth and Emma linked arms on each side of their father as they walked on the cobblestones toward home.

Children were out jumping rope now that the rain had quit. They chanted,

> "'Oranges and lemons' say the bells of St. Clement's.
> 'When will you pay me?' say the bells of Old Bailey.
> 'When I grow rich,' say the bells of Shoreditch.
> 'Pray, when will that be?' say the bells of Stepney.
> Here comes a candle to chop off your head.
> Chip chop, chip chop, the last man's dead."

Emma chuckled at the horrible words which meant nothing to the children. She knew that at "the last man's dead," the children would double the rope speed until the hapless child missed, and it was the next child's turn.

As if in response to the rhyme, bells from churches in all parts of Poplar, Limehouse, and London chimed the hour. Their sounds floated on the air like cherry blossoms falling off their springtime trees.

John glanced at the sky as if he were searching for the chiming tones.

Emma saw his look and ventured, "The sounds are like leaves floating in the wind, aren't they?"

Often, her father was in his own world of Rumford Baking Powder, ordering refined flour, or new cake techniques, and she never knew whether he really heard her. She was delighted when he answered, "They are."

Encouraged, she continued, "Funny how each bell has its own tone and its own pitch, but when they ring together, they're not discordant at all."

Elizabeth agreed. "They sound beautiful together! I've never noticed before."

It occurred to Emma that people often didn't notice things until they were about to lose them. After tomorrow, their father wouldn't hear the bells of Old Bailey or Stepney or Shoreditch or the great bell at Bow. After tomorrow, he would be too far, and then soon after, they would be, too. Emma hugged her father's arm, and said, in a moment of self-pity, "I don't think there are many bells in America."

John countered, "But they have other things." John patted her hand that rested on his arm. "You will see, daughter, other things will compensate."

Her father comforting her was a rare occurrence, and Emma liked it very much.

Before Emma could acknowledge it, Elizabeth sputtered, "I will come over to the house and see you before you leave tomorrow."

"It will be early, dearest."

"I know. But I'll be there!" Raising up on tiptoes, she kissed her father on his cheek. "See you tomorrow, Papa."

He hugged her lightly and then let her go. She went up the stairs into her own house, and he and Emma continued down High Street.

Inside their home, he would share the story with his wife and younger children of his missionary effort on his last day in the bakery. Hearing his recounting made Emma realize she would like to do the same thing. She'd like to share her testimony with someone.

In the morning, John was prepared to venture out in his traveling vest, coat and hat. Valise packed, he gathered his family together— even drowsy Martha and Richie—and they knelt in prayer in their common room.

Emma listened to his resonant male voice—her father's voice and the priesthood holder in the family —invoking God's blessings on them. Her heart lifted as he charged God to keep all of them safe in their journey. Surely God would honor his plea!

John left with many hugs and tears from his wife and children. Emma was happy to see Elizabeth keep her promise to say goodbye to their father. She had hurried down the street before William had to be at the shipyard.

Tears streamed down Emma's cheeks as her father hugged each child in turn, declaring with surety, "I'll see you in Florence."

The memory that Emma kept closest, though, was seeing her father kiss his wife, look deeply into her eyes, and pledge to see her soon in America. Emma prayed with all her heart that nothing would interfere with that pledge.

The First Train

POPLAR, ENGLAND

TUESDAY, MAY 13, 1862

A few weeks later, Emma tried not to trip over the plethora of boxes strewn on the stairs and sidewalk as she walked down their townhouse's steps. The time had come for the rest of the Horspools to leave Poplar. As she lifted her blue skirt to step carefully over another box, Emma breathed deeply of the scent of her neighborhood. For several days, there'd been no rain to mask the smell of spring, and the scent of wisteria and locust blossoms now blended oddly with the sour smells from the street. She didn't mind the oddity. The smells represented home to her.

Today the sky was blue—an unusual occurrence in May. Emma saw the clear sky as a portent of happiness and hope. She had been the main force for emigrating in the family for years. Yet now the day was here, she found she was as tentative and cautious as a crocus opening its head through the snow.

Even though it was unseasonably warm, Emma's stepmother had each child wear a jacket or cloak so there would be less to pack. One other thing Emma and Eliza had taken great care with was their excess funds. Each had sewn 100 sovereigns into her cloak lining, feeling it was wise to keep the bulk of their money away from prying eyes or quick hands.

Looking at the boxes stacked on the curb, Emma commiserated with her mother. "I'm sorry you couldn't sell everything. I know you worked very hard at it."

Eliza was frantic with so much to take care of this morning, yet she still fretted over the many knick-knacks and pieces of furniture that hadn't sold. She pointed to them in distress. "The large couch. The end tables and the coffee table. And I can't believe no one wanted these two Gothic Revival chairs. They're beautiful!" Her lamenting continued. "And clothing. Well-made clothing."

In a soothing voice, Emma said, "I'm sure *someone* will appreciate them. Think instead, of the good you'll be doing for other people."

Huffing, Eliza said, "I guess that's one way to look at it. At least Brother Berrycloth agreed to buy the bakery. He also gets the royal designation: the' King's Baker'."

"That should help him in his new business." Emma grinned. "He can always make chiffon cakes if he doesn't know how to do anything else!"

That finally got a bit of a smile from her mother.

Hattie, in her mint green dress walked down the steps, watching over her little sister. Martha, bright and clean in her new pink flowered dress, put two tiny feet on each step with arms outstretched as she maneuvered the stairs. As soon as she landed on the sidewalk, she scurried to a box and started to lift out one of the treasures. Hattie hurried over, leaning down to pull the tiny girl away. Emma giggled. For some reason it reminded her of a green crane hovering over a small pink flamingo like the ones she'd seen in the London Zoo.

Hattie's one thick braid fell across her shoulders as she reached for the baby, and Emma noticed the end was tied with a shiny brown ribbon.

Smiling, she said, "I see Georgie finally returned your ribbon."

"Yes, but I had to wash it and iron it. Ugh! It had been around a toad or something. I can barely bring myself to use it!"

"Sounds horrible," Emma said with tongue-in-cheek sympathy.

"Yes, but he had to dry my dishes for two nights," Hattie looked at her slyly, "so it was worth it in the end."

"Ah! That's why he was spending more time than usual in the kitchen."

"When are we going?" asked the person they'd been discussing, hopping down the stairs and then using the boxes for leapfrog.

His mother quickly responded, "As soon as the carriage comes that Elder Lyman ordered. George Alma, quit jumping over those boxes. At least we can leave these items unbroken for the neighborhood."

Richie stayed at the top of the stairs, hanging onto the railing like a monkey. Eliza saw that he had taken off his coat in the heat. "John Richard, pick up your jacket so you don't ruin it. It's the only one you've got."

Will was the last one out. Looking up the street, he noted, "Here comes Elizabeth and family."

Walking briskly, Elizabeth pushed a perambulator carrying the twins. Fourteen-year-old Eloise held little Frederick James's hand, while Sarah, Tildy, and Liam trailed behind. Oldest brother, Jack, had stayed behind, saying he disliked goodbyes.

Elizabeth's children immediately found the cousin who was closest to their age. Eloise complimented Hattie on the pretty pattern of dots and paisley swirls in her new dress, while Hattie playfully chucked Frederick James's nose. The three-and-a-half-year-old ducked his head and batted his long eyelashes with a bashful grin. Sarah, ten, felt she was too old to play with the "little kids" and stood by Eloise and Hattie. Georgie and Richie, meanwhile, enlisted Tildy, eight, and Liam, six, into a game of tag.

With relief, Emma ran over and hugged her sister tightly. "Thank you for coming." Her emotions, which had been close to the surface all morning, now broke free.

Emotions were close for Elizabeth, too, and a tear ran down her cheek. "Of course," she said, hugging her back.

Emma tried hard not to cry. "This is the first time we've been separated in our lives."

Lightening the mood, Elizabeth kidded, "What do you mean?

We've been separated for two years—unless you thought I was hiding in a closet in your house, and you never saw me!"

Emma nudged her. "You know what I mean. But you've been just up the street, and now you'll..." She couldn't finish the thought.

"I know," Elizabeth sighed, wiping away her tears.

The children had been told not to run in the street and were now rummaging through the piles of goods to be given away. "Tildy, put that down. Liam, you, too." She raised her eyebrows to the boy, shaking her head with a smile. "You can't have those. Grandma Eliza put them in boxes for other people."

Eliza said, "Right now, Grandma Eliza wishes she could take these two yummy morsels with her!" One by one, Eliza had picked up each sleeping twin from the baby carriage. Nuzzling them, she savored the smell and soft feel of the sixteen-month-old girls.

Looking at her mother while grasping Emma's hands, Elizabeth went on brightly, "We're coming right after you. We'll be less than two weeks behind you!"

"I wish you were on the same ship," Emma sighed.

"I do, too." She looked again at Emma. "But we have to go on the ship that hired William."

Emma nodded in understanding, "You know President Purdy was also hired as a shipwright, and his family went with him, too."

Will quietly interjected, "They're already gone."

Hattie watched her mother lean one of the babies down so Martha could touch her cheek gently. "Yes. The *Manchester* was supposed to leave Liverpool on the sixth of May."

Elizabeth nodded in understanding, "The neighborhood feels empty, but we'll manage." Then, rehearsing the mantra their whole branch had repeatedly said to each other, "We'll *all* make it, and then we'll be together in the Valley." She held out her hands, beckoning Liam and Tildy to her.

Emma's shoulders relaxed, and she grasped Tildy's hands, swinging her back and forth. "Yes, the Valley of the Great Salt Lake!"

Elizabeth beamed her heartening, big-sister smile. "And then we can take an excursion out to the Great Salt Lake itself and go swimming..."

"Where I hear..." Emma went on, her heart lightening.

The three sisters, Eloise and Sarah, fairly sang to the children clustered around them, "... one can never sink!"

That made everyone laugh. The Great Salt Lake, they had read, had so much salt in it that people and objects were buoyant. It was impossible to sink! Will shook his head and sighed at all the girls' silliness while Tildy and Liam raised their arms and twirled around.

Elizabeth giggled, "Can you imagine such a thing?" The solemn, responsible, rail-thin young mother giggled out loud.

"That's what they say!" exclaimed Emma. "I can hardly wait to get there and see for myself."

"Knowing you," smiled Elizabeth, "you won't just swim in the Lake, you will *dance* in it! And you, young lady," she grinned at Hattie, "will write stories about its beauty!"

Hattie laughed, and Emma hugged Elizabeth again. The sisters cried, "I love you, Elizabeth!"

"I love you, too, Emma. I love you, Hattie."

As Eloise and Sarah pulled Tildy away from the intriguing boxes, Elizabeth hugged her mother and brother. "I love you, Mother, and you, Will. I'll see you in the Valley!"

Amid the hugging, Liam tugged on Elizabeth's skirt with his own 'dance' and a desperate look in his eyes that said he needed the necessary right away. Elizabeth quickly gathered her children while Eliza patted the babies who were back in the pram. Then the Kidman group darted off.

At the top of the hour, the carriage arrived with Elder Lyman. Reminding the children that they would need to stay close to their mother in Liverpool, he and Will loaded their belongings. Members of the Poplar Branch who weren't emigrating converged on the sidewalk.

Eliza gathered her brood around her as, in the distance, the bells of London started chiming, each with its own tone and its own timing. Emma again noticed the sounds blending like many different birds flying in the same sky.

With Elizabeth gone, a sadness settled over Emma. Maybe it was the mournful sound of the bells, or maybe it was their neighbors who congregated on the street. *I've always been excited to go to Zion, but now the time is here, I don't know what to think. My heart feels so heavy, like there's a big hole in it.* She wished she felt differently.

Emma smiled half-heartedly as the branch members stood and sang the song all British Saints sang as loved ones left England:

> "Yes, my native land, I love thee.
> All thy scenes I love them well.
> Friends, connections, happy country,
> Can I bid you all farewell?
> Can I leave you, can I leave you,
> Far in distant lands to dwell?"

After more hugs, the family climbed in. The coachman called "Forward," clicked to his team, and the horses started clopping west on the cobblestone road. Hattie and the younger boys waved wildly out the back window, but Emma just looked out the side, tears falling onto her cheek. Leaning her head against the glass, she continued murmuring, "Can I leave you, can I leave you?" as their home on High Street fell far behind.

Liverpool Docks
LIVERPOOL, ENGLAND

MAY 13, 1862

As the railway rolled them west across the open, green English countryside, Emma's melancholy melted away. The view was beautiful and peaceful—far different from Poplar or London. Other than Harlington, she'd never seen such a wealth of green. The farms stretched out one after another, connected by low stone walls.

By the time they reached Liverpool, Emma had allowed herself to become excited again. But now at the harbor, she found herself divided. Part of her wanted to look everywhere to see things she'd never seen before, and part of her wanted to hold still to remain invisible from possible dangers that swirled about them. The harbor was so chaotic, it would be easy to lose luggage or even children!

Planting herself next to her mother, who was the anchor for their family group, she held tightly to Martha with one arm while she carried a heavy bag with the family Bible in the other. She took a breath and looked around. Such sights, such marvels were here at the dock! The ships with their tall masts, gangplanks going up to the decks, and huge apparatuses that swung enormous packing crates from the dock onto the ships. The mass of people walked every which way, each intent on their own business and each carrying an assortment of items in bags, boxes, and baskets. One man carried a large, ornate picture frame with a dignified person painted inside it. *He must love his ancestor to bring that huge thing,* thought Emma. One man even carried a straw mattress balanced on his head!

In addition to the strange assortment of belongings, there was a curious assortment of people. Based on their style of clothing, she cataloged the immigrants to Martha as if the toddler could understand her. "Most of the people here are English, but that family is Irish or maybe Scottish. And that lady is surely Welsh—I've seen pictures in *The Cornhill Magazine* of their tall hats and shawls. Oh, there's a man with a tall Welsh hat. I wonder if they're married. And that large group with delightful red and green embroidery on their jackets and bags—well, I don't know if they're German or Scandinavian. Their embroidery is so similar. Look, sweetie, there's a black man from Africa, and those people wearing flowing silk robes and veils must be from India. We saw a few of them in London."

She paused in the middle of her litany, thinking, *I wonder who I will meet on the ship?* The idea of meeting new people caused a hitch in her breath, and she glimpsed just the glimmer of possibilities that stretched before her. It wasn't just meeting new people; it was being new herself! She liked who she was—a daughter of God, a reader, a dancer, a bit of a singer, a seamstress, an embroiderer—but she could still become someone new. She had always thought of this trip as a way to get to Zion, as a way to be with a larger congregation of the people of God, but now she realized it could be more.

Martha noticed Emma's intake of breath and touched her cheek with her little hands, turning her face toward her. Using her name for Emma, she queried, "Mimi?"

Before Emma could answer, she turned sideways, holding the toddler tighter as one of the many embarking passengers bumped into her shoulder with a "Sorry! Pardon me." Emma smiled at such enervating, overwhelming bustle around them.

"It's noisy, isn't it?" Emma smiled again at the little girl. There were whistles, commands, horse neighs, yelling, frantic calls, and fractured imploring all tumbling over each other like squirrels in a forest. She had previously thought the shouts and mechanical sounds at the Thames shipyard where President Purdy and her brother-in-law worked were loud, but they were nothing compared to this din!

And the smells! Horses and their dung, sweat from the stevedores and sailors, grease and metal odors from chains and levers. She would have held her nose if she hadn't been holding Martha.

Emma was surprised to find she missed the stability her father would have provided but was grateful to have Elder Lyman as his surrogate. Mostly, though, she realized it was Eliza who was their solid rock amid the turmoil. Emma noticed that Will and Hattie kept their sights on their mother as much as she did. She was happy that Will was taking his assignment so seriously to guard the luggage.

In Eliza's assignments to tend to the younger children, Emma might have gotten the best end of the deal. Martha just stared placidly at the hubbub from the safety of her sister's arms. Hattie held five-year-old Richie's hand while he also grabbed onto her green skirt so fiercely she had a hard time moving, and Eliza held Georgie's hand because he was always a bit too spontaneous and might wander off at any given moment. Emma chuckled as her mother constantly pulled back the eight-and-a-half-year-old as he strained at her strong handhold.

Finally, the line they were in edged forward, and they were able to walk up onto the ship. Emma felt dizzy when she glanced at the water below, so instead, she resolutely looked forward, talking lightly to Martha as they went.

As soon as Emma stepped onto the deck, a grin split her face. Looking at Will and Hattie, she was suddenly as giddy as a court jester. She was here! She'd made it onto the boat. After all this time, a ship was taking her to America!

The ship was the *William Tapscott*, a sailing vessel that had already taken well over fifteen hundred people to America, many of them Latter-day Saints.

Will leaned over to Emma and pointed up. "That's the captain," he said. "Captain Bell."

"How do you know?" she asked.

"I heard some people call to him as he walked onto the ship."

"Ah," Emma nodded.

"Not only that, but you should also see the way he walks. Like he was born on a ship!"

Emma thought she was observant, but it looked like Will was observing different things than she did. Indeed, the captain stood on a high deck overlooking the boarding, arms folded and legs apart, as a seaman did to balance himself. Captain Bell looked to be a rough, ruddy man, but there also seemed to be a kindness about him. *I hope so. Time will tell what kind of man he is,* Emma thought.

The LDS Saints were assigned berths below the deck they were standing on, and one even lower than that. The Horspools received their number and went below. Lanterns lit the dim interior, but they soon found their three berths, one on top of each other, secured to the wall of the vessel. Eliza said she would share the bottom one with Martha and Richie, Emma and Hattie would have the middle one, and Will and Georgie would share the top. The older boys climbed up like monkeys, smiling broadly as they got out of the way of their mother, who immediately started arranging their family corner. Richie wanted to climb up with his brothers, but Eliza wouldn't allow him to climb so high. Hattie clambered up to her berth. She immediately reached down her arms for Martha as Emma held her up to get the toddler out of their mama's way.

That evening, the European Mission presidency came on board. Not wanting the small children out of her sight and needing Hattie to help her, Eliza asked Emma and Will to go up to the meeting. Thus, Emma and Will milled on the deck in the middle of the mass of Saints who were to receive instructions from Apostles Amasa Lyman, George Q. Cannon, and Charles C. Rich.

"Will, can you see Elder Lyman's father? And Apostle Cannon?" asked Emma.

"There are a lot of people here!" he grumbled, scanning the deck.

Craning her neck, she continued, "Do you remember what Apostle Rich looks like?"

Just then, Will pointed to the spot previously occupied by the captain. "There they are."

Emma joined the crowd in looking above them.

Apostle Lyman held up both hands, calling, "Greetings to the Saints of Zion from the European presidency! We have desired to greet you before you leave tomorrow. We are also on our way to New York. We're only sorry not to be sailing *with* you."

Apostle Rich grinned, "Yes, we are going on the fast steam vessel, the *SS Kangaroo*. So, we're going to 'hop' across the Atlantic before you!" He laughed at his little joke, as did his audience.

Bright-eyed, Emma looked at Will. "That's the same vessel Father took!"

"Then it will be fast!"

Apostle Cannon said, "In addition to applauding you for embarking on this great journey, we've also come aboard to organize this mission."

"I didn't know being on this ship was a mission," Emma whispered.

"Hush."

"The mission presidency of the *William Tapscott* shall be Elder William Gibson, President, with counselors Elder John Clark and Elder F. Marion Lyman, all returning missionaries."

"Putting Elder Lyman in charge again will make Mother very happy." Emma was chattering as much as Hattie, and Will raised his eyes to quiet her.

Apostle Lyman then said, "There are eight hundred and seven of the Latter-day Saints aboard out of a total of nine hundred and thirty on the ship. Our desire is that you have faith, good behavior, and obedience to your mission presidency and to Captain Bell."

"See, it *is* his name," said Will.

"Hush."

Apostle Cannon gave some general rules, and then Apostle Rich divided the 807 into nineteen groupings called wards. There were about forty-three people in each ward, with a leader over each group. Often, the leader was an Elder returning to Utah from a mission in Great Britain.

Emma looked around at her fellow Saints. Everyone in the assembly seemed to be smiling. Her own eyes lit with anticipation, Emma reached over and eagerly grabbed Will's hand. "Can you *feel* it, Will? The Spirit of the Lord is here in abundance!"

Will looked down at their joined hands. Emma did, too, giggled lightly, and gave up her hold. She thought, *That was rather unlike me to grab onto my brother, but he didn't seem to mind. Maybe I'm changing already.*

The business taken care of, Apostle Lyman started singing a hymn in a strong baritone, and soon, hundreds of voices joined him.

> Redeemer of Israel, our only delight,
> On whom for a blessing we call.
> Our shadow by day, And our pillar by night,
> Our King, our Deliverer, our all!

Emma joined her voice to the group and smiled at Will. Not being a singer, he looked around, his face a study in astonishment. After a couple of verses, he nudged Emma, jutting out his chin to point her attention to the sailors. Most were barefoot, and many bare-chested. Some held ropes hanging limply in their hands, and some just stood with their arms hanging down, but all held stock still as they watched the Saints singing. The men high above who had been bouncing from line to line on the rigging had stopped moving. All the sailors appeared dumbfounded by the overwhelming sound of so many unified voices and the magnificent spirit their singing created.

After President Gibson gave a prayer to close the meeting, Will said, "The crew didn't know what to think of such power."

"Besides hearing, I think they *felt* something, too." Emma unconsciously put her hand over her heart. "Will, the Lord approves of our crossing the ocean."

Sister and brother went below to their berth to attempt conveying, somehow, the majesty they had just felt up on deck.

Departure and Seasickness
THE ATLANTIC OCEAN

WEDNESDAY, MAY 14, 1862

After staying in the dock that night, the *William Tapscott* was pulled out into the ocean the next morning by a steam tug. So it was on Wednesday, May 14, 1862, that the full-rigged sailing vessel weighed anchor and set sail for America.

All the Horspools and most of the Saints were up on the deck, enjoying the whole undertaking. Using the cant of the times, much to the dismay of his mother and Emma's raised eyebrows, Will exulted it was "a banner day!"

Nevertheless, as Emma looked at her native land falling farther and farther behind, the lines of "*Yes, My Native Land, I Love Thee*" ran through her mind. "Can I leave you, can I leave you, far in distant lands to dwell?" Pausing, she thought with determination, *Yes, I can leave you.* Before she became teary again, Emma mentally said goodbye to England and turned her face toward the ocean.

About noon, Emma's family was still on the deck, enjoying the free feeling of being on the wide ocean. She called to her brothers, "Look! There's the steamship *Kangaroo*. Let's see if we can see Elder Lyman's father."

Georgie and Richie quickly looked up from playing a game of Mary Mack.

Will said brightly to his younger brothers. "That's the same boat Father was on. It's so fast it's already gone to New York and back! Look, there they are!"

All three members of the European presidency stood at the railing of the *Kangaroo*, waving to the Saints on the *William Tapscott*. Emma thought she heard a "Godspeed!" over the distance, and then their faster speed took them out of sight.

Impressed with the boat's speed, Will said to Emma, "They'll get to New York long before we will."

Missing her father on this voyage, she replied, "I hope they find Father when they do."

Shortly after, almost all eight hundred Saints became seasick, including Elders Lyman and Clark. Each set of berths had a slop bucket attached, and everyone was grateful that they had one close to their berth!

Half of the Horspools were sick, and half were not. Hattie and Will were fine. The roiling seas didn't bother them, so they took turns entertaining Martha, who also felt well. The rest of the family lay as still as possible, hoping that the dreadful heaving in their stomachs would pass. Georgie groaned as if he were dying. Richie kept his eyes closed and said shutting his eyes stopped his stomach from rolling over. Eliza was stoical, keeping her unease to herself. As for Emma, she wished she had her own personal slop bucket positioned right by her head.

Eliza, however, had come prepared; she managed to sit up long enough to rummage in a bag to find some ginger root. She gave each of them a hard biscuit and a bit of the root, asking them to chew slowly and see if having a little something in their stomach helped. The combination did seem to help.

Emma thought it strange that their berth area was called a mess, but she gladly stayed in their mess all that day and paid very little attention to what anyone else did in their ward. She heard the rustling in the mess across the aisle when those folks came back after watching a marriage performed that very first day by President Gibson. She also heard a child's cheery voice waft up from the deck below as he sang folk songs and hymns in some language.

Meanwhile, their corner of the kingdom was blissfully uneventful. Emma was almost sorry when her mother revived enough to issue cautions again. "Our leaders have advised your children, and especially you girls, to stay clear of the sailors. You can watch them do their work, but from a distance. Mary Emma, Harriet Marie, you take that to heart."

Emma and Hattie assured their mother that they would, indeed, stay far away from the sailors. Emma noticed that Will made no such promise. She heard him tell Georgie that two stowaways had been discovered and were being made to work with the sailors to pay for their passage.

"Is that true, Will?" Georgie asked weakly. The bed above shifted as the boy moved on the berth.

"It is!" Will sounded altogether too energetic. "Maybe we'll meet them after you get better."

I hope you don't introduce Georgie to two stowaways, Will, Emma thought. She surprised herself by realizing she was like her mother in wanting him to stay away from the sailors.

The next morning, Emma was still too sick to care what sailors or anyone else on board was doing, but Will had investigated the ship and come back to tell her. Hattie sat cross-legged on the lower berth, entertaining Martha on her lap with the corner of a blanket for peek-a-boo, while Richie snoozed next to her, cuddled against his mama. Georgie stretched out on top.

"Do you want to hear how things go around here?" Will asked Emma, climbing up by her.

"Sure," Emma groaned agreeably, not even sure she could say the word without upsetting her equilibrium.

"The morning bugle sounds at six o'clock."

"I heard it. It was loud and blaring," she complained.

"Just because you're seasick." Being perfectly fine, Will didn't have a lot of sympathy for anyone who felt nauseous. "But it does warn you that morning prayers will be held in each ward in two hours."

"For those who can stand up," Emma moaned.

"Yes, for those. Then, food is cooked sometimes by the ship's cooks and sometimes by someone in a mess. See, there's a ten-foot galley up top, and they keep a fire in it. Well, under it. When someone in a mess cooks, they take the hot food down to their group. And, of course, salt pork and sea biscuits are available any time of the day."

"Don't even mention food, Will."

Ignoring her pleas, he went on, "Have you eaten those sea biscuits? They're huge! They're the size of my hands—splayed out."

"And they're as hard as a tabletop."

"When they're dipped in a stew or tea, I'm sure they'll make do. We'll have to get used to them. Anyway, our day is finished with ward prayers at nine..."

"Do we have to hear the bugle again?"

"I'm afraid so. After that, we shuffle back to our bunks..."

"Berths."

"Sure, and say our own prayers, and we're in for the night."

"Remember, Eliza said not to get friendly with the sailors."

"She was talking to you girls, not me. I'm going to wander this whole ship, Emma. There's too much to see that I'll never see again!"

"Well, just don't get too friendly with the sailors."

"I'll be fine," the boy said defensively.

Emma could tell she had ruffled his feathers. "Just be careful, Will. They're a rough crowd."

"I know," he said a little less testily. Then, climbing up, he pushed Georgie aside, saying, "Move over. You're taking all the space."

A COUPLE OF DAYS LATER, Emma was finally well enough to leave her berth. She asked permission to go up top with Hattie, and their mother happily granted it. Hattie gratefully set down her poem book to accompany her sister.

"Maybe you can meet some of the other young people in our ward," Eliza said. "I know some other young women are in the mess across the way, but I haven't met them yet."

Emma said they would look for others to meet.

As soon as Emma stepped foot on deck, the chilly breeze caught in her collar and ruffled her hair. It felt so good, and it smelled sea-salt-fresh after being below deck with the persistent stench of retching and mold for days. The tang of pitch, damp wood, and fish almost stung her nose, but the breeze wafting around her wove everything together into one word: "Ship!"

Emma pushed back the tendrils of her shiny dark hair that had pulled loose in the gentle gust, relishing the pleasant feeling of having a calm stomach again. *Maybe I should have worn my hat,* she thought. She realized that being in the berths in their little Horspool corner—where one didn't wear so much as a cap—felt like being at home, so she wouldn't have thought twice. *Never mind,* she thought as she again pushed a stray strand away from her face. *This feels good!*

As Emma stood drinking in the fresh scent, Hattie pointed to a group of young women standing at the port railing, looking at the undulating waves far below. Emma was relieved to see that none of them wore hats or bonnets, either.

"Do they look familiar?" Hattie asked.

"A little. Maybe we saw them during morning or evening prayers," suggested Emma.

Emma and Hattie walked over to the young women. A dark-haired girl who was about Emma's short height turned and noticed them. Hand on the railing, she stood with impeccable posture, wearing a well-tailored dress of a rich navy-blue material that Emma knew her stepmother would approve of. She greeted the sisters as smoothly as the waves lapping below the ship. "Hello! My name's Rosetta Liver-more. People call me Rose."

Emma couldn't help smiling. She liked how the LDS Church changed previously accepted British constraints. No more did one have to wait to be properly introduced; you could do that yourself. And no more did you have to call others by titles like 'Lord' or 'Duke'; the church equalized everyone to brother and sister. Of course, it was 1862, and times were changing all over. Still, the Church was hurrying along those changes.

Feeling an association had been made, Hattie asked, "I think I've seen you. Are you right across from us?"

"Yes, we're near the stairs," concurred Rose.

Emma asked with a furrowed brow, "Did you hear a child's singing come from the lower hatch?"

"Yes!" answered Rose. "We found out it was a little Welsh boy who'd fallen down an open hatch and broken his leg."

"I'm told he was still in good spirits, bless his little heart," said the fragile-looking girl with frothy blonde hair who was about an inch taller than Rose.

Rose introduced her demure companion. "This is Annie Yeates."

Annie nodded shyly and said, "Hello."

"Hello, Annie," smiled Hattie.

"Glad to meet you, Annie," Emma said.

The tallest of the three young women then introduced herself. In a smooth voice, she said, "I'm Lizzie Gentry." Towering over her two smaller friends, the dark-haired girl carried herself with regal confidence.

Hattie was immediately taken with Lizzie's classic beauty; it was as if a Grecian statue had come to life. She watched, mesmerized, as Lizzie's delicate earrings danced in the morning breeze.

Emma introduced the two of them. "I am Emma Horspool, and this is my sister, Hattie. And we are *very* happy to finally be over the seasickness!"

Hattie jabbed, "I wasn't sick. I was fine the whole time."

The three girls laughed, and Rose replied, "We know what you mean. Some in our mess are still feeling the effects of the moving ocean beneath us."

Annie's eyes startled slightly. "Yes, it never stays still, does it? They didn't really warn us about that, did they?"

Lizzie laughed, "No, they didn't. Although my William spent years on a ship and tried to warn me."

Emma cocked her head. "*Your* William?"

"Yes, my intended, William Wood," Lizzie smiled bashfully.

Hattie almost swooned. "Oh, you're engaged. That's wonderful!"

"He's in charge of our mess," Rose explained.

Emma asked, "I believe I saw William. Tall? Lanky?"

"Yes, and goofy!" Lizzie grinned. "He's very philosophical, and he's always coming up with new ideas."

Emma hugged her sister's shoulders, "Well, he would get along very well with this one. She is full of ideas and is very philosophical, even poetical."

"Ah, then she *would* get along with your William," Rose smiled up at Lizzie. "All his poems..."

All three young women shook their heads and rolled their eyes in chagrin, thinking of William's crazy, original poems.

"Are you from London?" Annie asked, changing the subject.

Hattie nodded. "Poplar, actually."

"It's a suburb of London," Emma hastened.

Rose said, "I've heard of Poplar. That's where the docks are for the Thames, correct?"

Both Horspool sisters nodded.

Rose went on, "I'm from Essex, over on the east side. Well, Lizzie and I both are. I've grown up around ships and water my whole life. I used to play in the estuary with my brothers."

Emma asked, "And you, Annie?"

"I am from the west side of England—Worcestershire."

Lizzie beamed, "Well, we represent all of England, then, the east, the west, and the middle."

And just like that, Emma and Hattie made new, lasting friends.

Annie asked, "Who is in your mess?"

Rose interjected, "Mess! Isn't that a silly thing to call it! Who made up that name?"

"I thought the same thing!" Emma quickly agreed. "What a ridiculous name."

"Sailors, surely," Lizzie said, deprecatingly looking at the crew working the lines and ropes. "Mess indeed!"

Tentatively, because she was obviously the youngest there, Hattie said, "I think it's French for dish." The other girls looked at her in amazement, while she shrugged. "I've studied French."

Annie picked up the idea. "Sure. It's like a mess hall that soldiers have; a place for eating."

"There you go!" Hattie nodded pertly.

Emma laughed, "Well, our mess is our family. There's our step-mother, me—I'm nineteen—and Hattie."

"I'm fifteen," she added brightly.

Lizzie offered, "Rose is twenty, Annie is eighteen..."

"Almost nineteen," Annie interjected.

"I am seventeen," Lizzie said.

"Ah, our brother Will is seventeen, but he's not ready to get married!"

The girls laughed, and Emma went on, "Then there are the little ones: Georgie is eight-and-a-half—the half is important! Richie is five-and-a-half, and Martha will be turning two any day now."

Annie smiled, "Martha's the little one with blonde hair, isn't she? I've noticed the children across the aisle. They're a cute bunch."

"And lively!" Lizzie added.

Emma said, "Well, not so much for the first part of the week. Richie, Georgie, and our mother, and I didn't fare so well, but we're well enough to come up for some fresh air now!"

Annie looked around. "Speaking of fresh air, Lizzie, where's your intended?"

Lizzie looked around as if William would magically appear.

"Would you mind telling us how you became engaged?" Emma almost surprised herself by asking such a personal thing, but the Church helped people feel an almost instant connection.

Lizzie blushed as she answered with some reticence, "Yes, I'll tell you."

Keeping their hands on the railing, they continued looking out to sea or up at her as she began.

"William was gone to sea for five years with the British navy. He went everywhere, and he'd seen everything! When his service was through and he was back on land, he was of an age to marry. His employer thrust his sister, a Miss Gipp, upon William. But she was not a member of our church, and he was not going to marry someone who didn't believe the eternal truths that he did. The only way he could escape that uncomfortable situation was by leaving his employment and going elsewhere."

"Oh, that's too bad," Emma empathized.

"He's a butcher, you see," explained Annie. "That was his job on the Navy ship."

Lizzie nodded, continuing, "He ended up finding employment at a butchery in our town in Essex, which is Maldon."

"My same town," added Rose.

Lizzie continued, "William got to know my father, who was the president of the Maldon Branch, so when he met me on Sunday, he knew that I was also a member of the church. We were immediately attracted to one another, and after that, it was history!"

Rose nudged her, "No, no, you're not getting away with that short version! Tell us *how* he asked you."

Hattie broke in, "And when did it happen?"

Lizzie ducked her head, replying, "It was actually just earlier this very year: 1862—a banner year!"

Emma smiled at Lizzie's use of the same new phrase Will had used but simply asked, "Where did he propose?"

Looking at the horizon, Lizzie smiled as she remembered, "He borrowed my father's carriage, and we drove out to old Beeleigh Abbey. The ruins are ancient—it was a monastery built in the 12th century. The grounds are very lovely. Lots of plants and flowers and hedges."

"Yes, it's beautiful!" Rose heartily agreed. "I've walked there many times."

Harriet persisted, "How did he propose?"

"He proposed in a poem. William is so witty and clever!"

"He is, indeed!" Annie chuckled. "I am forever laughing at him in our mess!"

Emma tilted her head, asking, "Do you remember it?"

Lizzie laughed, "Not right off. But it's written down; he gave it to me." Looking upward as she tried to recall, she took a breath and said, "The ending was something like:

> ...Till the end of time,
> in every land and every clime,
> I want to have you by my side,
> as on God's good earth we do bide."

Hattie sighed, "Oh, that's beautiful."

Annie said wistfully, "Yes, and it's wonderful how a marriage sealed in the temple takes us till the very end of time—how it doesn't stop with 'till death do us part.'"

Lizzie smiled, "Yes, to think of spending eternity with him is a delightful prospect! William is such a sweet, charming person. His poem made me very happy. I was quite taken with it."

"May I ask something very personal?" Emma tentatively asked. Lizzie looked amenable, so Emma went on, "Why didn't you marry before you came on this voyage?" Again, she surprised herself by asking this aloud.

Hattie asked excitedly, "Or even now? President Gibson performed a marriage on the ship on the first day!"

Rose answered for her. "They're going to wait until they reach Zion and can be married in the Endowment House. Some people like to do it right the first time. Since the temple in the great city of Salt Lake isn't built yet, the Endowment House is!"

Lizzie smiled, "Of course, we know it's God's priesthood authority that binds us, not the location. And I don't fault those who got married beforehand or who get married on the ship. William and I just decided to wait until we can do it in the Endowment House."

Then Emma turned to Rose. "Do you have someone special that we haven't seen yet?"

Rose blushed, touching her perfectly coifed dark hair as if it were coming out of its pins, which it was not. "Well, he's not on this ship. He's already in America."

Answering for her, Annie said conspiratorially, "His name is Samuel Smith, and he went to Zion last year with Charles Penrose."

Hattie brightened. "I met Charles Penrose. He came to London with many other missionaries, and we had a parade for them. I got to give him a rosette."

Rose nodded. "He was a great missionary."

Wanting to stay on the subject of her possible love interest, Emma asked, "What's Samuel like, Rose?"

Smiling broadly, she settled in for a contented response. "He has fiery red hair, and he's tall and thin and handsome."

Annie laughed, "Of course, he's handsome!"

"He is!" Rose protested. "He's charming and very active in the church, and he sings everywhere he goes. He has a beautiful tenor voice."

Annie asked, "Rose, do you think you'll marry Samuel when you see him?"

Rose soberly said, "I really don't know. We've corresponded a bit, and he knows approximately when I should arrive in the Valley. But we don't have an official understanding. I was just fourteen and a half when I first met him after I was baptized, and he's nine years older than I am." Then, sounding resigned, she added, "He may have already found someone in the Valley."

Reassuring her, Lizzie patted her hand, "Rosetta, he couldn't find anyone better than you."

Hattie, the romantic, said, "I think he'll wait for you."

Emma smiled at her younger sister, thinking, *She has absolutely no basis for saying that! But it made Rose feel better, so I guess it was worth saying.* Aloud, she said, "Rose, nine years is nothing. My older sister married a widower who is twenty-one years older than she. He's a year older than our father, and they are very happy!"

Not wanting to get her hopes up more than they were, Rose shrugged and said, "We'll see."

The young women looked behind them as children gathered noisily. The sea was calm enough today that the young ones could jump rope or even play marbles on the deck—quite a feat on an ocean-going vessel. Two little girls who looked like sisters about Georgie's and Richie's ages wandered past with large sea biscuits filled with salt pork in their hands. Emma watched them arrange themselves on an enormous coil of rope. *Smart little girls,"* she thought, wishing she knew them. *They can watch what's happening on deck from the safety of the side.*

Rose turned back to Emma and asked, "What about you? Anyone special?"

Emma lifted her head up, laughing, "No, no one special at all! I was baptized when I was almost eight, and I'm nineteen now. We had a large house, and many missionaries stayed there over those—what?—

eleven years. I had an attraction to a few of them, but not enough to marry."

Annie asked, "What of the young men in your branch?"

Emma smiled, "I went to a couple of dances with two brothers. One is my age, and the other is a year older."

Hattie interjected, "They're the sons of our branch president."

"We mutually decided that we worked better as a brother/sister arrangement! Another fellow I know is Edward Cash from the London Conference. He's two years older than I am, barely taller than me, coal black hair. He's on our ship, by the way. He's a knife grinder—scissor and axe sharpener by trade."

Lizzie said, "Oh, I've seen him: quite spare, bright brown eyes, long side shavers?"

"Yes, that's the one," Emma agreed.

"So, no sparks?" Annie guessed.

Emma chuckled, "No, no sparks. Ed is a most amenable fellow, and I like talking with him, but he needs someone other than me to be his lifelong and eternal companion! My older sister says I have 'the power of discernment.' She believes it's one of my gifts, and I'll be able to tell right away when the right man shows up for me. So, no, no one for now."

Rose teased, "Not even any of these handsome sailors, eh?"

Emma threw her head back with a hearty chortle. Glancing at the tough crew working on the ropes and rigging, many without a shirt on, she thought momentarily that the rough nature of most of these men matched the hardness of their lives. She answered, "No! Afraid not!"

Lizzie then said, "Ladies, while we've been talking, the Coolbears have been cooking our lunch." Turning to Emma, she explained, "David Coolbear and his mother are part of our mess." Looking at Annie and Rose, she said, "I think it's time we get back."

Rose said, "And we have to make a stop first at the water closet."

Annie shook her head, "If only it *were* a closet! The WC is terrifying!"

Rose's dark curls bounced as she vehemently shuddered, "A bar across an empty space, and when you look down, you see the ocean frothing beneath you! It's enough to make one want to wait until the voyage is done to even use the necessary!"

Emma and Hattie agreed. Shaking their heads, they waved good-bye, "Good luck with that!"

As soon as the three young women left, Hattie looked at Emma. "Power of suggestion: now I need to use the closet, too."

Emma nodded, "It is a scary place to go. I'll hold onto you!"

Stormy Waters

SOMEWHERE ON THE ATLANTIC OCEAN

JUNE 1862

Emma couldn't predict the weather. Rough weather and turbulent waters were followed by calm skies and still waters. Then the cycle would start all over again. She'd go up on deck for some fresh air, but when the breeze grew chilly, she'd go below. Down in her berth, the air was stuffy and stinky, and she wished for the fresh, cool breeze again.

Sunday, June 1st, the day was cold and stormy. It was too rough for a general Sabbath meeting with everyone up on deck, so four meetings were held at different ends of the ship for any who could attend.

The next day was just as rough, which was a shame because Emma had hoped for pleasant weather for Eliza's 38th birthday. Back in England, the Horspools had not had large celebrations, but they *did* like to make note of the day. The family, however, was once again confined to their berths, just trying to keep down breakfast. Emma roused enough to nudge a weary Hattie while she poked her brothers above her to sing a couple of hymns Eliza liked. "We Are Marching On To Glory" was too lively, so they opted for "On Jordan's Tides the

Prophet Stands" and "Before All Lands in East or West." After that effort, they all sank back onto their cots, exhausted. Their songs were the best birthday present they could muster, and their mother thanked them for their efforts.

By Wednesday, the sea had settled, and, to their great relief, so had their stomachs.

On Thursday, Will and Emma escaped their berths for the fresher air on the deck. The sky lowered with gray clouds, and a wind whipped up, tugging at her dress and tousling his hair.

Will looked at the wake bubbling behind them, "The ship's going at a good clip."

"Thank goodness," Emma remarked. "We're sweeping along nicely. But Will, this changing nature of the ocean—I never get used to it! I don't know how the sailors do it."

"Watch out!" Will grabbed her elbow as she lost her footing for a moment. "Are you all right?" Then, spotting two sailors across the way, he said, "I think those are the two stowaways. I'm going to talk to them."

Left by herself, Emma looked around for her friends. She hadn't seen them in their mess but didn't see them up here, either. Strangely, she didn't see any female passengers. She only saw a few male passengers and sailors scurrying to do various tasks. Ignoring them all, she walked to the railing, instantly mesmerized by the vast expanse of gray, roiling ocean. The sea was much livelier than the last time she had viewed it.

The water arched and dipped as far into the horizon as she could see, cresting and flattening in never-ending and always changing patterns. Painting had never been her strong suit in school, but she wondered, if she were an artist, how she could ever convey such majesty and changeableness!

Emma's gaze shifted close to the dark waves crashing right beneath her. White foam brightened the tops of the dark waves, only to dissolve like steam sizzling off a hot iron. The frothing crests were like live urchins haphazardly hitting the ship, dissipating immediately like the storyteller's Little Mermaid, who became mist evaporating into the sky when she died. So many, many busy urchins that her eyes became bleary.

Without her being aware, the dark, rampant waves morphed into the solidity of the narrow alley, and the churning seas became its gloomy, confining walls. The images pulled her down until all she could see was the water's manic motion. The wild urchins became her, young Emma, running doggedly between gray stone buildings. Would this be the day a monster found her? Would this be the day her legs gave out? Would this be the day the family's money was stolen? Her little legs pumped as fast as they could, but the demons always lurked, and the walls always closed in. At times, the terrifying memories were so vivid, she swore they must be real.

Wrapped in her unconscious brooding, Emma became oblivious to her surroundings. She didn't realize the intensity of the storm had increased ten-fold, she didn't see how rapidly the sailors were pulling in sails and ropes, and she didn't even feel the rain whipping her hair around her face. She certainly didn't notice all the other passengers had gone below.

Her trance-like state was broken when a sailor hurriedly approached her. "Miss, you need to get below."

"What?" Emma shook her head, looking around through the dimness and wiping droplets off her face, only to have more fall on her. She *was* the last passenger on deck. How had that happened? Only then did she truly notice the heaving seas and the ship's lurching from side to side.

Water came from every direction—rain pelted from above and the sea splashed over the sides. She began moving, but her footing was precarious. The sailor grasped her arm before she could get to the hatch. He glanced about him as if to find someone else to help with this errant woman. Shaking his head in a disgruntled way, the man ushered her carefully to the opening. He showed her how to slide her feet carefully along the deck, not minding the water sloshing, but always maintaining contact with the wood. Right foot, left foot, right foot, left foot, carefully forward.

Holding onto her arm, he yelled over the storm, "It's a howler, all right!"

She glanced at him quickly, but found she needed to keep looking at the deck to keep her feet under her. In that glance, however, she saw other sailors tying themselves with rope, and that alarmed her more than the constantly splashing seawater. *More than a howler,* she thought as she stretched her booted foot forward. *This is no ordinary storm.*

Her breath hitched as the large ship crested a wave and then fell into a trough. She stumbled and looked up suddenly, even though she didn't want to. To her utter alarm, she was looking down at the surface of the sea. It seemed there was no ship, only water! Darting her startled gaze forward, she saw they had reached the stairs. The sailor almost shoved her ahead. An angled thought thrust itself upon her: *He needs to find a rope to tie himself down.* Grasping onto the railing, she held her skirt high and started down quickly.

When she was only halfway down, the hatch abruptly closed. No one else would be going up while the storm lasted. She was suddenly cloaked in darkness blacker than anything she had ever known. *Of course, no lanterns could be lit while the ship careens this wildly,* she thought.

Overcome by the sudden blackness, Emma's knees buckled, and she grasped the railing with both hands as if it were the lifeline the sailors used. Unbidden, her conversation with Elizabeth came to her: "Only when I'm in confined, dark spaces." The stairs felt like a confining box she couldn't see her way out of, and she surprisingly found she missed her birth mother terribly. Her breath caught. She was in danger of fainting. She thought of sitting on the stairs to rest for a moment, but realized they were sopping wet, and she didn't want to soak her skirt any more than it was. Another tremendous heave of the ship shook her out of her reverie. Mustering her courage, she thought, *I am nineteen, not nine. I can do this.*

Slowly she reached a tentative toe downward, finding the next step, and as she did, gratitude for many of her blessings in life washed over her. *I have a sturdy railing, I have sturdy boots (although they're wet right now), I'm out of the rain and the wind, and I have a family to go to.*

Suddenly, the last few steps didn't seem so onerous.

She straightened and reached the landing. Immediately, she was flooded with an oppressive and suffocating sensation. The odors of sweat, bacon grease, mold, and wet wood were enhanced in the darkness. A more present stench indicated many people had used their retching buckets, and she prayed she wouldn't step in any of them. A loose pot banged against her shin as some silverware tumbled across her boot, frightening her as if they were a big rat and tiny mice running loose.

The ship rocked fearfully again, and she heard the sailors above shouting and tramping. Somehow, Emma kept sliding each foot and slowly picking her way to her family.

I hope they're huddled together in our mess, she thought. And, even in the moment's dire situation, one tiny part of her couldn't help but smile at the sailor's jargon. *Mess, indeed!*

Groping in the darkness with one hand outstretched while covering her nose with the other, Emma called, "Where is the Horspool family?"

"Here, Mary Emma! Here!" Her stepmother shouted over the stomping on the deck above, the creaking of the wooden ship, and the metallic banging of the loose pans and boxes that skittered along the floor. Emma groped forward with her hand until Eliza grasped it in relief. "There you are!" Eliza exclaimed. "I was about to send Will back for you."

"Oh, good. He's here?" Emma bumped into the bunk above her mother's, with a resounding, "Ow!"

"Yes, but what were you doing?" asked Harriet worriedly from the berth above their mother's.

Little Martha Jane repeated, "Doo-ning?" from the security of her mother's lap. The little girl didn't sound put out at all, even though she couldn't see her big sister through the gloom.

"I was wool-gathering, Hattie. Just lost track of time, and suddenly, the storm was upon us."

Eliza tsked, "It's fortunate that you are here now. It sounds like a gale."

Emma said, "They wouldn't let Will go up, anyway. I was the last passenger down, and they closed the hatch behind me."

Hattie leaned over from the upper berth. "Come up here, Emma. Come hold my hand!"

"You might not want me," Emma warned. "I'm soaking wet." Nevertheless, she gathered her wet skirts and started to clamber up.

"What's going on out there, Emma?" asked Georgie excitedly from the uppermost berth. The boy who loved thrilling, moving things, like pirates on ships, knights on steeds, or trains on tracks, didn't sound scared by the storm in the least. In fact, he sounded a bit put out that he hadn't been up top.

Emma stopped climbing for a moment to answer, "As one end of the ship goes down, all you can see are the waves. It's an amazing sight, Georgie! The ship seems engulfed by the sea, but somehow it stays on top! And the next minute, the other end of the ship goes down, and then all you can see is water again on that side—just mounds and mounds of water! I can't even explain how terrible and majestic the sight is!"

From next to Georgie, Will's voice sounded eerily disembodied in the dark. "I wish I'd seen it! I came back too soon. It sounds astonishing."

Five-year-old Richie piped up from the other side of their mother, "It sounds scary!"

Emma smiled, picturing his eyes wide with terror. He didn't have Georgie's boldness, little Martha's calmness, or Will's nonchalance. He liked to have his mother's skirts handy to always hold onto, and luckily, that's exactly where he was.

"Some sailors are tying themselves with rope, and some are up on the rigging, pulling the sails tight shut. They'll be all right, Richie, and so will we!"

Just then, the ship lurched violently to one side, throwing more containers and baskets that had not been latched securely. Emma's foot slipped, and only by holding on to the upper berth did she not become part of the flotsam on the floor. Hattie found her hand and guided her to their berth, hugging her tightly as she finally sat beside her.

"Next time we have a storm, everyone needs to latch their goods," Will said loudly.

Holding tightly to her two youngest, Eliza called up to him, "I hope there won't *be* another storm!" Another swell picked up their stomachs and dropped them just as suddenly. She called, "Hold on!"

Will must have done what his mother wanted because Georgie exclaimed loudly, "Ahh, that's too tight, Will!"

"I like tight." Richie's muttering was barely heard above a set of pans that tumbled across the floor.

On the middle berth, Emma and Hattie clung to each other and to the bunk bed. "I hope...," Hattie gulped in air as the ship shifted again, "we don't... fall off!" She grasped Emma even more tightly.

Emma held her securely. "We will not fall off. But we *are* going to hold on for dear life!" Emma guided Hattie's hand to a metal ring attached to the wall of the ship, making sure she grasped it securely. Emma grabbed another one while holding Hattie around her waist. "We'll make it through!" she told her younger sister as if saying it loudly would command the ship to hold itself together. It took all her concentration just to hang on and to comfort Hattie. She knew sweet Hattie had such an imagination! Yes, she was a dreamer and often made more of situations than they were.

But this *was* a dire circumstance—here in the middle of the ocean, down in the belly of a ship, in darkness like the inside of a beetle, and with fearsome sounds all around them. And above them—squeaking of wood, stomping of feet, muffled yelling, and other jumbled noises. She wished her new friends across the aisle could bolster Hattie, but it was too chaotic in this creaking din to even think of hollering across the aisle.

She found herself wishing her father were here. The thought surprised her, because he wasn't normally her first choice for comfort. No question that he was a good person, provider, and a great speaker in church, but he was generally aloof and removed from her day-to-day experiences. Right now, though, she wished for his priesthood to bless them in this grave circumstance.

Well, he wasn't here, and for just a moment, Emma hoped he had not undergone a similar horrifying experience as he crossed the ocean.

Hattie was sniveling, and her father wasn't here, so Emma decided to diffuse her worries by being absurd. "Hattie, I figure we are being swallowed by your great white whale from Mr. Melville's novel," she said loudly. "When was it published? Nine years ago?" Sounds of boxes cracking and the ship creaking competed with her voice.

Hattie took two halting breaths and then joined in Emma's silliness. "Moby Dick? It was ten years ago. And no, this is even worse than a great white whale. This is probably..." she took another gulping breath, "a Norwegian Kraken. Huge. Red. With a hundred tentacles!"

Will called out from above, "Or maybe it's Poseidon, the Greek god of the seas, wreaking havoc on tiny people who should stay on land!" He must have decided it was better to take part in some silliness than simply to imagine the worst in the dark.

Emma could finally hear the smile in Hattie's voice as she responded, "Yes! What were those crazy people *doing* in the middle of the ocean? They should be on land!"

Another voice cut through the inky blackness, a calm, mellow, low one. It was Elder Lyman. This man had lived in their house, eaten with them, and taught them. They knew his voice. They trusted and loved it.

In a pleasant, comforting tone, with no angst whatsoever from the storm, he inquired, "Who do we have here? Ah, it's the Horspool family."

"Elder Lyman!" Georgie called through the gloom.

"Elder Lyman?" Richie echoed with Martha following, "Myman?"

Emma could hear him groping in the dark for a hold on the berths while setting each foot carefully and using his shoe to swish aside anything treacherous to stand on (or in). "President Gibson is still ill, so I'm visiting on your level, and Elder Clark has gone below."

"I'm scared, Elder Lyman," said Richie timidly. Emma heard his small voice directed hopefully up toward the Elder and could imagine her brother's wide-eyed stare.

"I know, Richie." His voice was warm and pleasant, with no fear. "But you know what? *We* are on the Lord's errand, and He won't let us fail. What I need from you is faith that we'll be all right. Can you give me that?" Emma heard his voice lifted to each layer of berths. "Can you do that, too? Can you?"

The children all murmured their assent.

"Then let's pray. Dear Heavenly Father, we are in the middle of the ocean in a precarious spot, but we know something sure and true: we know Thou art the God of creation and of miracles. We know Thy Son walked on water, and turned water to wine, and fed the five thousand with two fishes and five loaves. And we know we are on Thy errand, coming to America to build up Zion in preparation for the Second Coming of Thy Son. So, Father, we would be much obliged if Thou wouldst temper the elements, calm the seas, and help this ship make it through to New York. We will be obedient and do our part and praise Thee forever. In the name of Jesus Christ, Amen."

"Amen," each member of the family said, with little Martha echoing 'Mah-men' loudly. Emma could feel him patting Hattie's hand, saying he knew it was hard for her to travel without their father, but how proud he was of her. He encouraged the children to listen to their mother, asked them all to be faithful, and then pleaded with them to stay in their berths, no matter how the ship lurched. As he moved on to the next group, the comfort of his presence and his priesthood blessing stayed with them.

Meanwhile, Hattie's hands grew stiff from holding on so tightly. Emma's fingers were stiff, too, and her body was tense from doing double duty—holding onto her sister as well as to the iron ring.

"I'm cold," Hattie said loudly over the din. By her side, Emma could feel her shivering.

"Me, too," commiserated Emma. "I think the darkness makes it feel colder. Here, lean against me again. I'm drier now." Hattie changed her position and scrunched tightly against Emma. Emma wished they could see!

What a silly notion, she thought. A *falling lantern would set the whole ship on fire!* She sighed, stopped her quixotic thinking, and concentrated on holding on.

From below, their mother's voice rose to them, half a plea, half a command, "Hang on, children! Just like Elder Lyman said, we'll get through this!"

"We'll get through!" repeated optimistic Georgie, with the final echoes from Richie—"Get through!"—and Martha, "Froo, froo."

In the dark and the turbulence, Emma lost track of time.

Finally, after an interminable period, the waters calmed, the ship stabilized, and the sailors must have reset the sails, because they continued sailing smoothly through the rest of the night.

In Emma's family, stomachs were so sore from tension and nausea that no one even thought about eating. With Hattie tucked next to her, she eventually fell asleep, the ship at last rocking them gently like a cradle. As she drifted off, Emma was once again astounded at how inconstant the sea was and how strange and ever-changing life was aboard a ship!

Emma's Friends

SOMEWHERE ON THE ATLANTIC

JUNE 6, 1862

Emma stretched next to her still-sleeping sister, grateful she could see light coming through the hatch. She was glad she had been able to finally sleep and extremely happy her stomach was not complaining this morning. She climbed down from their bunk, aware she would stay all day in the dress she had slept in. At least a fresh breeze from up top could air it out a bit.

"Good morning!" she greeted her stepmother. "The children made it through?"

"Yes, thank goodness. That storm was really something!" Sighing heavily, Eliza added, "I hope we don't have to go through that again!"

"At least *next* time we'll know what to fasten down!" said Emma wryly.

Reclining on the bottom berth with two sleeping children by her, her mother looked at her just as wryly. "You *do* remember William Francis said the same thing last night? You'll excuse me if I don't laugh at your joke. I am too exhausted!"

Emma smiled at her. "Thank you for understanding it was a joke." Changing the topic as she pinned up her loose hair, she asked, "Will you let the children go up on deck this morning?" In addition to games like tag, marbles, hide-and-seek, hopscotch, and jump rope, some of the older, adventurous ones would even climb the rigging—urged on by the sailors.

"No, I don't feel comfortable just yet letting them go above. Maybe later. Why don't you go, though, and see what's happening? Quite a few people have already gone."

Emma ascended the stairs, her dark hair curling about her head in the fresh breeze as soon as she reached the top. She wasn't worried anymore about whether to wear a hat on this voyage. Most of the Latter-day Saint women didn't wear headwear here on the ocean. On a morning like this, she felt it was a wise choice. The wind ruffling her pinned-up hair felt so freeing.

She opened her arms, relishing the breeze. The morning air was quite chilly, and she wished she'd brought a shawl. The shawl she pictured, though, wasn't hers. It was Elizabeth's yellow paisley shawl that was her engagement gift from William. *Funny that I thought of hers,* she thought, *instead of my own.*

It was refreshing, though, and the air carried an after-rain scent instead of a fishy-sea smell. The ocean had already forgotten its furor from the previous day and was as smooth as Eliza's wall mirror. The sky turned bluer by the minute, and white, billowy clouds popped here and there high above like angels surveying yesterday's pandemonium.

She was surprised to run into the captain right there on the deck. "Good morning, Captain Bell," she said.

"Morning," he nodded, greeting her in his scratchy, low voice.

She looked around, noticing a congregation of people. "Why is everyone gathered?"

"I have something to tell the passengers. You're just in time."

Emma looked around as people assembled. Black-haired Ed Cash came and stood by her, standing only a couple of inches taller than she. She greeted him pleasantly and then looked for her friends from William Wood's mess.

Captain Bell plowed through the crowd and then took two steps at a time up to the forecastle. Standing still on his stocky sea-legs, his beefy hands held the railing in front of him as he overlooked the congregation. Raising his voice, he announced, "I want you people to know that was the worst storm I have witnessed in twenty-five years. My crew and I have been through some terrors, haven't we?" He looked at the first mate, who nodded his grizzled head. "We know what to do up here. But below decks—that's where the problem often lies. I want you to know, it is *only* because the Latter-day Saints are so well disciplined that we survived. Any other passengers would have rushed about in a panic, and the ship would have sunk. I thank you all." Then, with a twinkle in his eye, he added, "You know, there has never been a ship lost that was carrying Mormons. I *like* carrying the Mormons!"

The crowd laughed and shouted, "Huzzah!" and "Hurrah for Zion!" The women raised their hands, men slapped their friends' backs, children jumped up and down, and Emma and Ed grinned at each other. The captain nodded his head in profound but humble thanks, then waved dismissively in embarrassment, calling, "Have a good day."

He turned his shoulder away just as someone in the crowd started singing.

> *"Now let us rejoice in the day of salvation*
> *No longer as strangers on earth need we roam."*

Emma joined in with her pretty voice. Then one after another of the Saints joined in, until the wood on the deck vibrated with their sound.

> *"Good tidings are sounding to us and each nation,*
> *And shortly the hour of redemption will come."*

The small knife grinder finally joined the chorus in his raspy voice. What he lacked in pitch he made up for in enthusiasm.

> *"When all that was promised the Saints will be given,*
> *And none will molest them from morn until ev'n,*
> *And earth will appear as the Garden of Eden,*
> *And Jesus will say to all Israel, "Come home."*

When all three verses of the hymn had been joyfully sung, Ed turned to her. "Sister Emma, you have a very lovely voice."

"Thank you, Brother Ed. That's very kind." Looking up at the fore-castle, she said breathlessly, "That was quite a pronouncement, wasn't it?"

"It was, indeed. And I've heard the same from other people in the London Conference, so I guess it's true."

"That a ship has never sunk that carried the Mormons?"

"The same."

"That gives great confidence, doesn't it?"

"It does. Yesterday's storm *was* terrible, but, in fact, I was never really worried."

"I was kept busy trying to calm my sister. At one point, she was even afraid that a knothole would pop open, and water would pour through!"

"Oh my!" His eyebrows rose. "Were you successful?"

"I held her hand constantly. But what really helped was Elder Lyman visiting our mess. I can't conceive *how* he managed to walk through the ship in the dark, but he gave us a priesthood blessing that provided considerable peace."

Ed nodded. "I'm on the lower deck, and Elder Clark did the same thing down there. Very reassuring."

"We are fortunate to have the priesthood in our midst," Emma concurred. Changing topics, she asked, "By the way, have you found anyone here on the ship who needs knives sharpened?"

"I have found that a moving vessel is not such a good place for sharpening. When we get on the plains, I think people will be more likely to need my help."

"I'm sure you'll find clients," she answered. "It's a good service you provide."

A pleasant older gentleman walked toward them with a comely girl on his arm. She had fiery red hair that refused to be tamed in the gentle morning breeze.

Ed Cash smiled at the pair. "Ah, here's another Ed!"

The man's beard bobbed as he smiled broadly, saying, "Top o' the mornin' to you! That was quite a bluster yesterday, wasn't it?"

While Emma nodded in agreement, as did the young woman, Ed took Emma's elbow to introduce them. "Emma, may I present Brother Edward Batchelor and his daughter Harriet. Edward, Harriet, this is Emma Horspool. She's from my area near London."

"Happy to meet you," smiled Harriet.

Being the shortest of the group, Emma lifted her chin to look up at them. "And you're from Ireland?"

Lifting a strand of her auburn locks, Harriet smiled wryly. With a sweet lilt to her tone, she quipped, "Gave it away, did it?"

Brother Batchelor leaned back and laughed. Looking somewhat like an overgrown, bearded leprechaun, he seemed the kind of man who welcomed every living creature into his life. Emma warmed to him and his daughter immediately.

"Ah, even being from the hardy island didn't help yesterday. This one...," he smiled lovingly at Harriet, "didn't feel too well." He patted her hand on his arm, continuing, "But now she's right as rain!"

"I'm pretty sure I know how you felt!" Emma replied woefully. "I'm glad you feel better, Harriet."

The redhead smiled gratefully, "As am I! Believe me, as am I!"

Brother Batchelor turned around and put his hands on the railing, looking at the calm ocean. "Quite a journey we've undertaken." The rest of them followed his eyes, looking at the expanse of still water.

"Did you hear what the captain said about the Saints?" asked Ed Cash.

"No. We came up just as he was leaving the forecastle. What did he say?"

Brother Cash proudly repeated the captain's words.

Brother Batchelor smiled, "Well, sure and begorrah, that's truth itself! We *did* hear the singin' as we came up. A tremendous sound, that."

"And you should've heard Sister Emma sing," Ed added. "The voice of an angel."

"Brother Cash..." Blushing, Emma demurred, dipping her head. Turning the focus away from herself, she looked at Harriet. "I'm sure you sing, too. They say if you're born in Ireland or Wales, you're a singer!"

Throwing back her head Harriet laughed, her red hair bouncing on the breeze. "They *say* that, but 'tis not always true."

Remembering something, Brother Batchelor pointed a finger at Ed, saying, "Brother Ed..." He stopped himself, smiling and tilting his head toward the two young women. "I like saying that—*Brother* Ed—and I like bein' a part of this Church of Christ's."

As the two girls chuckled fondly, he looked again at Ed Cash, "There's someone I'd like ya to meet. I came over to find ya. I think they can use your knife grindin'."

Happy to find someone who could use his services. Ed went off with the other. The two young women walked to the railing so they could view the ocean. The seas were so calm today that one could scarcely believe anything untoward had happened the day before.

The young women had only just discovered each was nineteen years of age when they were joined by the three girls from William Wood's mess. Tall Lizzie and petite Rose, their dark hair both pinned in place, looked as if they had just stepped from Harrod's in Knightsbridge instead of climbing up from the bowels of a stinky, wet ship. Annie's blonde hair, which looked like it never wanted to be contained, fluffed around her head in a cloud. Today, all three young women were very happy to be alive and not to be seasick!

"Ah, I was hoping to see you today!" Emma beamed.

"Are you doing all right?" asked Lizzie.

"*So* much better than last night."

"We felt pretty sick in our corner of the ship, too," said Rose. "We didn't dare move."

Emma went on, "One of the sailors called it a 'howler.' I'd say it was a sight more than that!"

"As the captain said! Did you hear the adulation he gave to the LDS passengers?" asked Annie.

"I did. It was wonderful!" Emma smiled. "Girls, I have someone for you to meet. This is Harriet Batchelor. She's traveling with her father."

Harriet was greeted all around with admiration for her luscious auburn hair and her lilting Irish voice.

"We just found out that we are both nineteen," Emma told them, smiling at Harriet. Emma loved making connections. "And Lizzie told us she is seventeen, the same age as my brother."

Harriet said, "I have a seventeen-year-old brother, too. He'll be coming next year."

Rose said, "I'm twenty. I'll turn twenty-one while we're crossing the plains. August 1st."

"Oh! And I'll turn nineteen a week after that—August 8th," Annie said.

"In our family, we'll have two birthdays toward the end of our journey across the plains, but we'll have one here on the twenty-first of June—little Martha," Emma commented. "I'm looking forward to that."

"How old will she be?" asked Harriet.

"The little tyke will be two."

Annie gushed, "She is so pretty and sweet."

Emma nudged Harriet, saying under her breath, "Blonde girls always stick up for each other!"

Harriet chuckled as the two other dark-haired girls nodded in agreement. Then all five turned quiet, simply standing at the railing looking out and drinking in the crispness of the morning air.

Suddenly, Rose pointed, "Look, a ship going the other direction."

"Ha!" Annie chimed in. "We're not the only ones on the ocean!"

Harriet agreed in her Irish brogue, "Aye, it usually seems as if we are. So lonely."

The passing ship suddenly gave a loud horn blare—just one short blast.

"That ship just said 'hello'!" Annie giggled.

The girls laughed with her, and Emma said pragmatically, "That was definitely a greeting, not a warning."

"Yes!" Rose agreed. "A 'we're-sinking-come-and-help' call would no doubt be a *long* blast."

"Or several. Bah! Bah! Bah! Bah!" Harriet added. She punctuated the air with horn-blasting sounds.

The young women giggled, grinning at each other as the sea spray gathered on their dangling arms.

Emma was surprised and delighted once again to realize how

quickly members of this Church could become friends. Their union in Christ gave them immediate purchase in each other's lives.

Lizzie pointed to something much closer. "Look there! See? Do you see those noses? Those heads?"

The other young women rose on tiptoes, gazing where she pointed until they, too, saw a cluster of large fish swimming near their ship.

"What are they?" Emma asked.

"I don't know," answered Annie.

"I don't know either," responded Rose, "but I think they're ugly."

Harriet said, "I think they're called grampus, a sort of dolphin."

"Well, they're as wide as they are long. I don't think much of their proportions," Rose scoffed.

Annie kidded her, "That's because you're a dressmaker, and you like beautiful proportions."

"Yes, you probably want them pinned in at the waist!" Lizzie teased.

Annie went on, using a 'grampus' voice, *"Oh no, where are my stays? Where is my whalebone corset?"*

Emma caught up with the quipping. *"I don't have a whalebone corset because the whales still have their bones and they're deep in the ocean."*

Harriet and Lizzie laughed while Rose sighed with friendly long-suffering. "Oh, you all are terrible!!"

The girls continued watching them leap over each other as they cavorted in the calm water.

Emma said, "I don't think they're going to hold still long enough for you to make dresses for them, Rose!"

"Seriously, Rosetta, when you get to the Valley, are you going to continue sewing?" Annie asked. To Emma, it sounded like the continuation of a previous conversation.

Looking at Annie, Rose answered, "I would like to, yes. It's what I've been trained in. What about you, Miss Annie?"

"You know my training was in making silk gloves." Then, to Harriet she explained, "I had to always be careful that my fingers were smooth, so they didn't catch on the silk."

Harriet said, "That sounds like very precise work, Annie."

Pushing blonde wisps out of her face, Annie said, "I enjoyed it well enough."

Emma joined the conversation by saying, "I'm a seamstress because my stepmother is. She does the main construction and often has me do the embroidering and the finishing touches, like buttons, frog fastenings, braiding, and such. She's amazing with styles and colors. She would be your cohort in getting those dolphins or grampus or whatever they are to wear the clothes you wanted, Rose!"

Rose smiled, gazing at the free creatures splashing below. Then, through slit eyes, she suggested conspiratorially, "Instead of clothes, what would you think of putting hats on them?"

"Hats?" Annie asked, taken aback.

"Hats?" Emma queried, her eyebrows furrowing.

Shyly smiling, Rose said, "I think I'd like to open a milliner's shop someday!" From the modest way she said it, Emma wondered if it were the first time she'd ever admitted such a thing out loud.

"Oo, it's my turn after the dolphins!" Lizzie's eyes danced. "Will you make me a fancy hat? With satin and feathers and perhaps a fake bird perched in a nest?"

Rose lifted an eyebrow regally as she arched her shoulder. "If you will order it, I will make it!"

Lizzie replied honestly, "Well, we'll see how William's butcher business goes. At least, I think that's what he's planning on. A lot could change by then."

Annie asked Harriet, "What about you, Harriet? What would you like to do in the Valley?"

Harriet pulled her fiery curls over her shoulder, contemplating, "Well, what I would like *not* to do is laundry. My mother did laundry while my father worked in a gravel pit. I was the one who had to make sure we got our jobs done, and our job was to take the cleaned laundry to people's houses and pick up the dirty bags, often at three in the morning."

Emma smiled. "It sounds like most of us have worked in clothing: we made them, and you washed them!"

"One time too many!" Harriet heartily agreed. She then tilted her head, thinking. "Since I was the oldest of six, I did a fair amount of mothering. Perhaps I'd like to be a teacher."

"That sounds nice," agreed Emma.

"Teaching is commendable," added Lizzie.

Looking at her diminutive new friend, Harriet offered, "Brother Cash said that Emma has a beautiful voice. Perhaps *you* could teach singing lessons."

"That is very kind of him," Emma demurred, "but I don't sing well enough for that. But what I would like to teach...." She waited for one breathless moment before she could say it aloud. Just like Rose, she'd never said this to anyone. "...ss the Gospel. That would make me very happy."

Lizzie nodded. "I'm sure you'd be very good at that."

"I bet you'd be wonderful, Emma," Rose concurred.

"That's something I could never do," murmured Annie.

Harriet quipped, "They could ask me, but I'm not sure the British or the Americans would understand me!"

The young women laughed. They understood Harriet's brogue just fine, but they could see it could be a problem.

Rose said, "When I was an apprentice at the Stratford Dressmaking School, it was well that the other girls could understand me. You see, many was the time we had to stay up all night sewing mourning clothes for a funeral the next day. Funerals always happen so suddenly." The other girls nodded knowingly. "The light was dim, our fingers were pricked, and we were so tired. I kept the girls awake by reading novels and poems to them." To Harriet, she said, "I was the only one who knew how to read."

Annie said, "I'm glad they had you, Rose. I wish my sister and I had someone read to us while we were sewing! It would have made the time go faster."

Emma turned once more to the ocean. The playful creatures were moving away from the ship. "They do have nice smiles. I felt comforted just having them swim near us."

"You should," Harriet sighed. "Sailors say they bring good luck."

"Even without their fancy swimming outfits?" Emma kidded.

Her friends laughed and turned toward the deck to see what their fellow passengers were doing this fine day.

Birthdays and Celebrations

SOMEWHERE ON THE ATLANTIC

SUNDAY, JUNE 8, 1862

The seventh Sunday after Easter was the day of Pentecost when the Holy Spirit descended upon Jesus's original apostles. It was marked with great festivity in England, where it was called Whitsun or Whit Sunday. Emma asked Eliza, who informed her they would not observe the holiday this year. She was disappointed but understood that life on a ship needed to be bare bones.

William Wood had other ideas. Emma jostled past him as he held something precariously under one arm. With the other, he held tightly to the railing while he ascended the ladder, as the sea had kicked up again and the ship rocked roughly.

"What have you got there?" she asked curiously, gripping the other railing.

Lifting the supplies in his arms, he confided as surreptitiously as a child waiting for the appearance of Father Christmas, "I'm making shepherd's pie as a special Whitsun celebration for my mess. After that storm on Thursday, I figure they deserve a special treat!" He nodded and moved past her on his way to the cooking galley.

Emma was surprised that the fire in the galley would be lit today because of the choppy ocean.

I guess the crew knows what they're doing. They certainly knew what to do in that storm, she thought and went back to her mess to relieve Eliza of entertaining Martha. Figuring it would take more than an hour for William's pie to cook, she watched for him to return to his mess across the aisle.

Dinnertime came, and Emma's family ate cold sliced meat on sea biscuits dipped in a cold, salty beef broth Eliza had made the day before. She also gave each of her children small pieces of candied ginger to settle their stomachs and asked them to eat everything slowly. Even Georgie obeyed her and slowed his eating. That's when Emma noticed tittering and then outright laughter from William's group.

"I'm going to see what's happening." Putting down the half sea biscuit she hadn't yet been able to swallow, Emma got up and walked over. Standing by William's mess with her hands on her hips, she demanded, "All right, you people, what's going on?"

Through tears, because they were laughing so hard, Annie, Lizzie, Rose, and David Coolbear alternated telling the tale.

"William made a big ole' pie for all of us."

"A surprise for Whit Sunday."

"He cooked it in the galley until the top was crisp."

"And golden."

"Well, almost burned!"

"But the rest of the pie didn't get cooked through!"

Here, they lost control again, throwing back their heads in hilarity or clutching their stomachs, covering their mouths with their hands, or pounding their chests with an open palm.

"It's stringy and tough."

"It's horrible!"

"It's inedible!"

"It's terrible!"

Emma looked at David's mother and the others sitting around the food. They all looked up at her, nodding in agreement. Lizzie lifted a forkful, and Emma wrinkled her nose at the stringy, uncooked mass dangling from the soggy lower crust.

Rose went on, "We're afraid we're all going to get sick to our stomachs!"

William shrugged and said in defense, "I just wanted something special for them after the storm. Instead, I think I've created a stomach storm."

Emma shook her head in disbelief and rolled her eyes. "Oh, William, William!" she said, looking at the lanky, earnest fellow sitting there with crossed legs.

"Do you want to try some?" Rose asked wickedly.

Annie, who was often sick from the roiling ocean but was well enough today to bite into a piece, tempted Emma. "We have salt and pepper."

Looking at them all, Emma retorted, tongue-in-cheek, "Normally I might take you up on your offering, but I'll pass today, thanks!"

Smiling and shaking her head, she turned and went back to her family. After seeing that, it was amazing to her how easily she could swallow the rest of her rock-hard, weevily sea biscuit!

FRIDAY, JUNE 20, 1862.

Ship life settled into a pattern of rough seas followed by calm seas, gray clouds followed by blue skies, chilly days followed by blindingly hot ones. Even though Emma could never figure out what was coming next, there was a sort of ennui to the pattern. Lots of reading, resting, embroidery, and visiting took place on the calm days.

Late one morning, Emma and Will rested on their respective berths while Hattie read her book of poems and Georgie and Richie played Cat's Cradle on the lower bunk next to their mother. Eliza darned stockings while Martha napped. Loud laughter and "huzzahs" from below interrupted the boredom.

"What's happening down there?" Emma asked.

From the top berth, Will said, "That's what I want to know."

At that moment, a familiar head popped up at the top of the ladder.

His fingers holding the precarious string design, Georgie looked up and excitedly said, "Here comes Elder Lyman. Maybe he knows."

Elder Lyman walked right over to the Horspools, which was the closest mess to the hatch. Before the youngster could even ask, the Elder pointed his head toward the opening, saying, "Ralph Wardle's birthday is today! Ralph Junior, that is, not his father. He just turned seventeen." Looking at Will, he said, "I believe that's your age, correct?"

Before Will answered "Yes," Emma saw Hattie's cheeks redden at the mention of Ralph Junior.

Hm. Hattie hasn't been infatuated with boys before now, she thought, *but maybe things are changing. She is fifteen, and Ralph Jr. is a strapping fellow with gorgeous wavy brown hair. Maybe she's noticed him."*

Not wanting to embarrass her sister, Emma turned the personal observations into something more general. "It sounded like the whole lower deck was wishing him well!"

Elder Lyman chuckled, "They were, indeed. They were giving him a 'Lancaster greeting'! You know their father was a canal boatman there. He sold all the property that came to him when his grandfather died, so he could take his family to Zion. The *whole* family, at one time. Quite an undertaking."

Georgie asked, "What's a 'Lancaster greeting'?"

"'May your name be *first* in the penny news, and may you travel to any town you'd like!'"

"So, they have a penny newspaper up there?" asked Emma.

"Evidently so. For a couple of years now." Elder Lyman chuckled, "And the family definitely is traveling!"

Emma had seen the Wardle's a few times. They were members of the London Conference, and the father and mother were older than her parents. The married children were all older than she was. The unattached siblings were Louisa, a dark-haired, delicate beauty who was Emma's age, Ralph, the birthday boy who was Will's age, and Ella, a girl about Hattie's age who was always wearing ornate lace collars. Emma found that to be a strange and fascinating choice because the ship was often sweltering and always smelly. *Why would you want to wear such nice things on the ship?*

Emma's ear turned toward the last of the reveling below. She wished Louisa and Ella would join their group of young women, which now included red-haired Harriet—she of the lilting Irish brogue. The truth was, the Wardles tended to stay together most of the time. They were a pleasant enough bunch, but they didn't readily interact with the other passengers. Since their berths were in the lower hold, Emma usually only saw them when they used the hatchway closest to her side to climb up to the open-air deck, or sometimes up on deck.

Georgie piped up, "Where would *you* like to travel, Elder Lyman?"

Eliza entered the conversation for the first time. Gently smoothing Martha's blonde hair as she slept, their mother said, "I think I know. Elder Lyman would like to return to the Valley of the Great Salt Lake to be with his wife again."

Elder Lyman looked down at the sleeping child. "Yes, and my baby girls." He touched her dimpled arm lightly. "One is a year older than you, little girl, and the other I haven't even met yet. She was born after I came to England."

Hattie said softly, "Oh, my!" Emma caught her sister's eye and nodded. Apparently, she had not heard that detail when it was mentioned at one of their family meals.

"Yes, their names are Alice and Ellen," he smiled wistfully.

Suddenly, Georgie had enough of this boring adult talk. Letting the string drop from his hands, he asked hopefully, "Do you have a peppermint, Elder Lyman?"

"Yeah, 'mint?" repeated Richie.

"Why, boys, I thought you'd never ask!" He reached into his vest pocket and procured two precious mints. Each boy stretched out a waiting hand, grabbing onto the treat Elder Lyman offered.

Shaking her head at her sons' boldness, Eliza said, "What do you say, boys?"

They both chirped in sing-song voices, "Thank you, Elder Lyman!"

Then he surprised the rest of them by handing each of them a peppermint as well.

"Thank you, Elder Lyman!" Their voices rang in unison.

Grinning, he waved goodbye, saying he was meeting Elder Clark to see how his rounds had gone.

SATURDAY, JUNE 21, 1862

The next day held another celebration. It was Martha Jane Horspool's second birthday.

"Good morning, munchkin!" Will hopped down from his berth and tickled his littlest sister awake. Sleepily she opened her large eyes and pushed straggles of fluffy blonde hair away from her face. He said with more energy than he characteristically used, "You have a <u>second</u> birthday on the <u>second</u> of June in eighteen-sixty-<u>two</u>. That will only happen once!"

Emma stretched and smiled. Usually, it was Georgie who was fond of numbers.

"Birt-day?" Martha asked.

"Yes," Georgie, now awake, piped up, his blond locks flopping over his eyes as he peered down from the upper berth. "It's your birthday today!"

"Birt-day?" she'd intoned again, not even knowing what the word meant.

Eliza had everyone dress, eat breakfast, and have morning prayer in their ward. After that, she told Will, "We have work to do down here today, and we need to do it without Little Miss two-year-old. Could you take her up to see if you can find any dolphins?"

Emma suggested, "Or see if you can find those sisters, Caroline and Anne West; she likes them." She had finally met the ten- and six-year-old girls, who often sat on huge rope coils eating sea biscuits. The girls had a great deal of freedom because the family accompanying them to Zion—not their own family—allowed them to wander the ship.

"Yes," he agreed, "I can do that."

Eliza added sternly, "But watch her like a hawk! And don't let her out of your sight for an instant. Georgie, you go along, so there are two of you to watch her."

Emma prayed her brothers *would* watch her carefully once they were up on deck with so much to see and do. Every time Martha had been above before, it was with her mother.

As soon as they had gone, Hattie pulled out the satin purse she was making for her little sister. "I've almost finished the embroidery on this."

"Do you need ribbons for the drawstrings?" Emma asked. "I bought them for her hair, but I have some extras."

"No, thank you. I brought cording."

Emma smiled lightly, "Well, look at you, Miss Prepared!"

Hattie grinned and kept stitching. "It didn't take any space at all in my luggage." Rolling her eyes, she amended, "The trick was remembering where I had put it! And now trying to see in this dim light. I'm never going to scorn sunlight again for my whole life!"

Their mother entered the conversation, "Indeed, where did I put it?" She was rummaging in the extra foods she had brought. She had wisely supplemented the ship rations of hardtack, bacon, and tea with her own raisins, dried currants, dried onion, brown sugar, and some odds and ends from the bakery, like herbs and tapioca. "Ah, found it!" Eliza triumphantly held aloft a tiny wooden box.

Hattie asked, "What's in that?"

Eliza opened it carefully to reveal two hard pink roses packed in straw. They were made from hard Royal Icing and were in pristine condition. "I had Papa make them while the bakery was still open."

"Mama! Those are beautiful!" Hattie exclaimed.

"Eliza! She's going to love them!" Emma declared.

Eliza, who always seemed straightforward and forthright, smiled almost sheepishly. "I wanted to do something special for her. I planned ahead!"

"You certainly did! I can hardly wait!" Hattie said.

Richie woke up then. He had been placed in Emma and Hattie's berth and peered over the side. "What's going on?"

Emma mussed his already mussed dark hair and said, "We're getting ready for Martha's birthday party. She's two years old today!"

Richie didn't care how old; he latched on to the only important word. "A party? We're having a party?"

Getting her ingredients ready to mix, his mother said, "Well, as much party as we can have on a rolling tub."

"What tub?" Richie looked around.

"The ship, silly," Hattie giggled while Emma handed him some breakfast.

That night, Emma's family had an early dinner. They sat in their mess circle, each with a bowl and a spoon, and ate a luscious meal of split pea soup with salt pork, to which Eliza had added some herbs for extra flavor. Of course, they had the hard, ever-present sea biscuits to dip into it.

Then came time for the party. They started by reminding Martha that today was her birthday. She still didn't understand what that was, but she did understand gifts!

Emma produced a small package carefully wrapped in a corner of tissue paper and suddenly wished her father was here to celebrate with them. Maybe he would have chanted his "Mary on the Gate" song again. Martha would have loved it. It had certainly made *her* laugh!

"Hold out your hand."

"Mimi," Martha responded as Emma put the tissue paper package in her small, outstretched hands.

Martha tore the tissue paper, revealing pink and cream ribbons.

"What do you say, Martha Jane?" her mother prompted.

"T'ank you," she said. Her blue eyes, framed by golden curls, looked up at her big sister.

Emma's heart flooded with love for this sweet little stepsister, and she beamed down at her as she gave her a hug. "You're welcome, sweetie."

Hattie next gave her the satin purse she had sewn.

"Duckies!" Martha chimed, digging her finger into the three embroidered ducks at the bottom of the bag. "Birdie!" she cried, touching the bird flying in the *sky* of the purse.

"Look," smiled Emma, "you can put your ribbons in it." She helped the little girl stuff the ribbons in, and Martha held up her bag triumphantly.

Meanwhile, Richie was bouncing up and down. He could hardly wait for his turn. At a nudge from his mother, he gleefully brought forth in his sweaty hand a hard candy, undoubtedly bought by Eliza and kept for this occasion.

"T'ank you," she said again. Martha was an obedient child and a quick learner.

Georgie produced a single white feather. "I found it on the deck! See—there haven't been any birds flying out here over the water; that means it's special!"

Hattie leaned down and said with mock solemnity to Martha, "You put it under your pillow, and at night you dream of your true love!"

Martha looked up at her with big, believing eyes.

"That's not real," objected Will.

"You just made that up, Harriet Marie!" Emma grinned.

Hattie shrugged. "I did. But it sounds good, doesn't it!"

"Love for a two-year-old? Oh, Hattie!" Emma laughed heartily at her sister, who was full of fancy.

Will then took the little birthday girl on his knee, had her close her eyes, and open them on the count of three.

"One! Two! Fwee!" the little girl said, uncovering her eyes with a grand gesture.

Will handed her a small rag doll, which she grabbed and clutched tightly to her chest.

"Beebee," Martha said.

"Baby?" he asked his mother, wondering if this was going to be the doll's name.

Eliza smiled, "No, Phoebe. She's naming the doll Phoebe."

Will's eyebrows scrunched together. "How do you know?"

"I speak two-year-old," Eliza shrugged.

Emma grinned at her mother's response, then looked at Will and said, "Martha will treasure the doll, Will. It's perfect."

Then Eliza smiled, "Now it's time for Mama's gift. Are you ready?"

Martha nodded her head excitedly with wide eyes.

Eliza reached behind her and pulled out a cloth-covered bowl. She removed the towel to reveal a fluffy tapioca pudding, complete with two hard pink roses.

"Pink! Pink!" Martha's little hands shot forward in delight to snatch the two crystalline roses. Eliza smiled and looked around at her family, delightedly sharing her daughter's surprise. Uncharacteristically bashful, she explained, "These are roses that were used on Queen Victoria's wedding cake—1840, I think it was."

"These very ones?" Will couldn't help teasing.

Eliza shooed her son with the dishcloth, "Oh, you!" Handing him the towel, she said, "Just for that, William Francis, you get to wipe out our dinner bowls so we can each have some of this. And Harriet, please get a serving spoon. Thank you, dear."

Emma and her family slowly ate the wonderful pudding, savoring every bite. After five weeks of salt pork and hardtack, it tasted like heaven. Many times in the past, when Emma had had to stand behind the bakery counter with hurting calves as she served the customers, she had rued the fact that her father owned a bakery. And, of course, running the family money to the bank's night drop had been a dreadful experience.

Right now, however, she was delighted to belong to a family of bakers!

Burial at Sea

ON THE ATLANTIC OCEAN, CLOSE TO NEW YORK

JUNE 22, 1862

Immediately after Martha's party, the wind intensified, making the sea froth and boil, causing the ship to rock ferociously. The Saints were again confined to their berths, and Emma fell asleep to the furtive, stomping sounds above her as the sailors and God once more worked their magic to save the ship.

The next morning Emma tried to ignore the early morning bugle, and was awakened, instead, by urgent voices across the aisle. She lifted on an elbow to see William Wood talking to someone, but it was too dim to see who. Finally, it registered to her that it was Elder Clark.

After the Elder left, William came across to the Horspools. Seeing Emma awake, he gave his message to her. "Brother Hardcastle from Sheffield died early this morning. A burial will be held in one hour. Anyone who would like to attend is invited up on deck."

"Oh, I'm sorry." Emma's eyes immediately filled with compassion, and William left to deliver the news to several other messes.

"Eliza, are you awake?" Emma asked.

"Yes. Good morning. I heard what Brother Wood said."

"What would you like us to do?"

She thought for a moment and then said, "I would like our family to attend. I know it will be hard, but it's the least we can do to honor someone who loved the Lord so much that he gave up everything to go to Zion."

An hour later, dressed warmly against the morning chill, Emma's whole family stood with a great crowd of Saints. The sky was mostly overcast, with the sun blinking occasionally through rolling, gray clouds. The ocean was choppy, and another storm looked imminent.

She looked around at those who had also come. To her right, she spotted the tall forms of William Wood and Lizzie Gentry, and assumed that their shorter companions, Rose and Annie, were likely beside them. To her left, she saw tall Brother Batchelor, and the splash of red hair to his side was undoubtedly his daughter, Harriet. She noticed someone wending their way through the crowd, and when she saw a chance sunray glint off shiny ebony hair, she knew it was Ed Cash. As he approached, he nodded to Emma and came to a standstill next to the Horspools.

Hattie put her hand in Emma's, looking into her big sister's eyes. Emma could see Hattie wasn't sure about this and needed her reassurance. Their mother firmly held Richie's hand while putting her arm around Georgie's shoulders, and Will stood next to them, holding sleepy little Martha. Emma was glad they were pressed so closely together because it allowed them to better keep their footing in these rough seas. It was a hard day to have a funeral.

Elder Clark took charge. The Saints sang "Come, Let Us Sing an Evening Hymn" by Brother William Phelps. Emma thought it an unusual choice for a morning funeral, but perhaps the "evening" meant the end of Brother Hardcastle's life.

"Come, let us sing an evening hymn
To calm our minds for rest,
And each one try with single eye
To praise the Savior best."

Elder Clark spoke briefly on the Savior and His atoning sacrifice. With great love, he spoke of Jesus and how, because of Him, all mankind would live again. "Even more than that," he went on, talking loudly over the wind, "we will be able not just to live again but to live with our Heavenly Father in the highest degree of the Celestial Kingdom—with *all* the glory that He has, and with *all* that He offers us! Of course, that depends in part on us and how we live our lives. I believe Brother Hardcastle will achieve that highest degree because of the righteous life he lived and because of his faithfulness in striving toward Zion."

Then Elder Lyman gave a few short words about Brother Hardcastle's faithfulness in uniting as a community in Zion to prepare for the Second Coming of Christ. "We must love the kingdom of God more than our lives, our property, our appetite, and all things else," he said. "All of us have come on this voyage to be united with our fellow Saints in Zion so we can better worship our God."

Smiling, Emma squeezed Hattie's hand. She hoped with just a simple squeeze to convey to her sister her assurance that Brother Hardcastle had chosen the right path, and they must, too.

In closing, the Saints sang *O God, the Eternal Father,* another Brother Phelps hymn. Emma's and Hattie's pretty voices blended with others around them. Emma marveled that the Elders would take the time for the hymns of Zion amid the turmoil of the elements swirling around them. Then she thought, *"Maybe it's* because *of the turmoil that we need the hymns."* The verses were about the Savior and His glorious Second Coming:

> *He is the true Messiah, that died and lives again.*
> *We look not for another, He is the Lamb 'twas slain.*
> *He is the Stone and Shepherd of Israel, scattered far;*
> *The glorious Branch from Jesse; the Bright and Morning Star.*

Meanwhile, Brother Hardcastle's body had been placed in a canvas bag. Noticing the rough stitching along the edges, Hattie asked with terrified eyes, "Who sewed him in there?"

Before Emma could answer, Brother Cash said in a low tone, "The sailors."

Will leaned toward her. "I think it's one of their jobs."

Hattie shuddered, and Emma slipped her hand out of her sister's and put her arm around her.

Then Emma looked at Will quizzically, thinking, *How does he know such things?* She knew he went to different places on the ship than she did, so it stood to reason that he learned different things than she did, too. It made sense, though—somebody had to sew his body in.

"The bag is weighted with a ball of iron at his feet, so it won't float," Brother Cash added.

Emma thought that was sad, too, but it also made sense. She wished Hattie hadn't heard, though, because she shivered again.

They watched as the body was put on a long plank, and four sailors dressed in their finest regalia reverently lifted the board over the railing. This was difficult, as the ship was canting back and forth, but they finally managed it. They then tilted the board, and the body slid into the sea.

Emma had a sudden, frantic desire to call it back, to stop its slide, to stop what was happening! *But why would I call it back? What would I do with a dead body?* she thought reasonably. *He needs to be put into the sea.* She took several breaths, securely tamping down her desire to stop the whole thing. What she could do was to continue supporting Hattie.

Then the only sounds were the whistling of the wind followed by a splash from far below. The splash was a small, distant sound, yet to her ears it sounded as present and clear-cut and gut-wrenching as a gunshot. In that moment, she felt as bereft as a single survivor in a shipwreck, holding onto a bare, floating plank.

The image of the canvas bag falling free, followed by its impact with the water, was cemented indelibly into Emma's mind. A picture popped into her mind of the train they'd taken from London to Liverpool, only the train kept going and going through the green meadows, never stopping, and not even needing tracks anymore. *"Stop!"* she commanded herself, lest she fall into the memory of the alley from her childhood again, like she had done before the storm. Holding tightly to her sister at that point was as much for her good as it was for Hattie.

A sailor dressed in full uniform raised his rifle to the sky and fired three groupings of shots. As the report from the rifle sounded, a new worry surfaced in Emma's mind. *Could this have happened to Father? Had he sickened on his voyage and died at sea? Had he been buried at sea? They would never know!* Her imagination stopped at the point where his body dropped into the ocean. *No, that was too awful!* She wouldn't allow herself to consider that. *We* will *see him again; surely, we will!*

She surprised herself with how desperately she *wanted* to see her father again. The last time she could remember wanting her father so desperately was when Uncle Jesse took her and her siblings away after her mother had died.

Emma was still squeezing Hattie's shoulders while the bugler played a short mournful melody. The notes died away like Brother Hardcastle's hopes for this life, and the ceremony was over.

Hattie grasped Emma's arm, whispering frantically, "I hope I don't die over the ocean. I'd feel so lost!"

Emma grasped her sister's hand, forgetting all the angst she had just felt in her need to buoy up her spirits. She said confidently, "You won't, dearest. Besides, remember, it's just his body. His spirit is with Jesus, his wife, and his loved ones. *He* is still living! I find that incredibly comforting!"

"Yes, I *know* his spirit is still alive," Hattie agreed reluctantly. "But knowing that is only in my *head*. It doesn't seem to be in my heart."

"Give it some time. This has been hard, and very sudden." Emma nodded goodbye to Ed Cash and turned Hattie toward the hatch so they could go down to the musty but soothing familiarity of their berth areas. "When it's time for the resurrection, the spirit will reunite with the body. It doesn't matter where it ended up; it'll all turn out all right."

Then, to lighten the moment in a macabre sort of way as they descended, Emma said, "Did they tell you in school that in India they cremate bodies?"

Hattie, horrified, looked at Emma. "They burn them?"

Emma smiled, "Yes. They figure they're going to turn to dust eventually, so they just hurry the process along."

"I guess that works. It's just different," Hattie conceded.

Pausing at the top of the hatch, Emma concluded, "I don't think we'll have that issue in America. I think they're like the English, and they bury their loved ones in the ground. But we will have many things that are different that we'll have to get used to. I wonder what they'll be?"

Thinking on that, they went below for a cold breakfast.

America
NEW YORK CITY

TUESDAY, JUNE 24, 1862

Emma woke Tuesday morning feeling the vibration of the ship under her like a series of rabbits running through a park. That must mean it was going at a good clip, and they were getting closer to New York!

She poked the berth above her. "Will! Can you feel that?"

"The ship?" he answered, leaning over. "There must be a good wind today."

Everyone in the family woke and dressed quickly. Georgie and Richie vied over who would see land first until Will overrode them with a certain, "I will," as only an older brother can do.

As organized as ever, Eliza had the children pack all their things so they would be ready to leave the ship. Then she had the whole family go up on deck.

Emma and Hattie swung their joined hands as they sauntered across the deck, breathing in the foggy, gray morning mist.

Hattie said, "The sky looks like the first wash on an art canvas."

"Did you learn that in the watercolor class you took at school?"

"Yes."

Emma countered, "To me, it looks like gray split pea soup."

"Split pea soup is green."

"I know. That's why I called it gray soup."

"It's so thick! I wonder if we'll even see land before we arrive?" Eliza said, holding tightly to her active two-year-old who kept tugging against her hand.

Georgie and Richie found Caroline and Anne West and talked them into playing "What Do You Spy?" Will found Ralph Wardle, Junior, and they talked animatedly to a sailor. They all pointed toward the horizon, squinting through the fog like diamond cutters looking through their loupes.

Emma saw Eliza look apprehensively from her oldest son to the sailor. Emma wasn't as concerned about the effect the sailors might have on Will as her mother was. She knew him to be a good boy. Although he vacillated between being quiet and energetic, between self-directed and go-along-with-the-crowd, she had faith he would not only choose the best path for himself, but that path would align with God's will.

The deck filled as more passengers gathered, each hoping to be the first to spot land through the swirling fog.

By eight in the morning, the mist turned into tatters, like long strips of ragged cheesecloth floating on the breeze. Just then, in between the ribbons, Will and Ralph saw something solid. They cried out at the same time, "There! Look there!"

Georgie and Richie heard them, left the game they were playing with the West sisters, and ran over. The little boys' eyes followed where the older boys pointed, and then they jumped up and down, holding onto each other's shoulders.

As the wind finally drove the fog away, Hattie spied the land. "It's New York!"

Emma whispered dreamily, "Yes, it is."

Hugging Martha tightly, Eliza sighed contentedly, "We made it!"

At four o'clock in the afternoon on June 24th, the Horspools gathered at the railing as the *William Tapscott* arrived at the mouth of the Hudson River. The ship had almost run out of drinking water, but no one seemed to care because they were too busy viewing the magnificent sight in front of them. New York, Brooklyn, and New Jersey all stretched in front of them like children's towns built out of blocks.

"Look how many buildings there are!" Georgie exclaimed.

"And how tall they are!" Hattie added. "What do you think? Five stories?"

Emma looked at her mother, who was trying to stop Martha and was circling around after the bow at the back of her dress like a dog after its tail. Eliza finally said, "It looks marvelous!" She picked up the little girl to hold her in one place, pointing to the shore.

"They'll let us walk around, won't they?" Hattie asked excitedly.

"Yes," Emma replied. "As long as we're at the meeting place at the proper time."

"And as long as we don't talk to any runners," Will said.

"What's a runner?" Georgie asked.

"It's a bunko artist."

"Watch your language, young man," was Eliza's immediate reprimand.

Nodding his head, Will explained to his little brothers, "It's a dishonest person who takes advantage of newcomers."

"Will they get us?" Richie worried.

"Just stay close to the family," Emma said with a reassuring smile. "You'll be fine."

At five o'clock, the ship dropped anchor, and they had officially arrived! They went below for their final dinner. Will carried Martha carefully down the ladder, and Georgie and Richie tumbled after Emma and Hattie. Trailing them, Eliza murmured more to herself than to her children, "Everyone stay healthy for *one more day* so we can get off this tub!"

Bright and early the next morning, there was an exuberant crush at the railings as the passengers watched the steam tug *Henry Binden* attach itself to the *William Tapscott* and pull the larger ship to the Narrows between Brooklyn and Staten Island. They saw a smaller boat that would ferry them to the land.

By the time they disembarked, they had been on the ship for forty-two days.

Because of Eliza's preparations, the Horspools were among the first group of families loaded onto the ferry. Eliza held Martha, Emma had Georgie, and Hattie was in charge of Richie. Will followed with the odds and ends of luggage.

Catching up her long skirt in one hand, and holding her bag and brother with the other, Emma carefully picked her way from the gangplank to the ferry, the White Goose. Her family squeezed into the boat with seventy other immigrants. There was an anxiousness to the crowd, uncertain as to what would happen once they got on land.

Emma and Will sought a place to stand at the tall railing where they could view the dock and the surrounding land. Next to her, Eliza held Martha so she could see the water moving under them. Georgie and Richie stood on tiptoe looking for fish, but, of course, didn't find any this close to land.

Half to Emma and half to himself, Will said, "Well, White Goose, fly us to land."

Emma grinned at him and then noticed the ferryman. He was dressed nattily in a dark shirt, vest, and flat hat, and he loomed larger than his medium stature would indicate. Steering with one hand, he cleared his throat, shaking his 'chin curtain', that is, his beard neatly trimmed in the current style. In a rousing voice, he boomed, "Welcome, one and all, to Ellis Island. This is one of three Oyster Islands—named for obvious, tasty reasons."

His little joke got a small laugh from his nervous passengers, making his chin curtain wobble in return.

"What's he doing?" Will nudged Emma. "We're not paying for this, yet he sounds like a carnival barker."

She'd been thinking the same thing. She said, "Look at the tie around his neck. It has the same name as the boat. I think this is *his* ferry. He probably just likes being in charge."

The man droned on, "This point of land is known as The Battery because a fort was built here in the 17th century."

A large round building came into view. Grasping onto the high railing with one hand, Georgie pointed over it with his other. "What's that?"

As if in response to his question, the ferryman intoned, "The building ahead is Castle Garden, formerly Castle Clinton."

"Well, now we know." The circular structure looked like a rust-colored three-layer cake.

Will said, "I thought the whole area was 'Castle Garden', not just a building."

"So did I."

The man's energetic voice continued, "It's built of sandstone quarried in New Jersey, as is the wall that goes all around."

The land was getting closer. Emma could see now that the wall and the building were built of multicolored stones in orange, red, brown, and beige. The variegated effect was quite becoming.

"The Swedish songbird, Jenny Lind, first sang here just twelve years ago, with six thousand people in attendance!"

The ferry bumped against the pier.

Emma smiled. *He has told us what he must consider to be the most important items, and he's timed it to finish right when we reach the shore. Clever man.*

"And here we are," he called, as other hands swung forward and brought the ferry to a stop. "Welcome to America!" Bowing slightly, he swung his arm out with a flourish.

The people nearest him applauded in appreciation, but most anxiously pressed forward to go across the gangplank.

Emma smiled a "thank you" to the ferryman and then waited until her turn to step out. Holding onto Georgie's hand, she waited behind her mother and Will.

Eliza directed, "Son, will you please get out first and help the rest of us?"

Will did as he was asked, offering his hand first to his mother and then to Emma.

Finally, she was on the ground. Blessed land—earth! There was no other feeling like it! The solid feel of land was short-lived, however, because the ground felt like it was rolling like a runaway wagon.

Grabbing her arm, Will said, "Watch out there! Do you feel like you're still on the ship?"

Laughing, Emma agreed. "I feel I'm still skating the ice pond at Poplar Park, even after my skates are off."

Georgie piped up, "That's how I feel, too!"

They laughed as Hattie and Richie joined them, all of them feeling the same rolling motion even though their feet were firmly planted.

After a time, the rolling feeling subsided and was replaced with exhilaration.

"We're here! We made it!" Emma exclaimed. Her face, normally so modest and reserved, split into a huge grin. Still holding Georgie, she swept him into a hug and pulled Will, Hattie, and Richie into an ebullient circle of laughter.

Almost dancing, Hattie grabbed Eliza, who handed Martha to Will. The child, a mass of fluffy pink flounces, patted her big brother's cheek with one hand while holding Phoebe with her other. She repeated, "Here! Here!"

Emma shook her head and smiled. *Family!* she thought. *I hope I am blessed with a family of my own someday.*

When everyone had calmed down and collected their luggage, they were ushered into the line for medical examinations. This was the line Eliza worried over.

Emma noticed her mother's euphoria from landing died the instant they stood in line. Emma looked with concern at her, and that encouraged Eliza to confide her fears.

"What if they find something?"

"Eliza, the doctors are checking for diseases that shouldn't be brought into the States. We don't have typhus or cholera or smallpox."

They moved forward a couple of steps. The people eight in front of them had apparently been allowed into America.

"Yes, but they might see that bit of floor burn Georgie got as measles, or Richie rubbing his eye as pink eye." Eliza had examined her own children acutely, trying to imagine anything the medical examiners might find out of place. "And Richie is so thin. They might think he has a disease. But that's just him!"

Resting her hand on Eliza's wrist, Emma reassured, "We'll be fine." She prayed she was right.

Each member of the family stood separately before a medical

examiner, except for Martha, who stayed in her mother's arms. The doctor didn't smile. He didn't talk. The same actions were performed perfunctorily with each person. He brusquely held each person's chin, turning the head this way and that. He skeptically investigated each face, searching eyes, eyebrows, forehead, ears, nose, and mouth. Then he scanned down the arms and the whole body.

It was unnerving.

Will was stoic—putting up with it as if he weren't standing there. Happy-go-lucky Georgie just waited for it to end, and Hattie stood nervously playing with her braids. Emma looked patiently pleasant, but that merely masked her uneasiness at the intrusion. Each of them finished and was moved on past a mark drawn on the floor. Evidently, they had passed the test.

Emma looked back to see Eliza nudge Richie forward. The little boy with eyes twice their normal size looked terrified. Emma looked at her mother, whose calm demeanor belied the fear she carried. Emma breathed high and fast, and she could tell she felt the same way as her mother.

The doctor bent to the boy's level, turning his head and looking at his thin little body. He performed actions on Richie he hadn't on any of the others. He lifted his arms and let them drop. He had him hop and then jump. Then he came back to his eyes, his neck craning forward, scrutinizing.

This is taking forever. Emma felt her nervousness tingling in her. *Why is he checking Richie so thoroughly?*

The boy nervously rubbed his eye again, and Emma took a quick breath. *Don't do that, Richie,* she commanded silently.

She looked again at Eliza and recognized she was holding herself together as if the strands of her mind and her sinews were all that was keeping her body together. Emma had a similar reaction back in the confectionery, imagining how she would act toward customers if a rat had been seen in the shop. That had never happened, but if it had, she would have held herself together and pretended everything was all right.

Finally, the doctor nudged Richie forward past the line. He had passed the test, too. He said, "The fog bothered you, didn't it? Try not to rub your eye, little man."

Emma released a breath she didn't know she'd been holding. She leaned down and gathered the little fellow into her arms, while Eliza stepped forward with Martha.

Perhaps Martha's blonde curls and pink flounces charmed the doctor, because he spoke again. "Who do we have here?"

His question may have been rhetorical, but Eliza answered, "This is Martha."

"I'm Marfa," the little girl said timidly, but rather hopefully, holding the doctor's eyes with her own.

Turning her chin, the doctor smiled at her, looking at her eyes and body. Then he stepped aside, nodding, "She's fine." He hardly gave Eliza a glance.

Eliza walked over the line to her children. Emma saw the relief on her face. They had passed the test! Emma reached out and gave her mother's hand a celebratory squeeze. They had made it through! They were really in America now.

They were next guided to the registry line where Eliza gave the officials everyone's names, ages, and birthplaces and told them that, yes, they did have funds, and yes, they did have someone already in America. Her husband had come before them.

Emma found herself crossing her fingers, thinking, *I hope he really has come!*

After receiving official entry papers, the family moved aside and gathered in a tight circle, setting down their luggage. Emma's eyes shimmered with relief and gratitude to Heavenly Father for a safe arrival. Hattie's were just as bright.

With thankful eyes, Eliza said, "Let's say a prayer of gratitude."

They clustered closer, hands on each other's waists and shoulders. She asked Will to say it, and he agreed.

With heads bowed, he said, "Heavenly Father, we give Thee gratitude for bringing us across the ocean and landing us safely here. Please bless us with the next things we need to do, and bless our leaders, too. In the name of Jesus Christ, Amen."

As Emma said 'amen', she silently added, *And bless Father, wherever he is!*

Setting Martha down, Eliza said, "Well. Are we ready to explore?"

"Yes!" exclaimed Georgie.

Richie clapped Martha's hands together. "Let's exp'ore!"

Martha repeated, "Pore!"

Their mother reminded them one last time, "Stay close!" She reinforced the point by saying, "One of our brothers had thirty sovereigns stolen from his pocket on the dock at Liverpool just before sailing on the *William Tapscott* because he didn't listen."

Will whistled. "Thirty!"

"Yes. And this part of the journey will be very difficult for him."

Duly chastened, they walked along the promenade of the nearby grounds called The Battery Park and bought bread from a street vendor.

Looking around with appreciation, Hattie said, "My! This is far nicer than Liverpool, wouldn't you say?"

"Yes," agreed Emma. "It's bigger. Prettier. Greener."

"Cleaner. More open," Will added. "The dock wasn't as dingy."

Eliza concurred, "Yes, it is lighter here. And it's certainly more spread out than Liverpool."

"Well, it's newer than Liverpool," Will conceded.

"True," Emma and Eliza both said at once, smiling at each other.

Along the promenade, they passed women in fluffy pale dresses with parasols, and men in dark suits, vests, and stylish hats. In Poplar, Emma had always felt stylish and presentable. Now the coats and shawls her family wore on a warm afternoon when they weren't needed shouted, 'Immigrant!' She felt provincial and underdressed and found she didn't like the feeling. She sighed, remembering she *did* have the one good dress. However, tucked at the bottom of a steamer trunk as it was, it wouldn't see the light of day for months.

Near the extensive lawn they also passed vendors selling scarves, umbrellas, necklaces, and natty bow ties.

"Mama, please?" was met with "Not today."

Eliza had planned specific uses for their money, and useless souvenirs were not on the list.

"Look!" cried Georgie. "A kite!"

Richie pointed out the floating wonder to Martha. All three younger children started to run toward the kite with its streaming tail, but their mother pulled them back. "We'll look at it from here. See? You can see it better when you're not so close."

Finally, after passing another kiosk selling shiny gold pocket watches, gold and silver bracelets, and handkerchiefs embroidered with the words "The Battery," she allowed each of them to have a hot meat pie. "Not as good as our English ones, but they'll have to do," she said to Hattie, taking a bite.

After swallowing, Hattie replied, "I think it tastes good."

"Mmm. Yum!" exclaimed Georgie and Richie, who obviously agreed with their sister.

Martha said, "More," reaching up her fingers for a tasty bite of crust.

They had just settled on a bench to nibble when from across the park, Emma saw four figures in the distance. It looked like her friends from the ship. Waving, she stood up, but they didn't see her. "I need to go see them, Eliza," she said, hoping her mother wouldn't mind her running over to them.

Her mother said to go ahead, but soon they needed to go back to the Castle Garden building where the Saints would meet.

The four friends finally saw Emma as she ran toward them. She engulfed Rose and Annie in a hug, smiling up at Lizzie and William who were walking arm in arm. "I'm grateful to see you!"

"We wanted to see you, too," said Annie.

"Everything got so hectic there at the end," Rose observed.

"I know. I didn't realize we had so much to clean up," Emma smiled. "I guess we spread out during the six weeks."

"It's easy to do," agreed Lizzie.

Chuckling, William added, "Unless half of your supplies go teetering across the floor during a storm."

Looking suitably shocked, Emma asked, "Did that happen to you, William?"

"No. But it did to others!"

Annie nodded, coughing suddenly. "It certainly did."

Looking at her four friends, Emma said wistfully, "I wanted to tell you how much I've appreciated your friendship. You made the voyage enjoyable. More than enjoyable—memorable. Special. I can't thank you enough!"

"We loved getting to know you, too," said Rose, then anxiously asked, "Will we see you in the Valley?"

"I certainly hope so! I don't know my father's plans, but I hope so."

"Of course, you'll need to find your father first!" Lizzie knew a bit about Emma's fears.

"Yes, well. He should be in Florence. That's where we're supposed to meet him."

"Then that's where he'll be," said William.

So simple. What a man decides is what will happen—from a male point of view, anyway, Emma thought. She voiced, "I would like to stay in touch with you, but I'm told Great Salt Lake City has over ten thousand people! Not as many as London, of course, but that's still a lot!"

Rose said with sudden earnestness, "Emma, remember the dressmaker I told you about? Naomi Brett." She said her name carefully. "She lives not far from Brigham Young. I will visit her and tell her where everyone is, so she'll be able to tell you where we all are. She can help us stay in touch."

Nodding, Emma repeated, "Naomi Brett." Then she hugged them again, and the tears started, like raindrops falling off a flower. "This might be goodbye. I don't know what situation we'll find ourselves in at Florence, and I must stay close to my family until we get there."

"We might see each other, and we might not," conceded Annie, raising her handkerchief up to dry her eyes.

Rose held Emma's hands firmly in her own gloved ones. "Hopefully, our wagon trains will leave about the same time. Then we can think of you on the plains at the same time as we are."

"Yes!" Doing the same thing at the same time sounded hopeful. Shaking off her tears, Emma laughed, "And William, no more making pies for you. You stay out of trouble!!"

Raising his eyebrows, the tall fellow with the big eyes held up his hands in surrender, while Lizzie, Annie, and Rose laughed and called out, "God speed to your family!"

Emma waved at them over her shoulder, smiling when they waved back. As she crossed the lawn to her family— her feet pressing down on the green blades of grass as lightly as rose petals falling on a pond— it startled her to realize that one part of her life was over. Gone, as surely as snow melting in sunlight. Gone, like the leaves falling off autumn trees. Gone, like ships that foundered and sank. She'd left England, she'd left her house, and she'd left the support of her sister, Elizabeth. These four friends had been a welcome boon to fill that void, but now they, too, were leaving. As a litany of other *leavings* crossed her mind—primarily the passing of her birth mother—she had an uncomfortable feeling that she needed to figure out life on her own and not wait for other people to keep filling that hole inside her.

She mentally listed what she still had. *I have my family, and I'll surely meet more friends on the trail and in Utah. I have the church, and I have its teachings. But most of all,* her brow furrowed in thought, *I think I need to have* me. *I need to rely more on myself.*

Her footsteps slowed as she pondered how to make that happen. *I need to be more reliant on the Savior and intentionally obedient, not just acquiescing to directives. I can help more with the younger children. I need to trust God's promises and trust that doing the right thing will give me strength.*

In just the time it took to reach her family, Emma became a new person.

When she reached them, Hattie asked excitedly if it was, indeed, their friends in the William Wood mess. Emma told her it was, and they wished the Horspools well.

Picking up their belongings, they started on their way again.

Emma thought about the future as they walked. Would Lizzie and William marry in the Endowment House? Would Rose's handsome, red-haired Samuel actually meet her in the great city of Salt Lake? And what of Annie? Would she survive the trek across the plains? She always seemed so frail. Even today, she was coughing. Wistfully, Emma admitted she might never know the answers. The truth was, she couldn't be certain she'd ever see any of them again on this side of heaven.

As the afternoon wore on, no hint of any 'bunko artists' they'd been warned about came near them. Heaven forbid! Con men were still undoubtedly out there, but no untoward person ever approached the family.

Finally, they wandered back to the sandstone building and found the Saints congregating in a noisy, overwhelming mass on the second floor.

Emma saw Eliza scanning the crowd, and realized with chagrin, *she* was searching the crowd, too—only the person she was looking for was her father. *What are you thinking?* she berated herself. *He won't be here.* He had planned to meet them in Florence, Nebraska, not here. Gathering her thoughts, she asked her mother, "Who are you looking for?"

"Elder Lyman. He's in charge of the next part of our trip, and I have something important to tell him."

Will's sharp eyes spotted him first, moving through the throng. "There he is, Mother."

Emma noticed his purposeful stride as he rapidly approached. Her mother waved him over.

"How are your plans going, Elder?" Eliza asked.

He smiled down at them, looking comfortable in this small circle of friends he knew so well. It was obvious to Emma he was busy, but he still had a confidence about him that assured order in the midst of chaos. "The biggest issue right now is separating the large steamer trunks for the Saints going to Florence and the ones not, but that seems to be going well."

"Excellent." Then, lowering her voice a notch, she disclosed, "I want you to know that if you ever find yourself in a pinch, the Horspools have funds. Unlike Brother Phillips, our sovereigns are safe." She patted her cloak with a knowing look.

Elder Lyman smiled, "I am glad to hear that, Sister Horspool. Very glad! Excuse me now. I need to check in with Elder Bales, who is handling immigration matters here in New York. We need to find trains to take us to St. Joseph."

"Of course." Eliza nodded at him and then at Emma, whose cloak contained the other half of their money.

Emma's heart swelled with pride at her stepmother's generosity—really, her parents' generosity. They would have decided such a thing together before her father left. Now holding Martha, Emma entertained her by pointing out a fake stuffed bird on a lady's hat. Inwardly she marveled that Eliza knew so much about their family finances.

It makes sense, she thought. *Father always allowed Eliza a say in the family business, and of course, she makes her own money with her sewing.* It dawned on her that it was *after* her father had married Eliza Bennett that they had built the retail confectionery at #149, and it was after that time that their total sales had skyrocketed. Turning to Martha again, she pointed out a little blonde girl, saying, "She has yellow hair, just like you!"

Martha pointed in the girl's direction, saying, "Lallow."

In the crush of people, Hattie became separated from her mother for a moment. Securely holding Georgie's hand, she darted around some taller individuals until she found her mother, Emma, and Will. "Why are there so many people?" Hattie questioned.

The eight-and-a-half-year-old lover of numbers looked up at her, responding proudly, "There were eight hundred and seven LDS people on board our ship, and that's a lot of people!"

"But it seems like there are even more."

"I overheard some people say something about the *Antarctic,*" Will said. "There must be people here from more than one ship."

Emma reached over and grasped Hattie's hand with a smile, lest the girl feel anxious in the press.

The domed edifice encased the crowd like a cathedral. An air of expectancy and a humming stillness pervaded the space as they waited for their instructions. Even the children, who had been so agitated outside, were quiet.

The New York agent, Elder Bales, greeted the Saints. "I hope you had a nice afternoon exploring Battery Park. I am told that everyone, except two passengers, was given medical clearance to leave the ship, and those two were not of our number. They will be detained for a while in a separate facility, and if they get well, then they'll be able to enter.

"Tomorrow at four o'clock in the afternoon, you will board a train to make the first leg of your journey to St. Joseph, Missouri," he told them. "Eighteen cars have been paid for. Until then, you are welcome to wander the streets of New York if you choose. Of course, be careful with your currency!" He explained some of the ploys of the ungodly so they would know what to expect, like someone acting ill on the side of the road, or someone coming up to them with a sad story. He said, "Some women have even been known to throw their baby at you, and when you're busy catching it, they'll pilfer your purse. Better to stay away from that sort altogether!"

Emma caught Eliza's eye and nodded. Staying together in their little family cluster and avoiding others was exactly what they'd been doing.

Elder Lyman then stood and said, "Besides joining our train at four o'clock, there is another reason tomorrow will be special to you. On June 27th, just eighteen years ago, the Prophet Joseph Smith and his brother Hyrum were martyred."

A surprised gasp rippled through the congregation—one saying, "Oh!", and another one saying to their neighbor, "That's right!", and still another saying, "I'd forgotten."

Emma realized she had been so intent on getting off the ship and through the official lines that she'd forgotten, too.

Elder Lyman went on, "As the Prophet Joseph was the one who helped restore Christ's correct and full gospel, I know you'll want to remember him with your families. It was Wilford Woodruff who said, 'The Prophet Joseph Smith has done more, save Jesus only, for the salvation of men, than any other man that ever lived in it.' That's printed in the Doctrine and Covenants. However, as wonderful as the prophet was, and as much as he did, I always remember that he was merely a conduit. The Head of our Church, the One who is facilitating the Gathering of the Saints—as we here are a part of—and the One whose name the church bears, is Jesus Christ himself. He is the center of our lives and the reason for our worship. I am proud that you acquitted yourselves like Saints on the ships the *William Tapscott* and the *Antarctic*. I know you will continue to do so."

The Horspools left the meeting to eat the evening meal that had been provided for them. Then, the seven of them squeezed into one tiny room for their night's lodging.

Will encompassed the room in one glance. "It's small."

"But it has a window," said Hattie gratefully.

"And best of all, we're on solid ground," Emma said. "To me, it's a palace."

"I can handle these accommodations for one night!" Eliza responded.

The next day, they enjoyed walking through New York, appreciating the wonders of this port town that boasted over a million people. Of course, London was much larger—three times its size. London, after all, was the capital of the largest empire in the world. But both were port cities that relied on shipping, so there were similarities.

"Stores, streets, statues!" Hattie said expansively. "Everything here is big and busy."

"And newer. Much newer than in London," Emma said with satisfaction.

"Look!" cried Georgie. "An organ grinder."

"And monkey!" added an excited Richie.

Martha pointed with every muscle in her two-year-old arm. "Kee-kee!"

"Please, Mama?" they both begged.

Even Martha begged, "P'ease?"

Eliza relented, giving each of them one American penny to put in the organ grinder's box. "Stay back and just watch. Don't touch the monkey!"

They laughed as the monkey did somersaults, climbed up a nearby post, jumped off, and did more somersaults. Emma thought the pennies were well worth the entertainment.

Walking along after, Emma said, "I'd like to remember things we've heard about Joseph Smith."

Hattie agreed, "Yes, this is a good day to pay tribute to him."

"Like Elder Lyman said," added Will, scuffing the walkway with his toe.

"My Sunday School teacher said he liked children," offered Georgie. "He played games with boys in No-woo... Nahboo... what's the name of that city?"

"Nauvoo," answered Emma. "Yes, I've heard that. And that he had a cheery temperament. I think that would be a nice thing to be known for." Looking down at her brother, she said, "You have a cheery disposition, Georgie!" He smiled triumphantly as Richie looked up at her hopefully. "You do, too, John Richard."

Hattie said, "I heard that it only took him three months to translate the entire Book of Mormon. He had less schooling than I've had, and I couldn't do that!"

"That's because it was a miracle," Will said. "God gave him His power. He didn't do it on his own."

The Horspools were proud owners of one copy of the Book of Mormon, given to them as a gift by an Elder who stayed at their house.

Eliza asked, "Do you remember hearing how Papa joined the church? You younger ones weren't alive then." Settling Martha with Phoebe on her lap, and looking up to collect her thoughts, she said, "Your father was coming home from work one evening when he saw a group gathered at the end of East India Dock Road. Usually, at that time of day, everyone went home, so he wondered why they were gathered. He went to check and saw a couple of men gesturing broadly. As he got closer, he heard words like "baptism" and "resurrection," and he thought, 'Oh, it's just some religionists,' and turned around. Then he heard one of the men say something like, "*Anyone* who desires may come unto Christ, not just the elite few." That stopped him in his tracks. What they said was different from what other religions had said. Later, he realized it was God's Spirit prompting him to listen. He rejoined the group and went that night to a preaching. They gave him a *Book of Mormon*, and he read it. The doctrine was not like any he'd heard in other churches, but it resonated with him. How he said it was, "It made really good sense." He went to a few more meetings and liked what he heard."

"What kinds of things?" asked Hattie.

"Well, that Christ talked to mankind through a prophet, just like in olden times, and that God talks to us through his Spirit."

"That's called revelation," Will said in a low voice to Georgie and Richie.

"I know that," said Georgie.

"Wev-**ay**-shun." Richie worked out the sound.

Martha wasn't listening to her mother's voice. She was trying to tie the ribbons on the doll's braids, but her little hands just kept circling them around. Unsuccessful, she handed Phoebe to Emma, who took the doll, tied the hairbows, and handed her back.

Eliza didn't let the boys pull her from her story. "And he liked their teaching that Jesus would come again and smooth out all earth's problems. He and your Mama Martha so enjoyed being part of a people who were preparing for Christ's kingdom and the Second Coming that, in 1846, they were baptized. Two years later, I was baptized, and that's where I met them—in the Poplar Branch."

"So here we are," Hattie jumped ahead to the conclusion of the story, "on our way to Zion."

"On our way to Zion!" Richie echoed.

As if realizing it for the first time, Georgie exclaimed, "We're going to Zion!" followed immediately by, "Look, a candy shop! Can we have one, Mama? Please?"

"Pwease?" Richie pleaded.

Shaking her head with a tolerant smile, Eliza said, "All right, just one penny candy each. And don't take too long."

The Second Train

THE EASTERN UNITED STATES

FRIDAY, JUNE 27, 1862

Late that afternoon, Emma's family arrived at the Hudson River Train Depot with their fellow voyagers from the *William Tapscott* and the *Antarctic*. It was a huge group, and, as Elder Lyman had outlined, the plan was to take them by train to St. Joseph, Missouri, and then by steamboat to Florence, Nebraska.

Emma smiled politely at several folks as she walked to the platform, but she didn't see Ed Cash, Brother Batchelor, and his red-haired daughter, or her four friends. It was hard enough just to keep her own family in view in the melee.

Suddenly, as Emma looked through the mass of immigrants in their dull colors, drab traveling clothes, and packages, a large group in blue caught her eye. Standing on the same platform was a militia in crisp uniforms, also waiting for a train.

Emma was shocked and, glancing at her mother, could see Eliza was also. "

"Who are they?" she asked Will, as if he should know.

He did. "They're the Union army. Their uniforms are blue."

Emma nodded, suddenly feeling very small—much smaller than her five feet three inches. She felt she was on the distant end of a telescope and was just a pinpoint in height. What was there about men in uniform that made them loom solid and confident, looking bigger than life and making her feel so minuscule?

Quickly, Emma realized she needed to release her own shock and fear to help her sister, for Hattie leaned over, clutching Emma's hand. Eyes wide, she trembled in alarm.

"Emma," she whispered, as if talking softly meant that the soldiers weren't on the platform right next to them, "they have rifles." Emma heard Georgie admiring the gold bands, shiny buttons, and crisp hats, but all Hattie could see were the rifles. The soldiers carried real rifles.

Emma tried to placate her with a calm smile. "You've seen soldiers in England with rifles, although their uniforms were red."

Hattie countered, "Yes, but that was in parades in Harlington or London. These rifles are for real." Speaking even more quietly, she added, "They're for— hurting people."

Emma put an arm around her sister's shoulders and breathed deeply. "I'm sorry they're so scary, Hattie. But these soldiers don't want to hurt us. I don't think they even notice us." As she spoke to her sister, she grew stronger. "We'll stay together with our family and the rest of the Saints, and soon we'll be far away from them."

"I hope so," Hattie shuddered.

Emma sighed. The reality of rubbing up against an army was vastly different from what she'd imagined on awaking this morning. She wondered what else would occur that was completely different from her preconceptions.

Then she thought of something that made her breathing go faster: the Army's policy of conscripting men. She'd read about it in the *Star*. They would forcibly take any man who could hold a rifle.

She couldn't mention her concern about Father to Hattie because it would worry her further. She also didn't want to increase any burden on her mother. Instead, she sidled next to Will again and whispered, "You don't think they conscripted Father, do you?"

His eyes focused intensely on hers. It looked like he had not thought of the possibility.

"I hope not," he said with a lowered voice. "He was traveling separately, though. It's one of the reasons Elder Lyman keeps us together in a large group. He doesn't want any of us pulled away for a cause we shouldn't be fighting for."

"I'm probably just worried. I find myself thinking often of Father and hoping he's all right."

"I know it's hard, Emma, when we have no idea where he is, but I'm sure he's all right."

"You're right. I'm sure he's fine. He's fine. I'll just be so glad when we're all together again."

"Until then, we are going to hold it together."

Both siblings nodded to each other in a solemn pledge to do their part for the family.

The Army took the train that had been scheduled for the Saints. Emma and Hattie were relieved they were gone, but that meant they went back to the stuffy depot until another train could be procured. Did they not open any windows in this depot? It was as hot and stifling as a bannock cooked in their oven.

It wasn't until seven thirty in the evening that a train came for their large group. By eight o'clock, Emma's family was herded into facing seats. She was anxious to get moving, mostly to further their progress, but also to feel a breeze through the windows.

She lifted the neck of her dress, trying to fan a little air down her dress, saying to Will, "This is a far cry from a London fog."

He agreed with her. "I keep looking around to make sure none of the older people faint."

She nodded. "Yes, it's that bad!"

At nine o'clock, their chartered train signaled its intent to leave with a loud, long whistle. Emma heard steam escape outside and the scrape of metal as the heavy wheels started slowly turning.

Hattie said, "It sounds like an old person having a hard time waking up and getting going."

Emma barely had energy to respond to her sister. "I think it sounds like a bear lumbering off looking for berries."

As the train rumbled along, picking up speed, a breeze wafted through the open window, reviving Emma.

"Oh! Now it's a cougar leaping," she said, as the wheels roared with a new, ongoing drive under them.

"No, it's an antelope speeding through the countryside!"

"Not that you've ever seen an antelope," Emma quipped.

"Not that you've ever seen a cougar," Hattie countered.

"I have." Emma quirked her head. "In *Elephants and Castles*."

"That doesn't count," Hattie scoffed.

The girls took off their hats and sat back, letting the breeze riffle through their hair and fan their faces and necks. After the interminable wait at the stuffy depot, it felt luxurious.

As the night progressed, their coach encased Emma in darkness like the den of a fox. Georgie sprawled on her, and Richie fell asleep on Hattie while her head lolled onto Emma's shoulder. Will balanced a slumbering Martha between him and his mother. The rhythmic clickety-clack, clickety-clack, clickety-clack of the tracks created a steady pulse underneath them that felt like a constant lullaby, albeit a loud lullaby. As if they were in one big perambulator, they fell fitfully asleep.

When Sunday morning cracked open its pale sun's eyes, they found they were traveling through the countryside. Hattie lifted her head off Emma's shoulder and stretched. Looking out the windows, she exclaimed, "Oh, it's beautiful!"

Emma opened her eyes, rolled her shoulders, and looked out, too. "So green!" They were rolling past a verdant countryside full of green grass and trees on every side. "Wake up, sleepy head." She nudged Georgie, who had almost fallen on the floor.

Hattie tried the same with Richie, but he stayed asleep, as did Martha.

"Where are we?" their mother asked, replacing some hairpins that had fallen out onto her lap.

"I don't know," Emma answered. "It's lovely, though, isn't it?"

"It's certainly better than train yards and the outskirts of towns."

Will stood up, shaking himself out and cracking his neck. "How long are we on this train?" He sounded like he dreaded the answer.

His mother said, "Trains in general: nine days. It won't be this one all that time."

"I don't know if my neck can take it, but, of course, it will." Groaning, he rolled his eyes in frustration.

"It's all for a good cause, son. Remember that. We're building up the kingdom."

"I know, Mother," he said contritely. "We're going to Zion."

The older ones leaned back on their benches and enjoyed the green landscape floating past them until the little ones woke up. Then Eliza produced some sea biscuits she had saved from the ship for breakfast. They broke off small pieces and took their time eating the hard bread.

"I wish I had some rhubarb jam to go with this biscuit," Georgie wished.

"I wish I had butter," remarked Richie.

Emma chuckled. "That would be good. But I've decided to be happy with what I've got. Thank you for thinking ahead, Eliza."

"It never hurts to be prepared."

At noon, the train jolted past a sign proclaiming Rochester, New York. The younger children had fallen asleep again from the incessant clacking of the wheels, but not Emma. She didn't want to miss a thing in her new country. She looked at every tree as if it were the first one that had been created in the world. Then she looked between the trees, hoping beyond hope to see one of America's elusive animals.

The countryside looked different, although she couldn't put her finger on it. When crossing the east midlands going to Liverpool, they had passed gentle, rolling hills marked by low stone walls as well as wooded areas. The woods sprang up dark green and close-packed as an area where a Robin Hood might ply his trade, and then suddenly they were gone and the landscape switched to open meadow dotted with white sheep. Neither infringed on the other. In the west midlands, they'd seen a flat flood plain and woods as well as moors.

Here it was wild grass, not meadow—*I haven't seen a single sheep. What do they do with all this land?*—and then solid forest, trees upon trees, deep, dense, and dark. The trees seemed different, too, although she couldn't identify why. She would get used to it, though. It was her new country!

The trees ended rather abruptly when they reached a sign marking the Niagara River. But then an even more astounding sight burst into view. She took one look and then hastily woke her family. "You have to see this!"

Emma's family woke, as did everyone else in their train car. Like a gust, the words "Niagara Falls" swept through the train car. Excitement built as the occupants spotted the Falls. With dropped jaws and stunned faces, they pointed at their majestic breadth. The tremendous roar of the Falls filled the car, even at a distance.

Emma heard someone exclaim, "Gallons every second!" and "Been there for thousands of years." and "America and Canada." Spellbound, Emma watched the wide expanse of pounding water emerge as a mist, bedewing their windows from even a mile away. *What power they have!* she thought.

Suddenly, her amazement turned into abject alarm as, without warning, she saw they would pass high over the river on a suspension bridge. Their huge, heavy train with its rumbling metal wheels was going to cross the deep chasm on feathery-looking iron ropes held up by only four huge pilasters. The bridge looked so fragile compared to their gargantuan train.

Not only that, but this bridge was a double-decker, and ahead, she saw wagons, horses, and people already on the lower portion of the bridge. Would they be smashed under their train? Would the train stay on its track? Would the train cars get across?

Suddenly—and most terrifying of all—Emma couldn't *see* the tracks! She couldn't see anything but air. How were they even crossing the ravine? She imagined the train as a tightrope walker, zipping along a slender rope of jute.

Hattie must have felt the same way, for she grabbed Emma's hand. Emma kept telling her, "Breathe, Hattie, breathe," but she was saying it to herself as much as to Hattie.

Georgie and Richie's faces were smashed against the window as the train crossed the chasm. Will's hands pressed onto the glass on either side of them while he, too, looked out. Emma couldn't understand how they didn't look terrified. She looked at Eliza, who looked like she was holding her breath.

And then they were over. The train drew out two whistles and chugged speedily on its way. Emma and Hattie both let out their breaths. Emma was relieved to see trees and ground again.

Georgie and Richie stayed at the window, hoping for another amazing view, while Will plopped down across from Emma. "That was above board!"

Emma had finally caught her breath enough to smile. "Sounds like someone spent time with the sailors."

"They had a lot to teach."

Ignoring the two of them, Eliza took a deep breath, agreeing, "That really was something!"

Even though the train did all the work for them, Emma could see from their faces that they felt they had just undergone something momentous.

For lunch, they had pieces of cheese Eliza had bought at the train depot with as many hard biscuits as they could stomach. They talked of the sights they expected to see when they crossed the plains.

Georgie said excitedly, "I want to see a buffalo. Elder Lyman said there are thousands of them!"

"Me, too," agreed Richie.

Emma asked the little guy, "Is there an animal you'd like to see here in America?"

"I wanna see a eh-phant."

"Ah, an elephant," Emma nodded. "That will be a trick, but maybe we'll see one. You never know!"

Martha perked up at the word "animal." Holding up the satin purse Hattie made for her, she dug her finger into the corner, saying, "Ducky! Ducky!"

"Yes, dear, a duck is a nice animal. What about you, Hattie?"

After thinking, she said, "Antelope. What about you, Mama?"

Eliza said prosaically, "Whatever animal I see, I'd like cut and cooked and put in a stew."

Groans of "Ah, Mama" and "Oh, Mother" filled their benches, after which Eliza cleaned up their area, and they went back to looking at the scenery for the rest of the Sabbath.

Monday grew hotter as they traveled past Michigan and Lake Erie. Across the river in Detroit, they discovered the Army had again appropriated their chartered train. They milled about in the train station all afternoon until, near twilight, they heard an enormous roar. Elder Lyman had finally found a train for them, and they were ushered out onto the platform. The engine screeched to a puffing halt, spewing smoke, gravel, and sound. In their tired state, the behemoth could almost be mistaken for a dark, prodigious dragon.

Will leaned back from the track and counted. Walking back up to the family, he said, "There are only twelve cars."

Looking worried, Emma said, "Last time there were eighteen."

"Are more coming?" Eliza wondered, looking in the same direction.

"If not, we'll be squashed," replied Hattie.

After the train stopped, Elder Lyman walked quickly from group to group, starting the boarding process. "Twenty more into each car!" he called repeatedly. To the Horspools he said in a low voice, almost in an apology, "This is all I could requisition."

As they neared their train car, a horrendous smell emerged from the open door. Emma choked, and Hattie doubled over, gasping, "What is that?"

Emma saw what it was. These were cattle cars! Their conveyance had been for animals. This train was particularly pungent, however, having a strong, musky smell. Emma had been around horses and cows at her grandpa's estate. She knew how those animals and their manure smelled—earthy and grassy. This was not that smell. This was horrible.

She had just come to her own conclusion when Will climbed in. He pointed out stiff bristles stuck against the door, his lip sneering in disgust. "You know what that is."

"Pigs!"

They were riding on a pig train.

The only seats were backless boards. Most of the men and the able children let the mothers with small children sit. Eliza and Hattie sat with Martha and Richie on their laps. Georgie was tucked between them. Emma and Will stood behind, balancing as the metal titan started up with a wheeze and a whistle and a rocking motion.

There were so many Saints in each car, there was no room between the standing passengers. If someone sneezed, they sneezed on their neighbor. If someone had to suddenly vomit, well... And what had been merely hot on the previous leg would now be unrelentingly suffocating.

Trying to keep a sense of humor, Will quipped, "If someone faints, they won't have to worry about falling. There's no place to fall!"

"Don't joke, Will. Someone is bound to faint, but it'll be the smell that does it!" Emma replied.

"What is the odor?" Hattie complained, looking behind at her sister. "It's awful!"

"Do you really want to know?" asked Emma.

"Do I?"

"It's pig urine, and I agree, it's horrible."

"I can't breathe, Emma!" Her grief-stricken face looked like her best friend had died. "I can't get away from the stench."

"Cover your mouth with your handkerchief, dear," advised Emma as she pulled out her own embroidered handkerchief, shaking the edges free. She had sewn the embroidery herself—blue cornflowers, pink rosebuds, and small green leaves in two of the corners. It seemed a crime to expose her beautiful hanky to such an awful setting, but the thin cloth did help.

She looked sideways at Will and saw that he had tied a knot in the corners of his man-sized kerchief and was pulling it over his nose and mouth like a bandit. They nodded at each other, their eyes registering relief that each sibling had found a small way to alleviate the smell.

Despite their handkerchiefs, the foul smell from the pigs' hairy skin and excretions was still deplorable. Emma lamented, "The car wasn't even swept before we came in."

Will shook his head. "Their reek is in every fiber of wood, every speck of hay, and every scrap of metal in the cattle car."

"It's in every breath we're taking."

"I don't know if I'll die of the smell or the heat."

"And my calf already hurts." She was reminded of the many times her calves hurt as she served customers in the confectionery, but she didn't even have room to reach down and rub it.

Eliza moved Martha to her other knee, shuffling her belongings as she dug for something in the salmon-colored satin reticule John's mother, Charlotte, had made for her. It was small, so only her most delicate or precious items fit in it. Finally, she triumphantly pulled out a tiny bottle of peppermint oil. "I traded a very fancy black moiré mourning dress for this oil," she told her children. "Everyone, put three drops on your handkerchief and cover your noses. It will help."

They each eagerly sprinkled three precious drops on their cloths and found that it did help. It didn't stop the smell entirely, but if you concentrated on the lovely peppermint scent, you could momentarily forget the fetid odor that permeated the train car. Nothing, however, covered up the smell of retching from passengers who were too hot, too humid, or too tired.

Sometimes, Emma thought, *it really is hard to remember that we are children of God's kingdom on our way to Zion.*

Emma grabbed Will's attention. She looked around at their crowded condition, pulled away her hanky for an instant, and said, "Moses," before quickly covering her nose.

Will looked quizzical for a long moment. Then he lowered his own kerchief just long enough to answer her. "Children of Israel? Hard times!"

Emma had often read that favorite Bible story to her family. Moses (well, God, actually) had freed the children of Israel from Egypt, but then the Israelites had wandered in the wilderness for forty years.

Emma lifted her hanky off again to ask, "Think we'll be on this train for forty years?"

His eyes danced wickedly, and he bobbed his head up and down zealously.

Emma laughed. Even in the dimness of a hot, smelly, jolting, uncomfortable hog car, Will could make her laugh. Emma felt their camaraderie shift. She felt he'd been an outsider to the tight-knit group of three sisters. Now it looked like he could be her confidant and friend. She found she liked that idea a great deal.

It turned out that they were not on the hog train for forty years. Not even forty days. By the next day, Tuesday, they had reached Chicago (which they thought was a fine place) and at noon were put on a different train where they were seated comfortably with plenty of room. The carriage windows were open, letting in the fresh breeze as the train zipped along the tracks.

But even with the clean air whipping in, poor Hattie said, as she did for three days after, "I can still smell the hogs every time I breathe!"

St. Joseph

ST. JOSEPH, MISSOURI

FRIDAY, JULY 4, 1862

With a shrieking metal-on-metal, the monster train ground to a halt in a terrifying flurry of smoke and dust.

"Children, we've arrived. We're in St. Joseph," Eliza announced to her family, as she shook each of them awake.

Emma stretched, rolling a reluctant Hattie off her shoulder.

"No more twains?" a sleepy Richie asked.

"No more trains," his mother reassured him, lifting him to his feet.

"Besides, this is as far as any train can go," Emma explained, gathering her hat, bag, shawl, and coat. "There are no tracks west of Missouri."

Finally awake, Hattie said, "The train needs tracks. It can't go on the prairie by itself, silly!"

Will nudged Georgie with his toe. "Wake up, sleepyhead. It's July the Fourth."

"Why, it's Independence Day in our new country!" exclaimed Hattie, who always looked through rose-colored glasses. Somehow, a holiday seemed the perfect start to the rest of their journey.

Georgie groggily lifted his head. By this, their ninth day on trains, everyone was exhausted. None of the Saints had had enough sleep, sanitary conditions, or sufficient food. At one stop, they had cleaned a village out of bread. Almost everyone was at least a little cranky.

Scratching his head with one hand while hanging onto his ever-present neck kerchief, Will looked around. "We're at the very edge of the United States. This is the dividing line between America and nothing."

"You're exaggerating, Will. It's not nothing." Hattie straightened her hat as she reached for her cape. "It's a frontier. Wilderness. There are animals out there."

"But not a lot of towns except for the ones the Saints built in the Utah Territory. Not until you get to California or Oregon. That's what I heard, anyway."

The family gathered their belongings and left the train. The slanting rays of sunset cast a luminous golden glow over the train yard, making the boxy shapes of train cars on the parallel tracks look more like swank hotels on shiny roads than the dusty, utilitarian things they really were.

Emma looked at her fellow Saints as they slowly emerged. Their hair and hats were skewed, clothing crumpled, and they all smelled vaguely like hog. *I'm sure I look as askew as they do,* she thought. *Luckily, it's getting dark. I hate for anyone to see me this way.*

The large group moved through the dust toward an enormous unused barn where they would spend the night. As she walked, Emma took in the town—St. Joseph on the Missouri River, called by some the Borders of Civilization. The United States of America stopped here. Most of the land west of St. Joseph was just one vast tract of emptiness.

The Saints had been warned that St. Joseph attracted the lawless and the rebellious, but they'd also been told if they stayed together, they would be fine. Emma held Georgie's hand, Hattie held Richie's, and Eliza carried a sleepy Martha. Will came behind, hefting their small pieces of luggage.

As they walked, Emma stared in amazement to the right and to the left. Townspeople were out in force—couples going into stores, men talking excitedly, or mothers strolling babies in perambulators on the dusty road. Emma noticed a cluster of women dressed in bright colors and overly bright makeup lounging in the shadows against wooden pillars, seductively gesturing to their group as they passed. With chagrin, Emma thought, *What are women of the night doing here? Do they allow that?* She was shocked beyond measure.

Some men were already drunk and staggering along the main boardwalks. Their jackets and vests hung sloppily, showing their suspenders with shirt tails untucked, and they were yelling, shooting their pistols into the air, and swearing loudly. With furrowed brows, Emma looked back at Will, saying under her breath, "Is this their way of celebrating Independence Day?"

Will replied, "Seems like it. Everything we heard about St. Joseph appears to be true."

Emma walked with Georgie in the middle of the road, away from most of the staggering figures by the buildings. She guided him away from a couple of Missourians who veered into the road, shouting, "The Confederate army is coming!" Others came toward them, glaring and murmuring, "Them damn Mormons." She never wanted to be alone here!

Suddenly, one of the drunken sots stepped out, purposefully stumbling toward her. His face was a leering mask of filth and lechery. Emma suddenly wished for her father. He would protect her. He would send this awful man on his way!

It overcame her at once—the dark, the noise, the unfamiliarity, the fatigue, and this obscene man looming in front of her. It was all too much. Instead of seeing a wide street, her vision narrowed to a dark, cramped alley.

She stopped walking. Georgie stopped, too, looking up at her, perplexed. Just as the man's menacing body and jeering face drew close, Will nudged her from behind, moving them past the reprobate. Will didn't look at the man but kept Emma marching ahead to the barn.

Her continued forward movement, the blessed feeling of Georgie's hand, and Will's hand on her back kept her from spiraling into that gray, walled place of the alley she had repeatedly run down as a child.

"Ow, Emma!" Georgie complained as she realized that she was gripping his hand too tightly. Only when her gaze shifted down to her little brother did the spell break completely.

"I'm sorry, Georgie," she said.

Then they were at the barn, safe inside with all the other Saints. It was warm and smelled pleasantly of straw (although Hattie swore she could still smell and taste hog). Will helped them bed down around their mother, and one by one they drifted into sleep.

Will and Emma were the last to nod off. "Are you all right?" he asked.

Taking a deep breath, she answered, "I'm fine. Thanks for getting us inside." To herself, she thought, *I never told Will about the alley, and yet somehow, he was able to come to my aid. He is very perceptive.* She was grateful to have him in her life.

"Absolutely!" he smiled. When she didn't say anything, he added, "They were really horrible out there, weren't they?"

"Yes. What they call festive, I call loud and angry. Quite an indecorous introduction to our new land."

"Quite," Will chuckled.

Emma thought how Will was becoming more of a man with each mile into their new country. Back home, he had gone to school and was quiet and polite, and that's about it. Here, he was taking responsibility for his family. She liked this new version of him.

As her eyes grew heavy, she thought about the past few days: New York, Lake Erie, Niagara Falls, the hog car, the cacophony of St. Joseph. She wondered what adventures the rest of the journey would bring.

River by Steam

STEAMBOAT UP THE MISSOURI RIVER

SATURDAY, JULY 5, 1862

At first light, Georgie awoke. He shook Richie, who mumbled and rolled against his mama. He knew better than to wake her, and he definitely knew not to wake Martha.

He shook Emma, who opened her eyes and looked at him quizzically. She had rolled her shawl into a pillow, put her jacket underneath her, and managed to sleep decently. She wasn't sure she wanted to get up yet, though. She felt protected in this barn with the high rafters, like it was a vast cocoon enfolding all of them in peace. She half-closed her eyes.

Not having any luck waking his family, Georgie shook Will next.

He rubbed his eyes, then sat up. "What is it, Georgie?" he asked groggily.

"A steamboat! We get to ride a steamboat today!"

"You've seen steamboats on the Thames. Why are you so excited?"

"I haven't *been* on one. Today, I get to!"

"Yes, for a couple of days, I believe."

"Two whole days!"

His voice brought Emma awake. She looked at his starry eyes and smiled. Evidently, the lad couldn't believe his good fortune!

When the light in the barn grew stronger, Emma's family woke and sat in a circle, content to watch as one by one, the other groups in the huge barn 'joined the living.' The Saints shared victuals, and then most went outside to the pump to fill their jugs and to visit the privy.

Finally, it was time to leave. Elder Lyman called them to order. "Those of you traveling on the *Omaha* will line up in a moment. Those embarking on the *Daniel Boone* will leave at midday. This is the last time we'll all be together as a group of Saints, so let's ask for a blessing on the rest of our travels. I'll say it."

The men took off their hats, and everyone bowed their heads while Elder Lyman prayed. "Heavenly Father, we, a group of Thy Saints, are grateful to have made it this far. We're grateful for the shelter of this barn. We're grateful for the steamboats that will take us to Florence, and we're grateful for the opportunity we have of going to Zion. Please bless us with continued health, continued safety, and kind hearts as we travel. And please bless our leaders, the missionaries in all parts of the world, and family and friends whom we've left behind. We are ever mindful of them. In the name of Jesus Christ, Amen."

Emma was comforted by Elder Lyman's prayer. She imagined it invoked a string of hand-holding guardian angels hovering above them, watching over them and tempering future events. As she had when her father prayed before he left them, she felt like she would be cared for and protected.

As her family left the barn, however, Emma hesitated. This building meant safety, and St. Joseph had not been kind last night. Will waited for her while she looked both ways. He did not look impatient, and she felt he was allowing her, in her own timing, to come to terms with the town. The summer sun was already high in the sky, sending down its hot July rays. The sky was bluer than she'd ever seen it. Taking a deep breath, it seemed to her the clear sky wiped anything negative from the city.

Looking around, she saw no sign of the debauchery of the previous night. No drunks lay sprawled on porches. No slovenly men shoved each other or fired guns. Instead, she saw carriages, horses, a woman in a crisp apron sweeping her stoop, two little girls in clean dresses playing hopscotch in front of a house, and several men in their stylish tall hats and dark jackets walking briskly. This morning, everything about the town looked industrious and full of purpose.

That woman is taking care of her home, and the children are well-tended, she thought. *The men look like they are going to a business meeting. I can almost forgive St. Joseph. It looks vigorous and prosperous in the daylight.*

Finally, Emma stepped out the doors.

As they walked toward the river, Will noticed a sign on some stables on Penn Street.

"That sign says this is where the Pony Express started," Will said. "It ended just last year, you know."

Noticing the excitement in his voice, Emma looked at the little wooden building. "There are still horses stabled here," she noticed. She wished suddenly she could take one of them and ride to Florence, Nebraska instead of spending two solid days on a hot steamboat. *I'd unpin my hair,* she imagined, *and the wind would fly through its tresses. Yes, that's the way to go!*

On Main Street, Eliza pointed out several large houses being constructed. "These people have done well for themselves," she commented.

Will said, "It makes sense that someone would. Here at the edge of the United States, everyone needs to be supplied to move further, and the suppliers make a lot of money."

That conclusion surprised but delighted Emma. *Will thinks more things than he says out loud. I wonder what else he's hiding in that head of his.*

One newly built home with five tapered Greek columns in front had a yard area being landscaped.

Eliza chirped, "Daughter, go see what the sign says." She nudged Hattie toward the fence of the boxy, two-story house, and the girl came back, reciting "The Thomas J. Chew House."

"How many chimneys do you see?"

"At least four," Hattie answered, stepping back and looking at the roof.

Continuing down the road, Eliza sighed. "My! I certainly would like to see the inside!"

Before Emma had time to imagine what kind of wallpaper her mother was imagining, they were at the river. Before them sat their next conveyance.

"Wow!" Georgie breathed, reverently looking at the tall *Omaha*. Its two black smokestacks rose to the sky, and its two decks circled all the way around the boat. "It's big!"

To Emma it did, indeed, seem immense. But then, it needed to handle at least five hundred Saints plus other passengers.

"See the paddlewheel in back?" Hattie asked him.

Clearly awed, Georgie answered, "It will be so nifty to see it work!"

Emma chuckled at his language. *Apparently, Will isn't the only one to pick up the newest lingo.*

"Look!" he pointed. "There's a layer up there. What's that for?"

Hattie shaded her eyes, saying, "And there's a little glass box at the top. What's it for?"

Emma opened her mouth, but Will replied first, "I'll find out after we get on board."

Just then, she saw Elder Lyman muscle his way through the crowd toward them. Looking at Eliza, he said, "We have a situation, Sister Horspool. The agent says we have not paid for passage for the luggage, only the people. I know he's wrong. I know we paid the right amount, but *their* office has the papers, so I can't prove anything. Now, he's willing to let the people onboard, but he says all the luggage will have to stay behind."

Eliza protested, "We can't let that happen! All of us need the things we've brought."

"That's why I've come to you," Elder Lyman said contritely. "You mentioned you had funds should the Saints need them. I'm afraid that time is now."

"I understand, Elder Lyman," Eliza answered, with true consecration. "We have two hundred pounds. You can have them."

"Thank you. That's just the ticket!"

Eliza motioned to Emma and the other children, and they moved out of the way of the crush of Saints waiting to board. Finding a relatively quiet place, Eliza set her children and Elder Lyman protectively around them. Then, the women undid the seams of their cloaks, and each removed a hundred gold sovereigns. Emma and Eliza handed the coins to Elder Lyman.

He thanked them profusely. "I'll pay one hundred sixty to the agent now, and, if you don't mind, I'll use the last forty to buy food for those whose funds have run out."

"Certainly. Whatever you deem best, Elder Lyman," Elzia answered.

"Sister Horspool, this is to be considered a loan only, but I'm not sure when the church will be able to repay you."

Eliza waved him off, and he turned, his dark hair flying as he hastened away. The crowd quickly swallowed him, but he must have accomplished his mission, because shortly after that, boarding began.

The steamboat *Omaha* was beautiful. The Horspools, like most of the Saints, would stay on the lower deck, sitting on benches, exposed to the elements both day and night. A few families had purchased cabins on the second deck, complete with food service.

Hattie asked Eliza why they hadn't obtained any. "We could have done that, couldn't we?"

"Yes," her mother answered hesitantly. "But even though it would have meant beds and food brought to us, I didn't think it was a wise use of our money. We'll tough it out on this deck like most everyone else."

Emma smiled when Hattie sighed.

"It's just for two days. We can do this," she told her. She would have liked a bed, too, but it would just have to wait.

They stowed their baggage under a bench, claiming it as their territory for the next two days. "One of us has to stay on this seat at all times," Eliza ordered.

Hattie questioned, "Most of the passengers are Latter-day Saints. Don't you trust them?"

"Yes. But it's still a good idea to be wise in unfamiliar situations."

It wasn't long before the smokestacks began to churn out black smoke, the paddles started whirring, and they were on their way. As the steamboat slid out into the water, the movement brought a welcome breeze and the luxurious feeling of simply drifting like a leaf on a September stream.

Georgie and Richie sat obediently but not quietly on the bench by their mother. Their bodies were so wiggly, they may as well have been sitting on a pile of horseshoe nails.

Bouncing in his seat, Georgie begged, "Mama, I want to go see."

Equally wiggly, Richie chimed, "Me too."

It wasn't just the little boys; all the children were eager to see the water. With five sets of eyes on her, Eliza finally said, "I'll stay here with Martha. You children go ahead to the railing. Don't lean over!"

Released, they rushed to the rail like pigeons being let out of a box. They all looked in different directions at once.

"Look! There are steamboats going the other way," Hattie observed.

"Like when we were on the ocean and we saw another ship passing," Emma responded. "It felt so good to know we weren't the only ones out there."

"It did!" Hattie agreed.

"Hey, that steamboat has a little glass room on top, too," noticed Georgie. "What's it for?"

"I don't know yet, but I'll find out," Will promised. "Look at how we're always staying the same distance from the shore. The pilot must really know what he's doing."

Emma liked how Will wanted to know how things worked. Grinning, she thought, *In contrast, Georgie likes to do. He always wants to do, do, do! And Richie follows.*

Holding onto the railing as if it were one of her English dance partners, she leaned her head back, smiling with pure enjoyment. The gentle breeze ruffled her hair, and she wished again she could unpin it and let it stream down her back. That was unacceptable in public, so she just dreamed of it. At least she'd left her feathered hat under the bench and not on her head. With a certain amount of vehemence, she thought, *I am not putting it back on until we reach Florence!*

Richie pointed to some ducks flying in a V and she leaned down to tell him those were geese.

After a time, Martha grew restless and kept pointing at her siblings. Eliza called, "Hattie, Martha wants to see the water. Would you come sit here, please."

Hattie traded places with her mother. Eliza went to the railing and, holding the toddler tightly, pointed to the water that arched and twisted like cavorting dolphins.

Emma looked at Martha's eyes. She was mesmerized. Yes, water did that to you! *Water is ever running, ever going somewhere,* she thought. *It's magical. It forges a pathway ahead to some unknown place.*

When the toddler became restless again, Eliza took her back to their bench. Hattie rejoined the others at the railing.

"How long will we be on this boat again?" Georgie asked.

"Two days," said Will.

Holding his arms up, Georgie gushed, "I wish it could be more! I wish it could be forever!"

Jumping excitedly, Richie echoed, "Me too! Forever!"

Hattie raised her eyebrows. "Maybe someday, some author will write a book about two infamous river runners modeled after you two!"

Georgie pummeled the air in front of him with a swashbuckling thrust as he changed his mind. "Not river runners. Pirates!"

Richie agreed with an eager jab into the air. "Yeah, pirates!"

"Or maybe a riverboat captain!" Georgie said, having changed his mind again.

Emma leaned toward Will. With lifted eyebrows, she said quietly, "If they become riverboat captains, they might have to man their boat with crews like ours."

Will nodded. "Good luck with that!"

The crew was the only thing that had marred Emma's steamboat experience so far. They were a rough bunch. When she and her family had boarded, the men had been swearing at everything and leering at the women. Some were half-dressed, and some were strangely wearing a tattered vest with no shirt underneath it. Who did that? Some had no shirt at all, and their chests gleamed where drops of sweat pooled.

It wasn't just that. They were unhelpful and inconsiderate. Emma wanted nothing to do with them. She had shielded Hattie from them as they boarded, putting her between herself and Eliza.

"It's funny. Father serviced the dock workers in Poplar, and they were the poor and the rough," Emma said to Will. "But compared to this crew, they're genteel and refined!"

"The cream of the crop!" he smiled. "Hey, I'm going to walk around for a bit."

Emma saw Eliza watch him go. Apparently, she'd resigned herself to the fact that Will liked to investigate on his own.

Turning back to Hattie, Emma saw a dreamy look on her face. It was her 'I-have-a-poem-to-share' face, the same look she'd had when she gave Elizabeth her wedding poem. She wasn't surprised when Hattie said, "Listen to this:

> *Thou hast taught me, Silent River!*
> *Many a lesson, deep and long;*
> *Thou has been a generous giver;*
> *I can give thee but a song."*

"That was perfect, Hattie! Longfellow?"

"Yes."

"How ever do you remember poetry?"

The girl shrugged. "You know how Elizabeth said discernment is one of your gifts? I guess remembering poems is one of mine." Hattie walked back to the bench. "Mama, do we have water in the skin?"

"Yes, we do. I had Will fill it this morning." Eliza handed it to Hattie, who took a long sip.

"All this water around you makes you thirsty, doesn't it?"

Emma looked at the river passing by and laughed. "I should take a drink, too, while you've got it out."

After she took a sip, Martha and Eliza also took advantage of the skin. The little boys were too busy playing their pretend games to stop and have a drink. Every now and then Eliza called to them to calm down, and she did not allow any climbing or jumping.

Emma could see—even though Eliza seemed calm on the outside —she was wired on the inside. She was ready to jump into action at the first difficulty. Taking a drowsy Martha from her, she said, "Eliza, I'm amazed that you let us ride a steamboat. Are you all right?"

Sighing, Eliza dropped her hands in her lap. "I knew this leg would be hard for me. We're on the water, and none of us ever learned to swim."

Emma nodded. "The Thames was too dirty, and there was nothing closer." She nestled Martha against her shoulder, where the little girl's blonde head lolled.

"That's right. There was no need, and here we are, in a position where it would have been useful."

Reaching over with her spare hand, Emma patted her mother's hands. "We'll be safe, you'll see. We'll be fine."

Taking a big breath, Eliza said, "I hope so." Then, looking at her rambunctious sons, she finally called, "Boys! Over here. I want you to take a break."

Moping, Georgie and Richie obeyed. Once they sat on the floor by the bench, she gave each a sip from the waterskin.

Emma smiled. "I wish I had the *Elephant and Castle* game in my bag."

Richie misheard and excitedly asked, "You have it?"

"No, I wish I did. That would be fun right now."

Plopping down on the ground again, the little boy's shoulders sagged. "It would."

"Here!" Emma had an idea. "Reach into my bag and get the long string there. You and Georgie can play Cat's Cradle."

"Yea!" they both cried.

"Careful," she said while the boys vied with one another to reach into the bag hanging from her arm that held Martha. "Don't wake the baby."

A short while later, everyone joined Martha in a nap.

ABOUT NOONTIME, everyone woke refreshed, and Will had returned. Eliza passed the waterskin again, but the little boys didn't understand they should take only a sip. Georgie took a big swig and then handed it to Hattie.

"Georgie, it's all gone!" Two drops fell into her palm. "I'm thirsty. What do I do?"

Just then, a crew member happened past them. He nodded curtly to a pail near the railing. "Bucket," he said briefly, not stopping.

It took a minute for Hattie to understand his terse directions. Looking along the railing, she saw many such buckets, each attached to a long rope. She went over to the closest one, then called Emma and Will to help her. "All right. The bucket is attached to a rope. I guess you're supposed to lower the bucket into the river and pull up a pail of water."

"That makes sense. We certainly have no lack of it," Emma giggled.

"Let's give it a try," Will encouraged.

"I'll do it." Hattie claimed this task.

It was easy lowering the empty bucket down, but not so easy filling it with water.

"Aagh!" she cried. "The bucket's not filling. It's just bouncing on top of the waves."

Looking over the side, Emma said, "Maybe you bring it up half full. With whatever water you can get."

"Let me try," Will offered. He danced the rope up and down, dangling the bucket at different levels. Finally, it caught enough water that Will proclaimed it ready to pull up.

"Let me!" Hattie begged. "This is my job." She pulled on the rope, but now that the bucket was full, lifting was very hard. "All right." She was conciliatory. "I can use some help."

Will reached over and grabbed the lower part of the rope. Both heaved, and finally, they brought it up. It was only two-thirds full, but it sloshed as they set it down.

Going back to her mother, Hattie retrieved a tin cup that rested in their food sack. With a satisfied smile on her face, she dipped the cup into the bucket. She drank, only to spit the water out. "Gakk! This isn't water, this is silt! What are they thinking?"

Will grinned. "That must be why they call the Missouri 'the big Muddy.'"

"Is that what you heard on your ship investigation?" Emma asked with a smile.

"Yup. It looks like water, but it's a big soup we're on." Seeing Hattie's disgusted face, he said, "Nothing for it, sister, you're going to have to let it settle before you can drink it."

Hattie sighed, "How long is that going to take?"

"Dunno. I guess we'll find out."

She knelt on the deck, not paying attention to the dampness. "I'm not leaving it until it gives me water!" She circled it protectively, making the bucket seem like a pet.

Emma grinned at her little sister hugging the pail. It was a good half hour before Hattie could get a drink from the top half, and even longer before she let anyone else have one.

While the family waited, Will offered his newfound information. Strutting, he said, "Well, I found out what that glass structure is at the very top of the boat."

"What is it?" Richie asked excitedly.

"It's called the pilot house. The pilot steers from there. And guess what! The pilot is paid five times what the captain is. The captain's not the big man on this ship; it's the pilot!"

Georgie said, "Then I don't want to be a river captain. I want to be the pilot!"

"Exactly," agreed his big brother. "I also found that the deck above the second level is where the officers' cabins are located. You'll never guess what it's called."

"High deck," suggested Georgie.

"Nope."

"Third deck," Emma offered.

"Nope again."

"Officers' deck," said Hattie.

"Wrong again. It's called the Hurricane Deck."

Georgie's eyes went wide. "Maybe 'cause it's the one that will get ripped apart when a hurricane comes."

Emma wondered what on earth Georgie had learned in school!

Hattie asked, "Do they have hurricanes here?"

Richie asked, "What's a hurricane?"

"It's a great big, windy storm," answered Will. "But that's not what sinks most of the boats on the Missouri. The river is a treacherous one with snags and..."

"What's a snag?" asked Georgie.

"A snag is a huge dead branch from a tree that gets caught in the river. Sometimes even a whole tree! The river just snatches it up from the shore and churns it down." Will settled in to tell what he'd learned. "There aren't many rivers more treacherous than the Missouri. It's slow enough to meander, but fast enough to change course. And they never know where it's going to be next, so they don't know what depth they're running. How's that for a river?"

"That's crazy," said Hattie.

"Very different from the Thames," Emma agreed.

"That's right. Half of the boats sunk in the Missouri were from snags."

Will was not looking at his mother, but Emma was. Her face blanched with fear.

"Another thing that's treacherous about this river is the sandbars. They can appear anywhere, and they can hang up a boat for weeks."

Horrified, Hattie sympathized, "Oh, the poor people have to stay on a sandbar for weeks?"

"No, silly. They ferry them off. But the boat can't get off unless there's enough water under it."

"I guess those big paddles would just whirl in the air. That wouldn't do any good!" Emma remarked.

"Right. With the steamboat company losing money every day." Bringing Georgie back into the conversation (he'd been playing hand games with Richie), Will leaned over, saying, "That's why the pilot makes the most money on the boat. He's the one who guides the boat away from sandbars and shallow waters."

"Is he the one who sees a tree in the water?" asked the boy.

"That's my question, too," said Emma. "The water looks placid, but we're going at a good clip. A fallen tree or branch could tear a hole in the hull."

"Hole in the hull! Hole in the hull!" chanted Richie.

Martha picked it up. "Ho'e. Ho'e. Ho'e!" she sang while Georgie charged at the railing, pretending to thrust a sharp sword into the side.

Eliza had had enough. She asked Will to bring Georgie back to the family circle and to say the prayer over their meal. After the blessing, Eliza had everyone sit by their bench while she distributed bread, cheese curds, and jerky from the food bag.

"I want to see a snag," Georgie pronounced, tearing off jerky with his teeth.

His mother was stern. "That is enough, young man. No more horror stories."

Following her mother's desire to redirect, Emma said, "This is good. Where did you buy it?"

Eliza smoothed her skirt needlessly, trying to slow her erratic breathing. "At the last town before St. Joseph."

Emma cued Hattie with her eyes and a dip of her chin.

The girl said, "It's nice, Mama."

Georgie and Richie hardly ate anything. Instead, they argued over who'd had the longest Cat's Cradle turn. To quell them, Eliza produced a small apple for each of them, holding it out of their reach until they'd first eaten the food she'd brought.

I wonder how those boys survive? Emma thought. *They never eat anything!* Her next thought was, *I hope I'll do half as well when I'm a mother someday.*

The rest of the day brought more pretend play from the boys, more ship-wandering from Will, and more recitation from Hattie to Emma and Eliza, who were sitting on the bench with Martha, watching the passersby.

Fanning themselves with lace or silk fans, women and their husbands walked around the lower deck. Many of the women wanted to see the golden-haired two-year-old and stopped to chat for a while.

In this way, Eliza and Emma made the acquaintance of many other Saints. Eliza always politely asked where they were from, their intended destination, and if they had any family with them.

Meanwhile, Emma loved guessing where they were from by their clothing. She was generally gratified to be right. She had figured out

Germany, but she kept mixing up Norway and Sweden. Their embroidered clothing was simply too similar.

Emma's question to each was *how* they were getting to Zion. She hoped at least one of them would say they were buying their own wagon, which meant they might be in her family's independent company. Time after time, though, they said they would be in a church train, and that led to disappointment.

Finally, she stopped asking altogether. It was doubtful she would see any of these people again.

Snag

ON THE MISSOURI RIVER

SATURDAY, JULY 5, 1862

Twilight brought a completely fresh look to the river. The orange clouds reflected in the driving current, and the slanting rays streaking the sky bounced off the waves' tops like tiny yellow balls tossed hither and thither.

Holding Martha, Emma pointed at the shimmering water, saying, "Fairies are playing catch. When you see a glint of yellow that sparks and then disappears, it's river fairies."

Standing by her, Hattie smiled. "That sounds like something I would say."

"Maybe you're rubbing off on me!" Emma grinned.

The little girl didn't really know what her sisters were talking about, but she enjoyed being with them and looking at the colorful river.

Hattie pointed to a distant steamboat that was headed downstream. "It's funny to think there are people on that. It just looks like a black box."

"With smoking columns," Emma added.

Large birds like herons or snowy egrets landed near the shore with a flurry of wings, now looking dark gray instead of white. Geese (or ducks, it was hard to tell which) flew as dark silhouettes against the amber clouds.

The steamboat didn't stop for night, and as it moved on, it acquired a stillness that hadn't been there during the day. The noise of the boat continued—the paddlewheels flinging up water, gases and steam from the smokestacks, chains banging and creaking, and the crew bending and fixing things, always hurrying—but the boat sounds seemed to blend with those of the river, as did the boat itself. It glided smoothly and silently, becoming a part of the night as much as owls or ferrets or mushrooms.

Emma took Martha back to her mother, and the family arranged themselves for the night around their bench. The younger boys lay on their jackets on the floor. It was hot and humid, and they covered themselves with an extra shirt to ward off mosquitoes. Will stepped to the railing again to watch the night river. Martha, who had fallen asleep as soon as she was put in her mother's arms, was laid carefully on the bench, her mother's hand protectively over her so she wouldn't fall.

Hattie, a shawl over her shoulders against the insects (but certainly not against the heat), leaned against Emma's shoulder, and Emma's head rested on the wall behind her. She thought, *I'm the one who agreed with Eliza when she said, 'We can tough it out,' but right now, I think sleeping sitting up is as fruitless as threading a needle with a candy stick.*

Emma had just dozed off when she heard someone yell. She opened her eyes, but the night was black, and the ripples on the river were mere sparkles of silver moonlight. Seeing her brother still standing at the railing, she called softly, "Will? Did you hear that?"

"Yes!" he answered. "A crewman yelled 'Snag!'"

Emma sat up straight. She realized her mother had also woken and was on high alert. This was what Eliza had dreaded. This was the horror she didn't want to come true.

Another crewman shouted, waking Hattie. She lifted her head off Emma's shoulder, drowsily asking, "What's going on? Why's he calling numbers?"

"Direction or size," Emma responded hollowly, as she watched barefoot feet run past. Vests, torn trousers, and ropes flapped as the crewmen ran to the bow. Three carried long pikes, and their heavy breathing and haste only added to the terror of the moment.

A crewman pointed at Will. "You! Go sit down!" But he hastened on, not seeing if his directive was followed. As Will moved, another tripped over their bucket in trying to avoid him. Water spilled onto the deck, Will moved back to the railing, and Emma grabbed Richie before the water could wet him and plopped him onto Hattie's lap.

As if in one fluid motion, she scooped Georgie into her own lap. The little fellow who'd been so keen on conquering the world with his sharp sword was now a wide-eyed child who looked up at her, trembling in confusion.

Will leaned over the railing, calling back, "There's something coming fast. And it's big!"

The woman next to her screamed, and her children whimpered. The father told them to sit back down and be quiet. "Get out of the crew's way," he reprimanded them.

Tentatively, Eliza called to Will, "What does it look like?"

"It's dark. Spiked. Might be a whole tree!"

"Oh, dear, oh dear," Eliza fretted. "What do we do?"

"Let's pray, Mother," Emma said.

"Yes, let's pray. You say it, Mary Emma."

The women and the boys bowed their heads, and Emma offered a quick prayer of protection for their boat and wisdom for the pilot.

"Heavenly Father, please bless this boat. Please bless the crew that they will know how to protect it. And, Father, please bless us and our fellow passengers. We are in Thy hands, and we thank Thee for all our gifts. In the name of Jesus Christ, amen."

As she finished, Will called, "See, the boat is turning!"

Indeed, the bow of the steamboat had turned and was facing the errant tree head-on. One second later, they heard a watery crash and felt a shudder as the thing collided with the front part of the boat. Emma felt the jarring impact in her chest as if someone had thrown a heavy vase at her.

"They're pushing it away with those long pikes," Will called, followed by, "Uh-oh! All they did was turn it. The root system is away from us, but now the branches are coming on."

No sooner had he said this than they heard a grating sound like a metal brush on a barrel. Will jumped back from the railing just as the scraggly fingers of the dead tree scraped past. The woman next to them screamed again, and her children cried out.

Drawn by the downstream current, the jagged hazard continued past the boat and drifted out of sight.

Emma released a breath she didn't know she was holding, but thought, *It's still in the river. Now it'll just terrorize some other boat.*

The crying in the family next to them grew quieter, and Eliza called to Will, "Can you see—is there damage to the boat?"

Emma hugged Georgie until his shaking stopped, and Hattie stroked Richie's hair. Thankfully, Martha had stayed asleep the entire time.

After looking downstream, Will came back to the family. "I don't think there's any damage to the sides. The branches only scraped the paint as they went past."

Laughing shakily, Hattie said, "The sound was worse than the outcome?"

"Exactly."

Recovering, she smiled and said craftily, "You mean, its bark was worse than its bite?"

Will chuckled, kicking her leg with his toe. "Its bark, huh? Very funny, sister."

"Oh, I get it—bark!" Georgie said, and then everyone in the family laughed. Nervous laughter, but laughter still.

Taking Richie from Hattie's lap, Eliza hugged him fiercely, the action releasing her pent-up angst. "Thank you, Heavenly Father!" She looked heavenward, more like talking to a friend than an actual prayer.

"See, the front of the ship is built to withstand crashes," Will said. "That's why the pilot moved us to face the tree head-on."

Emma said, "And you learned this..."

"Talking to a crew member." Will lifted his eyebrows as if to say, "You already knew the answer to that, dear sister."

Eliza was businesslike again. "All right, the excitement is over. It's time for bed again. Down you go, boys."

"Mama," complained Georgie. "My coat is wet."

"Mine, too," echoed Richie.

Eliza inspected them and handed them back. "Here's a dry part. You can sleep on that."

The boys settled down, heads together and whispering. Hattie rested her head against her mother, and Emma walked over to Will at the railing.

"You know, Eliza has been really frightened on this voyage. She knew many steamboats had sunk before we ever came, and she's been worried because none of us know how to swim."

If he had sympathy for his mother's feelings, he didn't show it. Instead, she could tell he was smiling, because she could hear it in his voice. "Well, then, when we get to the Valley of the Great Salt Lake, we'll just have to learn!"

"Ah, yes." The danger was past. Emma was breathing normally again and felt comfortable. She smiled, even though he couldn't see it. "And we'll learn to swim in the Great Salt Lake because..."

Together they intoned, "... one can never sink!"

Laughing softly, they decided to try to sleep. Hattie had taken her place on the bench, so Emma lay on the floor by the little boys, pulling Richie to her. As slumber overtook her, she chuckled lightly, thinking of how good Will was and how good he was for her!

EMMA GRATEFULLY OPENED her eyes as soon as sunlight crept over the river plain the next morning. She watched her bedraggled siblings slowly wake after the sun touched the water.

After watching a stately heron fly by and saying a morning prayer, Eliza handed out jerky and cheese, saying, "I wish I were giving you deviled eggs instead."

"I do, too, Mother," said Will.

"One of these days, Eliza..." Emma consoled.

After breakfast was put away, they spent the early part of the morning quietly watching the scenes unfold on the river. Towns that had sprung up along the shore looked like toy blocks complete with miniature clotheslines, trees, plows, and horses. They saw the *Empress,* a hospital boat, in the middle of the river.

"What a unique idea!" exclaimed Hattie. "Bringing the hospital to the people."

"It's not for the people," Will corrected. "It's for soldiers."

Hattie didn't like to be reminded about the war, so she didn't ask any more about it.

They noticed swallows flying in and out of a rocky area and saw gaggle after gaggle of geese flying above. Georgie and Richie said they even saw fish jumping, although Emma and Hattie never confirmed that.

By midmorning, the little boys wanted to do something more active. Will found an unusual source of entertainment when he realized one of the nearby buckets lay unused. He told Emma, "It sat there all yesterday, so I figure no one needs it."

Instead of throwing the silt from the bottom half of their bucket back into the river, he put the leftover mud into the new bucket and let the children play with it. They were delighted and treated it like sand on a beach.

"Mother doesn't mind," he whispered to Emma." I checked with her first."

Emma's eyebrows lifted in surprise that she would let them play with mud, but said, "Well, it gives three little children something to do."

"It looks fun. I might want to join them!" he said.

Of course, he didn't mean it. With the children busy, and Hattie supervising the youngsters, Will vanished on one of his foraging expeditions.

Emma and her mother found diversion in watching the people who walked by, most of whom were Saints on the way to Zion. Emma noticed a pattern: if two couples sauntered past, the women invariably stopped to admire little Martha. The wives would sit by Emma and Eliza, chatting while they fanned their faces and necks. The ladies liked to share the latest news, and they were not averse to topping each other's stories.

"I heard that just two or three years ago, a steamer carried *nine hundred* passengers, and three-fourths of them were Mormons."

"I heard that most of the wagons Russell, Majors, and Waddell used for the Pony Express two years ago came by steamboat."

"I heard that this very steamer took five thousand sacks of corn to Kansas City."

"You don't say? I heard a steamer took five thousand fruit trees upriver to sell!"

"Where would you store all of them?" the first would ask, prompting laughter from the other. Their fans would gyrate wildly, and they'd finally get up, collect their husbands, and continue promenading.

It was all very entertaining, and Emma and Eliza would roll their eyes at such silly women. Were they trying to be cosmopolitan?

Meanwhile, their husbands in their jackets would stand leisurely discussing important matters—at least Emma assumed they were important because their faces exuded an aura of great earnestness as well as how they bent toward each other. *Why do they wear coats in this heat?* Emma wondered. Now and then, she'd overhear one group talk about the trouble with travel caused by the War between the States, and another about what effect the Crimean War (ended six years prior) had on them now. She even heard snatches of an unlikely conversation that the price of Missouri potatoes had dropped because shipment of potatoes from Nebraska by steamer was less expensive. What was the world coming to?

What Emma would have preferred was a good gospel discussion, but maybe that was too thought-provoking for Saints who were sleep- and food-deprived. They seemed to seek simpler diversions.

One of the most interesting conversations involved an older couple and a younger one. It started as usual, with the women commenting on Martha and petting her hair. "Oh, what a sweet little girl. What's her name?"

Eliza answered, "Martha Jane," and the women sat down to admire her.

The older one, a corpulent lady, opened her fan, vainly swishing away insects as well as heat from a face already dripping with the humidity.

The younger, more stylish woman noticed her fan. "Pardon me, but have you had that fan for a while?"

Stopping her wrist motion, the older woman looked at it as if it were a criminal in black and white stripes. "Yes, I've had it for six years."

The younger woman continued, "Did you happen to buy it on the steamship *Arabia*?"

"I did. We were visiting family in Missouri at the time. How could you guess?"

From her reticule, the younger woman produced an identical one. "Well!"

"I also bought mine on the *Arabia*."

Her husband joined the conversation at that point. Using a decisive voice like a lawyer making his case, he said, "One week later, it struck a snag that ripped a hole in its hull."

The older gentleman's double chin rippled as he said, "I remember reading about that. It sank quickly, didn't it?"

"I believe so. Rapidly filled with water. The newspaper said that the next morning only the smokestacks and pilot house were visible above the surface. Then they also sank down into the mud, and the boat was lost to view." His voice took on a funereal, almost ethereal quality.

Hastily looking at Eliza and Emma, the younger woman added, "The passengers and the crew were saved. But not the goods. You see, the *Arabia* was a floating store. It stopped at towns on the river selling food, fabric, hats, boots, coats—almost anything you'd need."

"Yes, rifles and guns, carpentry tools, and nails. And liquor. And seeds," he said.

Seeing that her audience was interested, his wife went on, "They sold children's toys and candles and beads. How delightful it was, just walking through a mercantile on the water! I wished I could buy some of their lovely blue and white china plates, but instead, I got this."

"Then, a week later, the ship was gone," the man reiterated in his soulful voice.

She looked at her husband wistfully. "Maybe I should have gotten those plates."

"Well, you got that fan," remarked her husband, as if it were a huge consolation prize. "Come, dear, we need to make a whole circuit of this steamboat."

The women stood, and the younger said, "It's been lovely chatting with you."

The older lady said in an aristocratic voice, "Yes, it has. I hope to see you in Florence."

As the four of them left, the older woman looked down and was heard to say, "Oh, my! Children playing in mud. I hope their mother is not numbered among the Saints."

The couples walked away with their stories and opinions wafting in their wake.

Flabbergasted, Emma and Eliza looked at each other. Emma covered her mouth and Eliza bit her lower lip to keep from laughing until the foursome was out of hearing. Then their merriment burst like water from a dam.

"What was that?" cried Emma.

"Oh!" Eliza gasped, holding her side. "If I had any doubts about the Missouri River being dangerous, those doubts have been laid to rest!"

"And I thought sandbars would be the worst of our troubles!"

AFTER A MEAGER SUPPER, washed down by silty-tasting water from the bucket, Eliza told the children there would be no more playing in the mud. The children moaned pitifully, but her word was final. Will's idea, though, had been a heaven-send. It had kept them busy for the better part of the day, and really, they weren't that dirty. Eliza looked at Emma's raised eyes and said pragmatically, "When it dries, it will be dirt, and we'll just brush it away."

"Yes, I guess so." Emma nodded reasonably.

The family ate dinner right there at their bench, and afterward, they played 'What Do You Spy?' until twilight's magical veil again cast itself over the river.

At that time, Georgie, Hattie, and Emma played a short game of Word In-between, where two people each say a word, and the third person tries to say a word that links them. For instance, if Hattie and Emma said "river" and "railing," Georgie might say 'steamboat' and get a point. Georgie—always up for anything—wanted to play for points, but Emma and Hattie were too tired.

"Besides, you three are too loud," Will said.

After a short time, that, too, fizzled, and everyone stayed remarkably quiet.

"By and large, this has not been a bad trip," Eliza said. "I think I might miss the river."

"Yes, it's beautiful," agreed Hattie.

"Riv-oo," Martha pointed.

"Yes, the river." Emma held her little hand in both of hers.

"Emma, would you and Hattie sing some hymns for us?" Eliza requested.

Emma was surprised and delighted. Her request would normally have come at a formal Sunday dinner with missionaries attending. It seemed that here her mother just wanted the peace the hymns brought. After looking at her sister, they started softly and slowly,

> *Israel, Israel, God is Calling, Calling thee from lands of woe.*
> *Babylon the great is falling; God shall all her tow'rs o'erthrow.*
> *Come to Zion, come to Zion, For your coming Lord is nigh.*
> *Come to Zion, come to Zion! Zion's walls shall ring with praise.*

Their sweet voices floated on the air as lightly as feathers falling on the river. Soon, other voices joined them, none loud or overbearing, just blending in a soft chorus of heartfelt sentiments about Zion—the land and the opportunity for which every Saint on that boat had given up everything.

After that song, Emma tentatively began "A Poor Wayfaring Man of Grief" and again, others joined in. She finished with "Adam-ondi-Ahman" and "Yes, My Native Land, I Love Thee." This time when she sang, she had no desire to cry, as she had back in Poplar. It was no longer a wistful longing for England. Over the couple of months, the song had changed into a hopeful, forward-thinking refrain where 'my native land' represented the new one they headed toward.

It grew dark, and Emma settled her head against the wall again. She'd try to get some slumber in. They still had hours to go before they arrived in Florence.

❦

EMMA KNEW she'd fallen asleep because the loud noises of the crew woke her. At her side, Hattie and her mother also stirred and opened their eyes.

"Boys," Eliza said, reaching down to the younger ones. "Time to wake up. We're here."

Will, sitting on the floor, his back against the bench, asked, "What time is it, Mother?"

"It must be midnight. That's when they said we'd arrive."

Even though she knew they had to disembark, the bustle surprised Emma. She was used to the late hour being given to calm sleeping, not activity erupting. She heard crew members relaying depth and draft to the pilot with loud, clear voices, and lanterns along the sides showed others pulling on mooring lines and preparing fenders that would cushion the side of the boat. Two men quickly walked the lower deck, pulling up the water buckets and making sure their long ropes were not trailing.

Emma saw several crewmen with long poles on the side closest to land. She said to Will, "Those look like the same pikes they used yesterday on the snag."

"I'm sure they are, but they're using them this time to push the boat forward as it tries to land. Guess what?" he asked the little boys with a grin. "What they're doing has a name."

"What name is it?" Georgie asked.

"Yeah, what name?" asked Richie.

"Are you ready for this?"

Emma chuckled as Will tantalized his brothers. When the boys were almost popping to learn it, he revealed, "Grass-hopping."

"Grass-hopping?" Georgie scoffed. "That's silly!"

187

Will spread his hands out, shrugging, while Richie added, "Yeah, silly."

"Will, you are a veritable fount of knowledge!" Emma smiled.

"What do you think I do while I wander the ship?"

"Now I know."

They were interrupted by a loud grinding noise.

"What is that?" Emma asked, her eyes suddenly wide.

Georgie stood by her side. "Yeah, what's that?"

"I believe that is the paddlewheels reversing to slow us down."

"It's loud!" remarked Richie, looking not at all pleased with the noise.

"We don't want to hit the dock," Will said reasonably. "See? We're slowing, and now we're going in at an angle. We're almost there."

"Everyone, gather your belongings." Eliza directed. "Georgie, you stay with Emma. And Richie, you hold Hattie's hand. Will, will you take Martha, please? You're more surefooted." Eliza directed.

"Are you all right with all these bags?" Will asked as Martha was put into his arms.

"I should be."

"Here, give me those two big ones. I've got a free arm."

Eliza slipped the bags over his arm and then directed the younger children, "Be polite and wait your turn. All the passengers don't need to get off the boat at the same time."

With a bump and a scrape, the *Omaha* landed at the dock in Florence, Nebraska. A gangplank was thrown between the ship and the land, and passengers, who were already lined up, immediately began getting off. Lanterns dimly lit the exit and the landing area, but darkness enveloped everything else. A wind arose, and clouds obscured the waxing moon that had given light the night before, so nature offered them no help.

The gangplank was wide enough for three people to pass. However, a crewman always seemed to take one (or more) of the lanes, as he hurriedly removed passengers' luggage.

It was Emma's turn to cross the gangplank. Holding Georgie's hand, she cautiously descended, the shadows betraying where they should step. Holding bags, long skirts and a brother's hand didn't help her balance on the slightly wobbly gangplank. A crewman barged past, a large portmanteau on his right shoulder. His right elbow almost struck her head, and his foot bumped hers. Emma stumbled and collided with Georgie. Luckily, he tripped into her, instead of toward the river, so they avoided dropping into the water. So intent was the man on his mission, he never stopped, never said 'sorry,' and never even looked their way.

Emma was outraged. This crew was horrible! When she had Will's ear, she told him, "They didn't care one bit. They were just trying to get rid of us so they could go get more paying passengers."

Will agreed. "You might be right. I think the boat is paid by how many passengers they take on. The faster they get rid of us, the faster they can turn around and take on new customers."

Holding Richie's hand, Hattie had the same experience coming down the gangplank. Looking at her sister on the wobbly board, Emma unconsciously held up a hand to steady her as one of those horrible men drove past them.

Even worse than using the gangplank as their own highway was the way the crewmen often took luggage off the boat. They simply hefted bags and threw them over the side, not carrying them carefully to the landing. Everything was just tossed as far as their strong arms could throw them.

The riverbank was soon a jumble of parcels. Bags, boxes, cases, and baskets were strewn among the willows between the land and the river. It was midnight and pitch black—other than that tiny bit of lantern light—and now five hundred people were bending over each other, scooting around each other, and pushing others aside, all vainly trying to find their belongings.

Eliza must have wanted to keep her children together more than finding their luggage, because she said, "We'll look in the morning. We each have our small bags that we carried, so use those for your pillows tonight."

Emma's family gathered in a knot, said a prayer together, and fell asleep on each other. She overheard the father next to them tell his family, "Just sleep on whatever luggage you find. We'll sort it all out in the morning."

Indeed, there was much to be done in the morning.

Storm in the Camp
FLORENCE, NEBRASKA

Emma woke to an odd sensation. She didn't know if it was from her body aching from sleeping on the ground, or that she woke in a half-light. The cloud cover from the previous night persisted, giving the landing a dim, gray-blue cast.

They were in Florence, Nebraska, but only the first hundred yards or so from the landing. The area, littered with luggage, looked like a horde of river birds had picked up sticks and dropped them randomly on the ground, with no rhyme or reason to where they landed.

The Saints, in little family clumps, looked like a series of random knots embroidered on dun-colored cloth. Slowly, the knots unraveled as people stood up and sifted through the pieces of luggage.

Eliza asked Will and Emma to look for theirs. She didn't want the little boys anywhere near the water, so she wouldn't let them go, and she needed Hattie to help tend.

The older brother and sister pulled apart piles of baggage, looking for their own in the indistinct light.

"Can you believe it?" Emma said, pointing her hand to the riverbank full of willows and tall grasses. "They just threw bags on the shore!"

"They're all soaked," he replied simply.

They took off their boots and socks so they could wade closer to the river. Emma lifted her skirt as high as she dared, but Will didn't even bother to roll up his pant legs.

Glancing at her questioning eyebrow, he said wryly, "They'll dry later."

They searched for half an hour and found all their luggage. After they dragged their things back to Eliza and the children, Emma told them what she'd heard from several other searchers. "They looked all over the landing and all over the riverbank, and they couldn't find their baggage anywhere. Apparently, pieces must have sunk or drifted away on the river during the night. It makes me so sad."

"Oh, that is sad," Eliza sympathized. "Things that people need—"

"And special mementos they brought from their home, never to be seen again." Hattie picked up the conversation with tremendous empathy.

Ever practical and ready to put a positive spin on things, Eliza reasoned, "At least they're here in Florence, where they'll be able to restock what they're missing."

"Yes, that's good, at least," agreed Emma, choosing not to think of her mother Martha's hair comb that even now safely sat in her bag of toiletries.

With luggage gathered, they sat on the ground in their family cluster.

"Look at us all," Emma gently berated her family as she sat on the ground. "We all look as limp as a pile of reeds pulled from the river."

Eliza nodded, but said, "We're just trying to figure out what happens next."

Emma turned her head, looking around for someone in charge. All too soon, she realized she was looking for a different person—the one person she had missed this whole trip—her father. She imagined him walking toward them, a big smile on his face. Then they would all be together and she would feel whole again.

She stood up, craning her neck, hardly admitting to herself that he was who she was looking for, but she didn't see him. She saw Elder Lyman, though, shaking hands with a squat, bearded man who was about her father's age.

"There's Elder Lyman and someone," she said, pointing with her chin.

Eliza stood up to look. "Oh, that must be Joseph Young. He's President Young's son."

"He must be. He looks a lot like the pictures of his father, Brigham."

"He does, doesn't he? I was told he's in charge of the landing process here in Florence."

"Too bad he couldn't tell the riverboat crew how to unload baggage," Emma said with a touch of vinegar in her voice.

"I imagine he's tried." Eliza shook her head dolefully.

Still watching, Emma said, "Elder Lyman is leaving. Why does he have a spring in his step?" Since Elder Lyman had lived in their house, Emma had seen him on sad days when his body drooped, and on happy days when he walked like he was now.

Eliza chuckled. "That young man has just handed over his commission to Brother Young. He isn't in charge anymore, so I bet he feels a little lighter!"

"I wish we could say goodbye to him," said Hattie, standing to see him go.

"Maybe we'll see him later," said Will, also standing.

Across the way, Brother Young relayed some information to a couple of people and then walked their direction. With arms wide open, he stood and called to the groups of people lounging, "Welcome to Florence, Nebraska! You've made it thus far, you glorious Saints! My name is Elder Joseph W. Young, and yes, I am President Young's son."

He's been asked that before! Emma thought with a smile.

"Stand up, boys," urged Eliza, holding up Martha so they could all see better.

"I am in charge of the staging grounds here in Florence, where you'll obtain wagons and supplies and be placed in trains to go west. For now, teams will be arriving shortly. When they call you, load your goods, and they'll take you to a campground not far away. You'll be provided with tents, and you'll be able to set up and be comfortable until the wagons arrive from the Salt Lake Valley to take you the rest of the way. Just put your belongings in whatever wagon comes your way first."

Perhaps because they were standing and looked ready to depart, a wagon pulled up beside them almost the instant he finished his announcement. Two men jumped down and introduced themselves with big handshakes.

"I'm Brother Stuart," said the one who was tall, thin, and balding.

"And I'm Brother Stewart," said the other, a man who was shorter, broader and brown-haired.

Both laughed, but Emma didn't know why until they explained the spellings.

"So, no, we're not related."

"But we are brothers—in the gospel." They laughed again, and Emma found she couldn't stop smiling. A difficult midnight disembarking had been the apex of nine trying days, and the laughter of these two delightful, helpful men released the angst she didn't know she'd been holding. With a lighter heart, she helped place the bags in the wagon bed.

"All right, who wants a ride to the campground?"

Arms shot up, and a chorus of "Me! Me!" was heard. Assuring Eliza they would go slowly, and the children would be fine, Brothers Stuart/Stewart allowed all the children who wanted to, to ride in the bed of the wagon.

"Want to ride!" Martha reached out to her siblings.

Eliza scooped her up. "No, little girl, not today. Mama wants you with her."

Emma walked beside her, to help carry Martha if the distance became too great.

Brother Stuart climbed onto the high seat on the wagon box, picked up the reins, and called, "Gee-up!" The mules started forward at a slow pace. The wagon jolted ahead, and no one had to tell the children to grab onto the sides.

Emma looked at her surroundings. The river with its willows and a few shady trees was behind them, and ahead was a vast flat acreage consisting of dirt and tamped-down grasses. There were no trees, no flowers, not even any large boulders—nothing to break the flat monotony. A vast network of tents were set up haphazardly, and here and there, a "covered" wagon sat, but without the cover. Instead, the wooden bars that would eventually hold the canvas arched from side to side. Bare as they were, and with four to six arches to a wagon, they looked like the ribcages of boiled chickens.

Walking beside Brother Stewart, she asked, "Why do you use mules instead of horses?"

"Ah, mules!" he grinned, running a hand through his hair and then repositioning his hat. "Mules work harder than horses. They eat less, and they need less water. Also, did you know their hooves are cloven and their two toes spread out? They pick out the path better on rocky trails. They're almost as good as mountain goats!"

"I did not know that. My grandfather had horses, but not mules."

"Well, if you ever have a chance to work with one, I'd suggest you use it. They are wonderful animals and not nearly as stubborn as people say." Reaching over to rub behind a mule's ear, he said, "You're a good pal, aren't you, Noggy?"

Emma chuckled. The animal plodded forward, ears twitching, but otherwise seemed completely unaware of Brother Stewart's accolades.

Brother Stuart stopped the wagon at a table where a person was stationed to assign tents. The camp mandated that eight to ten people share each tent, and since the Horspools had eight people, they were given a tent all to themselves. Theirs was loaded into the wagon amid much laughter as the children dodged out of the way of the heavy canvas. Then Brothers Stuart/Stewart took them to a vacant spot and helped them unload. Waving goodbye with broad smiles, they left to go help another family and lighten their load.

MAKING sure Richie and Georgie were playing with Martha off to the side, the four older Horspools set up the tent. They had just hammered the last spike into the ground when the sky turned darker than it had been all morning.

A fierce wind sprang up, turning the air surprisingly cold. Fat rain drops suddenly fell from the sky.

Eliza ordered, "Georgie, Richie, take Martha inside. Georgie, quickly!"

Will grabbed a large box while Emma swiveled another toward the tent opening. She called over the wind, "Hattie, help me get this inside!" Then the older two scanned the yard to see if anything else needed to be inside the shelter.

Once inside, Eliza, Emma, and Hattie sat on the large boxes, while the younger children sat on the bare ground where only a few slivers of grass poked through. The wind outside sounded as loud as a hurricane, and the chilly air whipped through the tent as sharply as Ed Cash's grinding knives.

"Brr!" shivered Hattie. "It got cold fast!"

"Here, let me find something for you," said Eliza. Putting down Martha, she stood and opened a large box, rummaging until she found a thin quilt. She tossed it to Hattie, who put it around her and Emma's shoulders.

Georgie, at nine and a half, didn't want to be classed as one of the "little ones," but Emma could see his thin frame shivering. "Georgie," she called, "would you please come and keep me warm?"

Georgie happily complied, climbing onto her lap. Martha and Richie were both cuddled in a shawl with their mother. Will held up the central pole to make sure it wouldn't collapse. No one was left to hold down the front flap, and it kept letting in the slanted rain and occasional sights of flashing lightning.

Something large hit the side of the tent with a jarring thump. For a second, it seemed as if the tent would collapse. How would they stay dry if that happened?

Richie looked up at his mother with large, frightened eyes. "Are there giants outside?"

Will said, "Something just hit our tent from the wind, Richie. There're no giants."

"Gi-nuts?" Martha repeated.

Eliza, looking down, replied, "No giants, sweetheart. Boys, this won't last too long—" Looking at the older children, she said loudly, "I hope. This is certainly heavier than we ever had in England!"

Will nodded, and Emma exclaimed, "It is! It's a deluge!"

Hattie agreed, "It feels like it's pouring buckets from heaven!"

Will said, "At least it's buckets of *clear* water, Hattie! Not like what you pulled up from the river!"

His statement lightened the mood in their cold, dim confinement. Emma grinned while Hattie made a face at him.

"Aghh!" Will yelled suddenly. Rain leaked through the top, right where he was holding the post. He sprang back and shook the water from his arms.

"I made the tent do that for making fun of me!" retorted Hattie. "Serves you right!"

"It's just water, little sister. I think I can handle that," he chuckled.

A minute later, he looked at Emma and said, "Moses."

It didn't take long before she answered, "The Red Sea."

He nodded. "We must be Pharaoh's army, though, because we're in the midst of it!"

"We're in for it, then! Everyone in Pharaoh's army drowned!" Even as she joked with Will, she hugged Georgie even tighter, hoping it would let him know he was safe.

The rain continued to drum over their heads on the heavy canvas like countless birds flying against a dark window. One by one, each member of the family lamented, "How long will this last?"

Eliza played peek-a-boo with Martha under the shawl's warm shelter, and Richie joined the game with many a happy, "There she is!"

Trying to find something positive, Emma loudly pointed out, "Maybe this will cause new grass to grow that our oxen can eat."

"What oxen?" asked Georgie.

"The oxen Father has bought to pull our wagon," she answered.

"How many?"

"Maybe four."

"What will their names be?" he asked.

"Do you think Papa will name them?" put in Hattie.

"Certainly." Thoughts of a fluffy chiffon cake suddenly intruded on the downpour. Smiling, Emma said, "He'll name them Butter and Cream, Royal and Icing."

Hattie said, "No, he'll name them after towns. Harlington, Poplar, Limehouse, and London."

From the wet, cold center post, Will said, "No, he'll name them after the scriptures: Matthew, Mark, Luke, and John."

They all groaned at that, and Georgie whined. "I don't like any of those names. Does Papa have to be the one to name the oxen?"

Reunited

FLORENCE, NEBRASKA

MONDAY, JULY 7, 1862

The wind shrieked and howled. Thunder crashed against the sky's roof, and the sudden, bright flash of lightning illuminated both the flap opening and the tent's opaque walls, like a lantern briefly switched on and off. It took a full twenty minutes for the violent storm to abate, and then it stopped as abruptly as it had begun.

Emma knew not everyone's tent had been raised and staked like theirs. She thought it a good idea if she and Will walked through the camp to see how others had fared. Eliza agreed, and as they moved to leave, she said, "Mary Emma, take that quilt with you. Someone might need it."

Emma nodded, and she and her brother bent as they stepped outside. Then they stood straight, aghast at what they saw.

Tents cantered off their poles at strange angles. Others were strewn haphazardly around the grounds like newspapers caught in the wind. Boxes, baskets, and packages lay on their sides, pushed up against debris or a standing tent. Water filled every hole and crevice.

"It looks like a war zone," he said.

"These puddles are as big as pools," Emma remarked, carefully skirting a large one.

"Watch where you're walking," Will advised, "I think that one's deeper than it looks."

They watched their fellow travelers, soggy and dismal, sift through their belongings. One swished pooled water off the top of one item as they righted another. Another lifted a soggy package, trying to shake out the excess water.

The July sun, hidden by the storm, suddenly emerged, now as hot as it had been cold a moment before. Some Saints walked—arms out to their sides—with no seeming purpose except to dry off. Will wandered off on his own, and Emma watched him set to right some blown-over barrels.

Emma came across old Sister Coolbear from William Wood's mess. Her cap had blown away, and her hair was wet and flat against her head. She looked disoriented and most definitely cold. Emma looked around, wondering where her son, David, was. Nevertheless, here was just the person who needed this quilt. "Here, Sister Coolbear, let's put this around you," Emma said gently as she wrapped the warm layer around the woman.

"Thank you, dear," Sister Coolbear said gratefully. "Now, who are you?"

Emma smiled. "I'm Emma Horspool. We were in the mess across the aisle from you on the *William Tapscott*." She wondered how she would find her son among the hundreds of tents that had been erected on the grounds. They walked here and there, talking about how much water the sky had poured on them.

"I haven't ever seen such a downpour," Sister Coolbear said.

"Neither have I," agreed Emma.

Across the way and in between wagons, Emma chanced to see David Coolbear and William Wood.

"David! William!" she called, immediately steering Sister Coolbear that direction.

Spotting her, they ran over.

A look of relief passed David's face. "There you are, Mother!"

"This sweet sister found me." She beamed at Emma.

"She walked away while I was adjusting the tent," David told Emma. "Let's get you back, Mother." He put his arm around her, helping to secure the quilt around her thin shoulders. Looking at Emma as she left, she said, "I'll make sure you get this back."

Emma beamed, "I know you will. We're back that way."

Emma then looked at William Wood, who was thoroughly drenched and seemed rather distracted. "William, what's going on? How did you and Lizzie fare?"

William answered with a wry smile, "We're in a tent with Rose, Annie, the Coolbears and two other couples you haven't met. Our tent was up, and David said the girls fared well. so I assume they're all right. It was the woman under the tent that you should be asking about."

"What woman?"

William smiled, "I had secured Lizzie in our tent when I went out to bring in a box I didn't want to get blown away. I chanced to see a tent blow down on top of a lone woman. She was struggling with it something fierce, as you can imagine—her arms flailing under the heavy material. It was almost wrapping around her. Well, I ran over to help, and that's when I discovered she wasn't just a single woman; she was a woman in confinement! Her time was almost upon her."

Emma's eyes shot up. "What did you do?"

William answered, "Well, I had to stay. The tent came in handy as a covering from the storm while she gave birth—rather quickly, I might add—to a healthy baby boy right there on the ground! She's doing fine, and I believe we'll continue to be great friends after a bonding like that!"

Emma shook her head in disbelief, chuckling, "William Wood, you never cease to amaze me! The stories you'll have to tell your children after you and Lizzie marry...!"

"And I plan on that happening as soon as we reach the Valley of the Great Salt Lake!"

"By the way, William, have you seen Annie?"

"She came with us as far as the steamship. We separated at that time. Emma, she's not doing well. I hope she can make it across the plains."

"I'll add her to my prayers." With a deprecating little laugh, Emma added, "She's already in my prayers."

Just then, her brother, Will, walked up to the two of them. "I just heard some bad news. Lightning killed two people – one was a wagon driver from Salt Lake, and one was from the London Conference."

Emma shook her head sadly. "I'm so sorry for their families."

"There's more," he continued. "Some cattle became frightened and stampeded down by the landing area. They ran into some unsecured wagon boxes, and they fell on Brother Young. He's severely hurt. They say his chest is badly bruised, and his head gashed open."

William said, "That's terrible. I'm sorry to hear that."

"There's a chance he could die," Will answered.

"We'll keep him in our hearts and pray mightily for him," Emma said sadly. "Let's go back and tell Mother and Hattie."

"Where is your tent?" William asked.

Will pointed in the general direction.

William said, looking at Emma, "I'll make sure you get your quilt back."

"Thank you. And tell everyone in your tent how much I love them!"

As they parted from their tall, lanky friend, Emma pondered over their upcoming trek across the plains. *What would happen? What would it be like? They were on the Lord's errand, and He was supposed to help them, right? But Brother Young was on the Lord's errand too, and look what had happened to him!*

And Father. Where was he? Everything would be better if they had Father. He was supposed to meet them here.

She was surprised at how much she had thought of her father ever since he'd left. All through her teen years, she'd viewed him as abrupt and not caring. Now he was the very man she longed for—the very man she felt would bring her stability and happiness.

They headed back to their tent, but Will outstripped her. Soon she was walking alone. She found her thoughts going in directions she didn't want them to, like rabbits hopping down countless warrens. *Had Father survived the voyage? Had he been unhealthy, and the doctor wouldn't let him land? Oh, what if he'd been sent back to England, and he was on one of those ships that passed them going the other way? How ironic—they wouldn't have known for months!*

Her thoughts spun round and round. *Had he found passage on the railways to St. Joseph, or was he knocked off his train like they had been? Or worse, had he been shot by one of those St. Joseph hoodlums in their idiotic ranting? If he had, he could be lying somewhere hurt or recovering right now, and they'd never know. Heavens, oh heavens! What if he had been conscripted into the Union army?*

Oh, why had they let him come alone? She had heard Eliza and her father talking, and their approach sounded so reasonable. But right now, it didn't seem reasonable at all.

She pulled herself away from her unwanted thoughts and refocused on where she was going. There were so many tents and empty wagons that she had to concentrate on her path.

Then, fifty yards away, walking between two wagons was a form she knew. At least, she thought she knew that form. It looked like her father. She quickened her pace, determined to find the man that she had barely glimpsed.

She walked between the two wagons, looking left and then right. No one was there. Well, not the man she was looking for, anyway.

A family sat in a small circle by one wagon and looked up as she passed by. "Hello!" they said cheerily. Apparently, the rainstorm hadn't bothered them much.

"Hello," she echoed, but didn't stop to make their acquaintance. Her eyes kept searching—she had a greater mission just then.

She rounded two large tents and saw a man's leg as he walked out of view. Thinking it might be him, she sped up again. *Why is he going so fast?* she thought.

There were enough people around that she hated to call out. She rethought that as she rounded a smaller tent, only to have the man go out of view again. Did she dare call out? Was she certain enough that it was her father? *Audentes Fortuna adiuvat* jumped into her mind—a phrase she'd learned in Latin class: 'Fortune Favors the Bold.' There was nothing for it, then. She needed to call out.

"Father!" She could see him now, but it didn't appear he heard her. "Father!" she called more loudly. She saw him look to the right, but he didn't stop. Taking a huge breath, she stopped and called, "John Horspool!"

The man stopped abruptly and turned. The familiar face of her father looked at her. Emma gathered up her skirts and ran to him.

"Emma girl!" he smiled, catching her in his arms.

She threw her arms around his neck and unabashedly hugged him fiercely, kissing him on his whiskered cheek. It may have been out of character for Emma-of-Poplar, but it wasn't out of character for Emma-of-Florence. "You're here! You made it!" she gushed.

"Well, yes, but I've been here for a while. It's *you* who are newly arrived," he smiled down at her, hugging her back.

Letting down her arms from his neck, she asked, "When did you come? Have you been safe? Are you well? Did coming early work out?"

"Whoa, there!" he chuckled. "You sound like Harriet Marie."

"I do, don't I?" Emma blushed. "I'm just so glad to see you!"

He looked at her closely. "You've been worried about me, haven't you?"

She looked back at him, her dark brown eyes luminous. She couldn't say a word.

Taking her by the hand, he faced forward. "How about you take me to the family?"

"Yes!" she agreed happily. "They're this way."

Rounding a couple of corners, she glimpsed a quilt drying on a tent pole. That was their quilt! This was their tent. She saw Georgie outside. Quickening her steps, she called out to him. "Georgie! Look who I've brought!"

He looked up from the box he was placing outside to see who she meant. It was his father! He dropped the box and ran to him. "Papa!" he called, launching himself at his father.

Laughing, John caught him, the momentum twirling them around.

Hearing something, Richie came outside, exclaiming, "Papa! Papa!" He grabbed onto his father's leg and held on for dear life.

"My, how tall you've grown," he said, placing a hand on the small boy's dark head.

"Me, too, Papa!" Georgie proclaimed.

"You too, my boy," he smiled at Georgie. "And in just two months!"

Hattie stepped out expectantly, her thick brown braid hanging over her shoulder. Seeing her father, she cried, "You're back!" Running to him, she latched onto his arm as if it were the solid frame of a bed. Contentedly, she settled her head onto his shoulder.

"You, my dear, are lovelier than ever," he remarked.

Her answering smile was brighter than the sun that was drying up the puddles.

Hearing the hubbub, Eliza stepped out with Martha Jane. "John! You're here!" she sighed gratefully.

"I am," he smiled with a loving look that Emma had seen only once when he was taking leave of his wife in Poplar. Before that smoldering gaze could turn into anything stronger, he shifted his eyes to his youngest daughter. "And who's this little charmer?" He reached out his arms for Martha, who eyed him suspiciously.

Eliza said—more of a statement than a question, "You remember Papa."

After thoroughly investigating his bearded face and scanning her siblings' beaming faces, she must have decided he was a safe bet because she finally put her arms out to him.

"Well, little one, you had a birthday." He bounced her in his arms. "How old are you now?"

"I two!" she said, enthusiastically holding out three fingers.

John gave her one more squeeze before handing her to Emma. Then he finally took his wife in his arms, unapologetically hugging her and kissing her forehead right in front of the children.

Eliza melted into his embrace, relief evident in every fiber of her being. Seeing this, Emma's happiness knew no bounds. She was gratified beyond measure at this completion.

Just then, Will came to the tent from the other direction. At the scene in front of him, he stopped dead, his mouth dropped open with a look of wonder on his face.

John left his wife and crossed over. "Now we're complete," John exhaled, holding out his hand to the youth and putting his other on his shoulder. "Thank you for keeping them safe," he said, looking in turn at all of them. "For keeping *you* safe!"

He reached out for Martha again and put his other arm around Eliza while Richie held onto his leg for dear life.

"Yes, we are all safe," Eliza nodded.

"But we've had adventures, Papa!" exclaimed Hattie, as Will and Georgie vigorously nodded their assent.

"Yes, Papa!" exclaimed Georgie. "It's been so exciting!"

Emma intervened before her brother got on a roll. "Come let's sit down. You tell us your adventures, and we'll tell you ours. Let's sit out in the sun!"

Eliza directed Will, Hattie, and Georgie to brings boxes out from the tent. Then, as fast as one could say, "Pussy cat, pussy cat, where have you been? I've been to London to visit the Queen," everyone seated themselves. Gathered in a circle, they looked eagerly at their father, and the stories began.

End of Book One

Acknowledgments

I would like to thank my editor, Troy Lambert, for his encouragement and for teaching me along the way; for Stacey Smekofske, who guided the publishing process.

I am thankful for my readers: Heather Moore, Jennifer Moore, Susan Easton Black, Debbie Youngberg and Eric Schetselaar.

Thank you to my cousins who trusted me with writing about a great grandfather and his two wives.

I am grateful for my neighborhood writing group where writing personal stories whets an appetite for detail.

I am thankful to my readers, who offered great insights.

Thank you to the readers of my first book, *Scott's Choice,* who told me they thought I was a good writer.

I'd also like to thank my walnut tree, whose branches and leaves enfolded me during my many happy hours of writing as a child.

About the Author

Having over fifty Utah Pioneers in her family line, Elaine loves all things historical. Dressed in period clothing at her town's Pioneer Village, the littlest of her twenty grandchildren ask, "Do you live here?" Author of bestselling *Scott's Choice*, Elaine has also been awarded first place standings in such contests as The Metropolitan Opera, San Francisco Opera, and NATSAA. She graduated Magna Cum Laude from the U of U, received an MM at BYU, and taught  elementary ed and singing lessons, as well as musical theater and storytelling through USG and the Utah Arts Council.

To learn more about Elaine and to sign up for her free newsletter featuring special giveaways and behind-the-scenes information, please visit: www.elainebrewster.org

Coming Soon

WALKING WITH EMMA • BOOK 2
CROSSING
the
PLAINS
BASED ON A
TRUE STORY
Elaine
BREWSTER

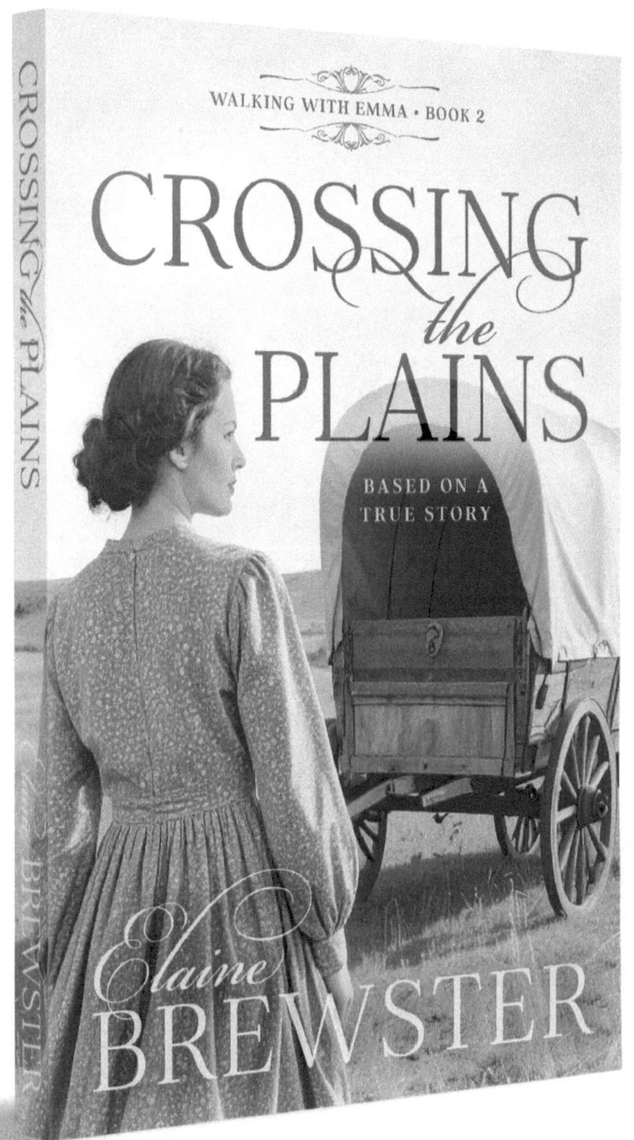

Book Club Questions

- The two oldest daughters had a close relationship. How did Emma help Elizabeth, and how did Elizabeth help Emma?
- In what ways is Emma a forward-thinking girl (even a feminist)?
- How does Emma feel about her father? Does that change throughout the story: How and why?
- Emma has a close relationship with her sister. When she doesn't have that anymore, what does she do? How does she replace that or does she?
- What images of the London area do you get from what Emma sees?
- During the trip Emma sees Will differently than she did back in Poplar. In what ways?
- Were there any places that frightened you in the story?
- Did Emma's scary memory of running down the alley remind you of a scary time in your life? What was it? How did you resolve it?
- Any similes and metaphors you found that you'd like to share?

- How was America different from England?
- In what ways does Emma try to be the conciliator, smoothing things over?
- The family's immediate goal was Florence, Nebraska. Were their expectations met?